Published by Fox Chase Books, L.L.C.

P.O. Box 5868

Midlothian, VA 23112

D1707055

Breaking
Free

A.M. Mahler

Fox Chase Books, L.L.C. – Richmond, VA

For my parents, whose support
Of my dreams of being a
Writer has been unwavering
And who, despite what I may have
Said growing up, aren't
Mean and nasty like some of
My fictional parents!
I love you!
(P.S. Daddy, please stop reading the
love scenes. It freaks me out.)

One

DOCTOR SEBASTIAN STUART stared across the desk at his father, smirking inside.

Take that, you bastard.

An unfortunate happenstance of genetics gave Sebastian the look of his father—same dark hair, similar facial features, and darker skin tone. The elder Dr. Stuart loathed Sebastian's closely trimmed beard. So, of course, Sebastian wouldn't dream of shaving it off. But thankfully, Sebastian didn't share his father's cold and calculating brown eyes. Sebastian's were a stunning blue he had inherited from his mother, who had been a frat party fling of his father's in college, which resulted in Sebastian.

His mother had split after Sebastian was born, and he was raised by his grandparents, since his father couldn't bear to be reminded of his existence. He paid for Sebastian's upbringing and care but never showed him any kind of love or affection. The man never even attended any of Sebastian's birthday parties or major school events growing up. Sebastian only saw his father when he came to Sebastian's paternal grandparents for holidays. He even had half-siblings by his father, but they couldn't be bothered with him either—unlike his siblings from his mother who showered him with love, attention, and genuine interest in his life.

Sebastian wished he was with those siblings right then as his father glowered across the desk at him. The elder Dr. Stuart was the chief of surgery at a large university hospital in Chicago where Sebastian himself was an up-and-coming surgeon.

Until he had tendered his resignation just now.

"It's out of the question." His father said before turning his attention to the paperwork on his desk. Sebastian knew he was dismissed, but this time, he wouldn't go.

Amazed, Sebastian shook his head at his father's immediate refusal to let Sebastian do anything that went against the man's plan for him.

His father's shrewd gaze snapped back up at his son. "Something amuses you?"

Sebastian was about to stop laughing and school his features into a serious expression. His father was a serious man. Sebastian couldn't remember ever really seeing his father smile—certainly not in his direction at least. Instead, he let the chuckle play out.

"I'm amused you think you have some kind of hold over me. I'm a grown man with a career. I make my own decisions. Grandma and Grandpa are settled in Florida now. There's nothing left for me here."

"Nothing left?" His father said with a sneer. "You have family here." Looking around the office, Sebastian noted the irony. There wasn't a single picture of his so-called family in his father's office. The mere fact that his father could use family as an argument in his favor was ridiculous. The man had forgotten the meaning of the word long ago.

"You haven't been family to me." Sebastian countered, clenching and unclenching his fists. Sebastian was reminded that he wasn't as strong as he thought. "And you haven't allowed my brother and sisters to be family to me either." Did he sound whiny? He definitely didn't want to sound whiny.

"I paid for your education." His father's attention returned to the file on his desk as if Sebastian wasn't even worthy of his full attention. Sebastian counted to ten. He was almost free. Just a few more minutes and he was done. He could hold out that long.

"Which doesn't give you the right to control me." Sebastian said, calmer now. Supporting me financially is your obligation as the man who fathered me."

"You'll speak to me with respect." His father barked. Sebastian had been waiting a long time for this moment—for the opportunity to get out from under his father's thumb, for the chance to look his father in the eye and tell him to shove it up his ass, and Sebastian was getting great satisfaction from the moment. With each passing minute, a weight was lifting off his shoulders.

His father had been even more distant and cold to Sebastian since he lost his bid for a state senate seat, but now Sebastian knew his father was making a run for the open federal senate seat. Originally, Sebastian was supposed to dig up dirt on his siblings on his mother's side, but he never did. He didn't have a relationship with his brother and sisters in Chicago, he didn't want that to be the case with his brothers and sisters in New Hampshire.

Sebastian lifted his chin to his father in defiance. "What are you so upset about?" he challenged. "I'll be away from you—out of your hair. You'll no longer have the constant reminder of your mistake to look at every day. I would think you'd be ecstatic to see me go. I could never figure out why you insisted on having me near you anyway. It certainly wasn't out of love." Silence followed as his father looked at him in a way no father should ever look upon their son. It was impossible to tell by his father's frigid gaze whether his words had hit a mark or not.

"And where are you going to go?" His father asked, ignoring Sebastian's comments.

Sebastian paused for a minute before answering, "Grayson Falls." The words fell between them like an axe. The muscles in his father's face tensed. His father's features all but turned to stone and the condescension Sebastian saw there amazed even him. Sebastian imagined a crack running down the man's forehead. Smirking on the inside, Sebastian put his hands in his pockets. *That's right, old man. The complete opposite direction of you—literally and figuratively.*

"I see." His father sat back in his chair. "You'd give up a lucrative job in a big city to practice small town medicine in Bumfuck, New

Hampshire?" Returning his attention to his paperwork, his father offered a parting shot. "I won't take you back."

Sebastian's mouth hung open before he let out a surprised laugh. "If this were the only hospital in the country, I wouldn't come back." He knew that was petty and somewhat immature, but his father had a tendency of making him stoop to new lows. "There are many traits of yours that I thank God weren't passed down to me—arrogance is one of them. I never asked to be born, but you treated me like a cancer from day one. Do you have any idea what it's like to grow up knowing you were a mistake and still viewed as one? No, you don't. Because Grandma and Grandpa are loving and attentive. You were so obsessed with forging a successful career that you completely missed how to be a man."

The room felt smaller every minute he was inside. What was normally a breath-taking view of the city seemed to move toward him until he felt like he was teetering on the edge about to be pulled down into the loneliness of the fast-paced city prison.

"That's uncalled for." His father snapped.

Nodding slowly, Sebastian began to back out of the room, stepping away from the life that was drowning him. "One day, you'll regret how you treated me."

Before his father could retort, Sebastian left the office. The secretary, obviously listening in, jumped back when the door opened suddenly. He couldn't bring himself to meet her eyes as she shuffled around the outer office trying to make herself look busy. Purposeful strides brought him to the elevator quickly. Keeping his eyes on the elevator doors, Sebastian shuddered against the tension forming in his neck and shoulders and the tingling sensation in his chest and back. He was being watched, but he wouldn't turn around to see by whom. He couldn't get out of there fast enough.

What did he expect? A tearful goodbye? An acknowledgement of past wrong doing? Sebastian knew he would never get either one.

But still, there was something inside him that had admittedly hoped for some sort of emotion from the man Sebastian spent his life trying to get attention from. But it was not to be.

Bursting through the hospital doors into the late-September sun, he breathed deeply, the smell of exhaust permeating his senses. Dropping his head back and taking in the clear blue fall sky above him—the kind of sky that looked like anything was possible—the sound of traffic amplified around him. He had done it. He wasn't officially free yet, but he could finally leave this stifling life. With a lighter step, he strode away from the hospital, pulling out his phone. He hit his brother Zach's contact, and Zach picked up on the first ring.

"Did you do it? How did it go?" Smiling at the concern in his brother's voice, Sebastian let himself feel the love coming through the phone. He did have family that cared about him—just none in Chicago.

"I did." Sebastian confirmed. "He didn't take it well. My big moment didn't feel as satisfying as I thought it would."

"Probably because you were secretly hoping he'd beg you to stay or tell you he was sorry for being such a dick your whole life." Zach said. "He's never going to do that. Tigers don't change their stripes, bro."

Though his brother couldn't see him, Sebastian nodded his agreement. He hadn't known his brother long, just a few short years, but these siblings knew him well. They had all migrated to Grayson Falls. Sebastian was the last one to relocate. He would have been there sooner, but he didn't want to leave his grandparents behind in Chicago. He had waited until they were settled in Florida.

When Sebastian had discovered he had five siblings from his mother, he had an unexpected reaction to the news. After his initial shock, he felt hope. His grandparents were always there for his every need growing up, but he had longed for a big, rowdy family—the family he imagined his Chicago siblings to be when he wasn't with them. When he did see his siblings on his father's side, they were cold and distant toward him, just like their father was. And his stepmother, well, she barely acknowledged him at all. Sebastian never did find out what his father had told his brother and sisters about him, but whatever it was, it wasn't complimentary, as they were very good at making him feel like a stain on what was outwardly a perfect family.

"So, when are you coming home?" Zach asked.

Home. Wasn't it strange that he thought of Grayson Falls as his home when he had never even lived there? The town fit him like an old friend—from its streetlamp lined sidewalks to the friendly faces you saw along the street and its small-town New England charm. He was leaving behind the concrete kingdom with its high-end restaurants, sophisticated women, high-power culture, and money for a town that had one movie theatre that could only play two movies at a time. Going to the theatre meant seeing a play at the old community playhouse. Even if the chief of police wasn't his brother-in-law, he'd still know Sebastian by name.

It was that magic that lured him now. He wanted nothing more than to gather his brothers and sister at Over the Hop Brew Pub for a beer and a burger, listen to Ryan and Jackie bicker, watch Ethan roll his eyes over it, and see Zach make goo-goo eyes at his fiancé, Piper. He longed to spend a quiet breakfast at the Liberty Diner with his sister Natalie, whom they couldn't acknowledge as such for safety reasons.

As a car horn blared and people rushed by him, Sebastian sighed. He had once excelled in this fast-paced environment. He fed off it. But that had changed. In a few short weeks, he'd be in a town with only one traffic light, and he wouldn't miss the city one bit.

"Hey!" His brother prompted. "You there?"

"Yeah," Sebastian said, running a hand down his face. "I have some surgeries scheduled I need to complete. My assistant was able to move most of them to other doctors. I should be finished in about two weeks, assuming the old man lets me linger that long."

"Sounds good to me." Zach said, his breathing increasing as Sebastian imagined him on the move. "Ethan just made me a bitchin' fire pit out back. It's a great place to unwind."

"You let our brother with only one good leg haul rocks for you?" Sebastian demanded. Their brother Ethan had been a working dog handler in the Marines. He was discharged after he lost the bottom part of his leg in a roadside bomb accident.

"I didn't *let* Ethan do anything." Zach replied, defensively. "We were supposed to do the project together, and I had planned to do most of the heavy lifting."

"When all of the sudden." Sebastian prompted.

"The weekend Piper and I went to Florida, he did the whole damn thing himself. And it's beautiful." Zach sighed. "I know you and Jackie worry about him, but seriously, man, there's nothing that guy can't do."

It was the doctor in him that worried about Ethan testing his limits. He marveled at the strength of the human spirit. Not only had his brother recovered from the horrific injury, he thrived in spite of it.

A tone sounded in Sebastian's ear signaling a text. Promising to keep Zach updated as to his plans, he disconnected the call, switching over to his texts.

The Sire: All your remaining surgeries have been reassigned. I will handle them myself. Your employment with the hospital has been terminated effective immediately.

Brows up, Sebastian stared at his phone. He supposed his father was trying to show him that he still had some kind of power over him, but that's not what Sebastian saw. Sure, the man was a rat bastard for firing his son, rather than accepting the resignation like a professional, and it bothered Sebastian, it really did. But it also gave him the freedom to leave. Most of his things had already been shipped ahead to Grayson Falls and currently sat in an unused bay of his brother Ryan's garage.

Sebastian opened up his text string with Zach.

Change of plans. I'll be there tomorrow.

He had just started walking again when Zach's replay came.

The Player: Roger that, bro. Piper's had the room ready for weeks.

Smiling, Sebastian continued along. The knot in his stomach loosened and the tension began rolling out of his shoulders. He finally felt like he could break free.

Two

TREES HAD BEGUN to show their autumn colors in Grayson Falls. As he approached the covered bridge that led into town, Sebastian remembered the first time he had seen it. He was terrified to cross it in his shiny, new Lexus SUV. But like the town, the bridge held up. An immense forest with soaring trees replaced the sidewalks and steel buildings as he entered the town.

The hospital he would be working in with his sisters came up first, and he pulled into the parking lot. Instead of a sprawling mass of brick with winding corridors and lots of people, the hospital was housed in an old white Victorian house. His sister, Jackie, was the town's only doctor—until today, that was, when Sebastian was joining the practice. The second and third floors held patient rooms, and the ground floor held exam rooms, a lobby, a very small surgery, and three-bed emergency room. It was a lot of work for two doctors, and his sister had been juggling it on her own with a covering practice of doctors the past few years.

He waved to their battleax of an intake nurse/receptionist, Terry, who greeted him with a single nod and a clipped, "Doctor." Sebastian always thought she would work well with his father. Their friend, Eric Davis, called her Nurse Ratched. Sebastian by-passed the exam rooms where they held regular doctor's appointments and stopped in the doorway of Jackie's office. His sister sat at her desk busy on the computer. Her long blonde curls were pulled up into a messy bun. She wore a black-ribbed turtleneck, and though he couldn't see her legs underneath the desk, he knew she would be wearing scrub bottoms.

Slamming her finger aggressively on a single key of her keyboard, she swore at her monitor. Sebastian crossed his arms over his chest and leaned on the doorframe to watch her for a minute. Jackie was their mother hen. She liked her family close, and now she would have everybody. She and Ryan grew up together on the stock car racing circuit with their famous driver fathers. They hadn't even known they were related until Jackie's father, Jimmy Reilly, died in an accident during a race and Ryan's father revealed they were siblings. After that, Jackie attended boarding school with Ryan, and the two grew close during that time. Ryan was highly protective of their sister—as was her husband, Danny McKenzie, the town's chief of police.

"Dr. Stuart reporting for duty."

When Sebastian finally announced his presence, Jackie's gaze shot up to his, and a big smile spread across her face. Scrambling out from behind the desk, she covered the short distance and threw her arms around him. One thing Sebastian was still adjusting to with these brothers and sister was how affectionate they were. Sebastian wasn't accustomed to sibling physical shows of emotion, but he would work on it.

"You're here! It's real! You're really moving here!"

Giving her a quick squeeze to satisfy her, Sebastian gently extricated himself from Jackie's arms. *This* was home. This family that loved him—that engulfed him with their entire being with their joy to see him. A warmth spread through Sebastian's chest as he watched Jackie wipe her tears away. Tears of joy to see him were shed here, not the stone cold glare he got in Chicago.

His sister stepped back into the office, and Sebastian followed. She looked around and shrugged. "I thought I had more time to get a second desk in here, so we'll have to share for a bit until we can arrange that."

"That's fine." He said. "Don't stress over it. A laptop and the couch work too."

"Maybe in the short-term, but if you're putting in the time, you rate a desk. There will be plenty of days we'll be here together."

"Jackie, I have the records for—" Their sister and Ethan's twin, Natalie, came swinging into the office and stopped short upon seeing him standing there. Natalie was one of the hospital's nurses and a damn fine one too.

"Dr. Stuart!" Her smile was radiant, but Sebastian sighed inside. Natalie had been born Sarah Currie and separated from Ethan. After graduating nursing school, she went on a trip with Doctors Without Borders and while in Mexico, witnessed an assassination by a drug cartel and had to go into the witness protection program. It was Eric Davis who had tracked her down. How he was able to do that through the Marshall's Service, Sebastian didn't know—and didn't want to know. However, he hadn't said a word about Natalie's true identity, only that she was in town. Jackie and Ethan figured it out on their own.

"Nat, don't ever call me 'doctor' again." Not a big hugger himself, Sebastian let his hands fall at his sides. A new doctor wouldn't hug a hospital nurse, even if they were friends first. "It's good to see you."

"You too." Turning to Jackie, Natalie handed her the next patient record. "Jimmy Wheeler is here in room three. Flu symptoms."

Sighing, Jackie took the file. "And so it begins." She gave Sebastian one last peck on the cheek before she walked out to see her next patient. Crossing her arms, Natalie leaned against the doorway, just as Sebastian had done a few minutes earlier. Sebastian put his hands in his pockets and rocked back on his heels, studying his sister. As a blonde, which was her natural hair color, she was a dead ringer for Jackie, but when her hair was brown, as it was now, she looked just like a female version of Ethan.

"So, Zach and I tend to meet most mornings at the diner for breakfast or coffee," she said. "I hope we'll see you there."

"Count on it." Sebastian nodded.

"The breakfast menu has gotten a lot better with healthier choices. Not that it seems to matter to Zach. I think he can eat plastic food containers and still thrive. Of course with the amount of miles he runs in the morning, he just burns it all off."

"Some of us are luckier than others in the metabolism department," Sebastian nodded.

"Well, I've got patients, and I'm sure you've got things you have to do, as well." She pushed off the door. "I'll see you around."

"Count on it." He said again, quieter this time as she left the room.

He looked around the empty office. There was plenty of room for a second desk, and they may even be able to keep the sofa. He noted Jackie took down some wall art, he assumed to make room for Sebastian's diplomas. Even cramped with two desks, it was bigger than the storage-closet-sized office his father had assigned to him at the hospital in Chicago.

Sebastian pulled out his phone and scrolled to his group text with his brothers and Danny and Eric.

Back in town. OTH?

His brothers were expecting his text, and as it was a Saturday, it was easier for them to keep themselves available—not that any of them had a structured schedule anyway. Zach was a retired major league pitcher, who was now working on a charity project. Ryan owned his own business designing stock cars, which he ran out of a second barn on Jackie's property that he had converted into a multi-million-dollar showroom and garage. And after Ethan was discharged from the Marines with his dog, he went to work lovingly nurturing Jackie's small farm back to life. He had expanded it now to include horses, pigs, chickens, and several fields of vegetables and herbs. Ethan had turned it into a nice little business. He had planned on setting up a small market stand down near the hospital where the long wooded driveway into the property began.

Sebastian's brothers' messages started popping up.

The Player: Already here, dude. Started early.

The Racer: On my way!
The Hero: Just about finished. Will meet you there.
The Cop: No nanny on the weekend. Need to bring the baby.
The Mystery Man: Same.

Smiling, Sebastian slid his phone back into his pocket and left the office. Since Over the Hop was only a few buildings down and across the street, he left his car in the parking lot. As he walked, he waved to various people who called out hello to him. From what he understood, small towns usually closed ranks against newcomers and outsiders, but not Grayson Falls. The quaint New England town welcomed him and his siblings with open arms. The women seemed especially fond of Ethan and Danny, despite his newlywed status.

The trees were an autumnal kaleidoscope of color. The air was crisp, and the town was preparing for its annual Pumpkin Festival and Parade. Sebastian had never attended, but he had heard the festival was the biggest and most popular in the area.

When he entered Over the Hop, Laurie, one of the owners, greeted him by name from behind the bar. Feeling like Norm from *Cheers*, he waved back with a smile and joined Zach over in the corner at a large table Zach had already reserved. Standing up with open arms, Zach gave him a welcoming man hug before sitting back down again.

"Where's your better half?" Sebastian asked, referring to Zach's fiancé Piper, who was a well-known artist and owned her own gallery in town.

"Painting," Zach said. "She said she'd see you at the house later. She's making ribs in her crock pot for dinner."

Nodding, Sebastian looked at the menu he already knew by heart. "Then I won't get them here. How are the wedding plans going? Did you decide on a date?"

"Well, since Ryan and Sophie stole Christmas, Piper wants July Fourth, on the baseball field in town, and she wants to hire a professional fireworks company."

Brows up, Sebastian sat back in his seat. "And what does our brother-in-law think of that?"

"What does your brother-in-law think of what?" Danny asked, as he approached the table with his sleeping daughter in some sort of over the chest contraption that freed up Danny's hands. He slid the diaper bag hanging from his shoulder onto the floor next to a chair then slowly eased down to sit.

"Nice purse." Sebastian smirked. Danny shot his middle finger up at Sebastian, as he looked down to make sure he didn't wake the baby.

"You're not talking about the fucking fireworks again, are you?" Danny grumbled.

"Not only will we pay for overtime, but we'll make sizable donations to the fire department and ambulance squad. And we'll also hire the extra security you seem to think a retired pitcher needs." Zach said.

"Dude, you'll have only been retired for a year," Danny reminded him. "Not only that, you weren't just any hack. You were arguably one of the best pitchers in baseball history."

"Aw, don't make me blush." Zach said. Sebastian chuckled. Danny shot his middle finger up at Zach and the baby stirred at the action which, caused Danny to glower more.

"You were also part of a very successful charity auction where your little lady sold paintings of various parts of your body." Danny continued. "There's going to be people showing up that weren't invited."

"The whole town is invited." Zach sat back in his chair, picked up his beer, and took a long pull.

"Exactly," Danny said. "That alone is a logistical nightmare without people from out-of-town showing up."

"It's what Piper wants."

"I know." Danny said, exhaling a breath. "Just give me some time to absorb it and think it over. You only just told me about it last week. Besides, Piper doesn't even like big crowds and lots of attention."

"No, you're right." Zach agreed. "But she wanted to give back to the town. She grew up here, and this town has been very supportive of her. She wants to show her appreciation."

Zach's fiancée lost her hearing during an especially bad illness that had her in the hospital when she was in college. But she was a strong, independent woman, and the people that knew her and loved her rallied around her to ensure she would be successful. Several business owners, including Jackie and Danny, had learned sign language so Piper could communicate with people with more ease. Since Zach fell in love with her, his siblings had also started learning it, as well.

Sebastian felt a hand slide over his shoulders. When he looked up to see who it was, Laurie, smiled back. "If it isn't Dr. Delicious finally come home."

"Don't swell his head." Zach said.

"What was that, Perfect Porter?" Laurie asked, squinting her eyes. "What can I get you boys?" Something caught her eye outside, and she looked up. "Here come the others."

Looking out the window, Sebastian saw Ryan, Ethan, and Eric with his daughter Emma on their way in. One of the things he loved most about his family was that they immediately came when called. They were there for each other, be it a homecoming, a baby born, illness or injury—or just in want of someone to have a beer and lunch with.

Eric settled his daughter Emma—currently dressed as some princess Sebastian couldn't identify—in a chair between himself and Ethan. Emma immediately flung herself into Ethan's arms. Ethan and Natalie, who lived together, frequently babysat for Emma when Eric was away on business. Ryan clapped Sebastian on the back and took the chair next to him. Once they were all settled, Laurie returned to take their drink orders.

Sebastian turned to Danny. "When did you hire a nanny?"

"A couple of weeks ago." Danny said, running a hand over the baby's back. Sebastian smiled. He delivered that little girl for Danny and Jackie. She was the first—and so far only—baby he had ever delivered. With the move, he had planned to change the focus of his practice to pediatrics and ease himself away from surgery. "I don't think you've met her. Her name is Megan. She used to work at the library, but they let her go when their budget was slashed. She's been great so far."

Sebastian wondered if it was the girl he had met in the library last fall. She was beautiful, but he remembered her eyes were haunted. She was also cold toward him. It was almost like she took an instant dislike to him. It was a strange encounter. He hoped she had gotten over whatever was wrong that day. If they were both going to be in close proximity to Danny and Jackie, he didn't want things to be awkward.

Turning to Danny, Sebastian waved his fingers in a "come here" gesture. "Give me the baby."

"No."

"I want to hold her in that thing." Sebastian was aware there was a near whine to his voice, but dammit, he had a connection to the little girl his other siblings didn't—well, other than Natalie, who also assisted in the delivery.

"When she wakes up," Danny denied.

"I delivered her," Sebastian argued, as Laurie served their drinks.

"I *created* her."

Sebastian curled his lip. "Let's not talk about that."

"She had a tough night." Danny said. "She needs her sleep. When she wakes up, *on her own*, you can hold her."

Sebastian let out a sigh. He reached out to stroke her little cheek with a gentle finger and scowled when Danny slapped him back. Picking up his glass, Sebastian smiled and shook his head. As he drank, his one thought was, *it's good to be home.*

Three

MEGAN MILLER UNLOCKED the front door of Danny and Jackie's house early and quietly let herself in. Pausing, she listened to see if anyone was awake and moving around yet. When she could detect no noise, she hung up her coat, changed out of her shoes and into her comfy faux fur-lined slippers, and padded into the kitchen. She didn't know if Danny or Jackie had a late night, but both cars were in the driveway, so she knew they were both still home.

At home in the house, she moved around the kitchen grabbing ingredients and various bowls to begin making breakfast. Cooking for them wasn't part of her job, but she liked to do it anyway. She was so grateful they had given her a chance that she tried to show her appreciation whenever she could. Turning on the kitchen baby monitor, she noted little Ally still sleeping in her crib and got to work.

It would be Belgian waffles this morning. Pulling the waffle maker out, she set it on the counter, plugged it in, then moved to the coffeemaker to get that going. Crossing to another cabinet, she pulled out her herbal tea. Not being allowed caffeine sometimes truly sucked, but she had gotten used to drinking the decaffeinated tea.

Movement on the monitor had her looking over to the screen. Danny had gone into the baby's room to check on her. Shirtless and wearing plaid pajama pants, he leaned down and rested his hand on the baby's back. Jackie truly was a lucky woman to have a man so engaged. Danny disappeared from the screen, and Megan moved to the refrigerator to pull out the fresh fruit.

She was just pouring the batter onto the waffle maker when Danny entered the kitchen wearing jeans, a hooded sweatshirt, and his police badge hanging around his neck. Danny only wore a uniform for official police events. He liked to be approachable to the people of the town, and she knew the people of Grayson Falls appreciated that.

"You're spoiling us." He retrieved a large coffee mug. "But hell if I'm going to stop you from doing it."

Chuckling, Megan took a sip of her tea and leaned up against the counter opposite her boss. "Rough night?" She asked when he ran a hand down his face.

"Not so bad," he shrugged. "It was just hard to get out of bed this morning." The light smile and dreamy look in his eyes told her exactly what kept him in bed that morning. The baby started to fuss, but before Danny could push off the counter to go upstairs, Jackie appeared on the monitor dressed in her own uniform of a long-sleeved shirt and scrub bottoms. Cooing, she picked the baby up and disappeared from view.

Smiling at Danny's dopey grin, Megan turned back to the counter and flipped the waffle iron over. Danny was the type of guy every girl dreamed of, at least in Megan's opinion. Handsome, attentive, charming, completely in love with his wife and daughter, with just a little bit of badass bad boy left over from his younger days. He was known amongst the women in town as Chief Hottie.

Megan plated the first waffle and handed it to him with a side of fruit. Just as Danny put his breakfast on the table, Jackie came in with the baby, who was already secured in a little chair that vibrated and bounced when she kicked. Jackie placed the baby and chair on the table away from the edge and moved to the kitchen. Distracted by his daughter, Danny walked over to tickle her toes and say good morning. Ally smiled broadly at her father. He then crossed to his wife to kiss her as she reached for a coffee mug, which he plucked off the shelf for her.

"Megan is making Belgian waffles," he said, before turning around and sitting down at the table.

"You didn't have to do that," Jackie said turning to Megan. Before she could respond, Danny replied, "Shut up, say thank you, and sit down and eat."

Jackie rolled her eyes at her gruff husband. "Thank you," she said to Megan. "We really appreciate all that you do. I just don't want you to think cooking for us is expected."

"It's my pleasure to do it when the schedule allows," Megan said. "I enjoy it."

Megan turned quickly before Jackie could look at her too long. Having spent her life in and out of hospitals, Megan grew uncomfortable around doctors. When she met one outside of their office, she always felt as if they were evaluating her, looking for signs of illness, even when they weren't. She was still getting used to Jackie and was determined to overcome her issues. Megan liked Jackie. She found her to be sweet, smart, and she didn't take shit from anyone. She was a strong woman loved by her family and her patients.

"Well, I'm especially appreciative this morning," Jackie said, taking her plate from Megan and joining her husband and daughter at the table. "My brother is starting at the hospital today, and there's still so much to do. He was supposed to start in two weeks, but he was able to come to us early."

"Your brother?" Megan asked, tensing up. "Is that Dr. Stuart? I thought he lived in, Chicago, was it?" Megan kept her back turned as she took a deep breath.

"Yes, but he's moving here. He arrived yesterday and is staying with Zach and Piper. He was waiting until his grandparents moved to Florida and got settled." Jackie explained, while taking a sip of her coffee.

Vigorously scrubbing the counter to keep her attention diverted, Megan thought back to her one and only meeting with the handsome doctor, who her cousin Laurie at Over the Hop dubbed 'Dr. Delicious.' Megan had been working at the library at the time, and Dr. Stuart had come in looking to apply for a library card. He had caught Megan on a bad day, and, of course, she assumed he was diagnosing her—in her defense, he *had* commented that she looked pale.

And given that she had just had an episode before he came in, it was no wonder. If he had been just five minutes earlier, he would have found her short of breath and trying to slow her heart down. The disease was progressing, and she had some difficult decisions ahead of her.

Stepping to the sink, she turned on the faucet to start the dishes. Danny plucked the plate she was holding and gently nudged her out of the way. "You are not the housekeeper. You cooked, we clean."

Megan stepped back and pressed a hand to her forehead. "Sorry. Habit."

"Thanks to you, we have plenty of time to clean up breakfast," Danny said, taking the sponge from her hand and gently easing her away from the counter.

Downing the rest of her coffee, Jackie rose from her chair. "Not me," she said. "Too much going on at work, and that's without the patients." Jackie placed her mug into the sink, pecked Danny on the cheek with a quick, "Thanks, babe," and moved to love up Ally before calling out her goodbyes and heading for the door.

"Dammit, she did it again," Danny said, watching his wife tear out of the driveway. Megan chuckled and leaned against the counter to drink her tea.

No sooner had Jackie left then the front door swung open again, and Megan's laughter died. Dr. Delicious himself strolled in, making a beeline for the baby. Right before he unclasped her restraints, Danny stopped him.

"Wash your hands, Doc," Danny ordered.

"I used hand sanitizer before I came in. I'm no dummy," Sebastian argued.

"Not in front of me, you didn't," Danny countered.

Sebastian rolled his eyes. "I feel sorry for the poor guy that comes to take her out on a date." He stepped in the direction of the sink but stopped when he spotted Megan. She watched in dismay as Danny left the kitchen to go finish getting ready for work.

Megan's heart began to beat faster, but for an entirely different reason. Taking deep breaths, she attempted to calm herself down. The last thing she wanted to do was trigger the doctor in him. It was a relief that not many people in town knew about her illness. She didn't want people looking at her with a wary eye or sympathy. She'd had enough of that in her life.

"Hello, again, Megan" he said, cocking his head to the side. "Do you remember me?"

Did she remember him? What kind of question was that? A girl didn't tend to forget someone that looked like him.

"Yes, of course, Dr. Stuart," Megan said, stepping away from the counter to allow him to wash his hands. "Welcome to Grayson Falls. I hear you're going to make this your home."

"It's been my home for a while now." Sebastian smiled at her. "Home is where the heart is, right?"

Now why did he have to go and say something so utterly charming?

Sebastian dried his hands and moved back to the baby. She cooed and kicked and waved her fists around when she saw him. Megan couldn't help but smile at the baby's excitement to see her uncle. Gently, he picked her up and placed her against his chest. The baby pushed back to grab at his face and hair. She seemed to like it when Sebastian rubbed his closely shaved beard against her sweet cheeks.

Pressing a hand against her heart, Megan sighed. *Boy, did that man look good holding a baby.*

Danny returned now with his gun strapped on, shoes on, and shoving his keys in his pocket. Stopping to press a kiss to the baby's head, he then ran a gentle finger down her cheek. Ally immediately grabbed onto her father's finger and laughed in delight.

"Damn, you're hard to leave," Danny said, then looked up at Megan. "I'll be by to check in later."

"We'll be here," she smiled. They didn't often leave the house except for walks in the stroller. When Ally was older, Megan supposed she'd start taking her to the park or the library for story hour, but for now, the baby was much too young for that kind of thing.

When Danny left the house, Megan was alone with the baby and Sebastian. She turned away to look for something to do. Finding the kitchen clean, she looked back at the man who seemed to take up the whole kitchen.

"You know, I delivered her," he murmured, as Ally laid her head on his shoulder and her eyes grew heavy.

"I didn't know that."

"It was the best moment of my career—of my life, really." He pressed a gentle kiss to the baby's head, and Megan's heart fluttered. Normally, that wasn't a good sign, but she knew now it had nothing to do with her condition. What was it about good looking men holding babies? They were as dangerous as men in uniform. "I was the first person in the world this baby saw. There's something amazing in that." He began to sway as Ally's eyes closed.

"You're good with her," Megan noted.

"Think so?" he asked. "That's nice to say." Gently, he laid the baby back down into her chair and strapped her in. Turning, he put his hands in his pockets, rocked back on his heels, and cocked his head to the side. "How are you?"

Her jaw and spine tightened, and her walls automatically went up. "And why do you want to know, *doctor*?"

"Okay, see, you did that to me last time we met, too," he said, pulling his hand out of his pocket and pointing a finger. "Asking you how you're doing was just the normal flow of conversation, 'Hey, how are you?' 'Good, and you?' I didn't mean anything offensive by it. In fact, I'm not sure how one can get offended by it."

Megan dropped her head and shook it back and forth. He was right. He couldn't know how that simple, polite question would touch a nerve. She raised her head. "You're right. I apologize."

"Is it all men or just me?"

"The truth is I tend to get on edge around doctors," she said. "They don't always have good news, you know?" She wouldn't explain anymore but would just let him draw his own conclusions.

"Delivering bad news is the worst part of the job," he said quietly. He didn't push, and she was grateful. "Well, hopefully, I can at least convince you not to paint us all with the same brush." He flashed a charming smile that gave him a devious, boyish look, and she had to admit, she softened. If she wasn't very careful, she'd fall under the charms of Dr. Delicious.

Four

SEBASTIAN'S THOUGHTS WAVERED back and forth between finding his rhythm at the hospital and his sister's delectable nanny. She wasn't his type—conservatively dressed, stand-offish, elusive. Sebastian had always dated the more sophisticated type, always put together, slim, well-dressed, rich. The type of woman that was more looks than substance—one he had no chance at having a real future with. He always thought that it was his hospital schedule that kept him from meaningful relationships, but he had discovered it was his intent not to stay in Chicago after his grandparents left. Until a couple of years ago, he wouldn't have thought he would end up in Grayson Falls—or even New Hampshire for that matter. He had his eye on Boston, which was only a few hours away now. It was funny how things could change so drastically, and yet, still feel so right.

"Hey, there," Natalie said. Sebastian looked up from where he had been crouched on the floor unpacking medical textbooks he brought with him.

Natalie approached him with her hands behind her back and a wicked gleam in her eyes. He knew her well enough to think she might be up to something.

"Hey, yourself," Sebastian said, straightening up. "Sorry I missed breakfast with you and Zach. I snuck over for some baby time."

"She's a hard baby to resist," Natalie nodded in understanding.

"What are you hiding behind your back?" Sebastian asked, gesturing behind her.

Natalie pulled a patient record out and presented it like Vanna White revealing the letter B. "This is the record of Esther Kennedy, but everyone around here calls her Nana Kennedy. She's a frequent customer. She comes in for every hangnail. We play along because we think she's just lonely. Her grandkids own Over the Hop, but they're busy during the day. However, Laurie is here with her now. She thinks Nana has an actual problem. It seems Nana has tenderness under her breasts, but she won't let Laurie see. Jackie thought you should start meeting our regular patients. She ran home to feed the baby."

Furrowing his brow, Sebastian glanced through the record. He knew appointments like these were par for the course in a small town. In fact, he welcomed it. He wanted to be the kind of doctor that knew his patients—one that saw them through every illness and injury, even if they were just scrapes and sniffles.

He looked back up at Natalie, who looked highly suspicious and all too amused.

"What's going on?" He was apprehensive. It would be just like his sisters to give him a little hazing on his first day.

Natalie shook her head. "You'll like Nana Kennedy, and she'll love you, *Dr. Delicious.*"

Groaning, Sebastian rolled his eyes to the ceiling. "Tell me that is not catching on."

"Like a wild fire."

Natalie's wide grin told him she was getting much too much enjoyment at his expense. Well, he determined, even sisters that wouldn't acknowledge their relationship to you could annoy their older brothers. No matter, he welcomed the interaction.

"All right," he said as he began to walk and waved with the file for her to follow. "You're with me."

"What, why?"

Gesturing to himself with the file, he said, "Male doctor, female patient. A female nurse has to be in the room."

Natalie led him to the appropriate exam room and stopped outside to squirt hand sanitizer on her hands before entering the room. Sebastian did the same. When they entered the exam room, familiarity greeted him. They were all the same. Exam table, desk, cabinets with supplies and rolling chairs. However, instead of the standard linoleum, these rooms had hardwood floors. Painted wainscoting along the walls and soft butter-yellow paint gave the room a more homey feeling than the standard impersonal feel he was used to.

Nana Kennedy was perched on the exam table with Laurie standing next her, running a hand along her grandmother's shoulders. A plump woman with gray hair and wrinkles, Nana had kind and loving eyes. Sebastian's own grandmother was spry and tiny. Still trim from her years of yoga, his grandmother had always believed once you stopped moving, you began to fossilize. Nana Kennedy looked like she had been fossilizing for a few decades now. Sebastian offered his hand, and Nana Kennedy took it, giving him a gummy smile.

"Nana," Laurie said. "This is Dr. Stuart. He's Dr. McKenzie's brother and has just moved here from Chicago."

Pausing, Nana began to rummage through her bag. When she pulled her hand out Sebastian saw she held her teeth. Giving them a good shake, she replaced them in her mouth.

"You're right, dear," Nana said to her granddaughter. "He is delicious."

Sebastian sat down on the rolling stool in the room and clasped his hands in front of him, determined not to react to the flirting. "So, Mrs. Kennedy, what brings you in today?"

"Oh, please, doctor, call me Nana. No one calls me Mrs. Kennedy anymore."

"All right," Sebastian nodded. "Please explain what's going on."

"Well," Nana let out a long sigh. "Things just hurt under the girls here. It's uncomfortable when I move around."

"How long has this been going on?"

"About a week now."

Sebastian stood up and reached for a pair of gloves and pulled them on. "Okay. I'm going to need to take a look. Are you able to undress on your own?"

"Laurie can help me," Nana said. She gave Sebastian a wink. "She's such a sweet girl, hardworking. And single." Laurie didn't even blush. She met Sebastian's eyes with confidence and even went so far as to mimic Nana's wink.

Sebastian suppressed the urge to react in any way. He was used to older women telling him all about their daughters and granddaughters and being blatantly flirted with. Doctors were still considered good marriage material—although Sebastian never understood why. They were always working and never home.

Once Nana had her shirt off, Laurie unclasped her bra in the back and gently pulled it down her arms. Nana wasn't the slightest bit shy or embarrassed about sitting before Sebastian topless. Women often were when exposed before a male doctor. They didn't seem to understand that the human body to a doctor was merely just that—the human body.

Just as Sebastian was about to move in for his physical exam, Nana reached her left hand across her body to cup her right breast. A quarter dropped out and rolled along the floor before coming to a stop in the corner. Shifting her breast up—to Sebastian's utter shock—she began to remove more things from under her breast with a wince and a hiss. Out came tissues, cash, a mint, a small battery. Under the other breast were more tissues, a hair tie, lipstick, and seventy-five cents in quarters. Sebastian ran a hand down his face and stopped, cupping his mouth. He wasn't sure if he was trying to hide his shock or humor, but this definitely ranked a first for him.

Natalie—ever the professional—opened a drawer at the counter and retrieved a plastic bag they gave medications out in. Wordlessly, she put all the miscellaneous items Nana Kennedy apparently carried around in her bra into the plastic bag. Laurie hung her head, shaking it back and forth.

"Seriously, Nana?" She asked. "That's what purses are for!"

"They hurt my shoulder." Nana waved off.

"And what if that battery had leaked?" Laurie challenged. Nana ignored her and looked back at Sebastian.

Wordlessly, Sebastian gently lifted the breast to examine the affected area.

"This is the most action I've seen in thirty years," Nana quipped. Sebastian chuckled Nana was definitely growing on him. Moving over to the underside of the other breast, the skin was red, raw, blistered, and even scabbed in one spot. It was amazing she could even tolerate wearing a bra at all.

Sebastian stepped back and removed his gloves with a snap. "Natalie is going to wash the affected area and apply a medicated cream. You are to do that every day, Nana, and refrain from wearing a bra for the next week. You have to give the skin time to heel. Save hiding cash in your bra for the strippers."

Nana threw back her head and shouted with laughter. "Oh, you are a rascal." She said with delight. Sebastian shook her hand again and ducked out of the room.

Jackie was in the hallway, giving one of their other nurses instructions. The hospital had five nurses that worked each day—the receptionist/intake nurse, two assigned to the exam rooms, and two upstairs taking care of the admitted patients. The hospital employed a total of seven nurses.

Sebastian walked over and leaned against the counter. "Be honest," he said. "Were you hazing me with Nana Kennedy?"

Shaking her head, Jackie smiled. "Afraid not. I really did have to go feed the baby. What was it this time?"

"I don't even want to go there."

"Well, Mr. Johnson is in room two," Jackie said, handing him the record she was holding. "He could use your considerable surgical skills, big brother."

"What's his story?" Sebastian tipped his head to look at the file.

"He fishes with Piper's Uncle Joe," Jackie said. "Today, he somehow got a lure stuck in his neck."

Sebastian studied his sister carefully. She looked completely serious. "Are you paying actors to come in here today with odd things wrong with them?"

Shaking her head, she pat his shoulder. "Welcome to small town medicine, Dr. Delicious."

MEGAN DROPPED DOWN onto a bar stool at Over the Hop, and Laurie put a glass of herbal decaffeinated tea in front of her. Taking a deep inhale, Megan propped her chin up on her elbow and slowly let her breath back out.

"Tough day with the baby?" Laurie asked.

Megan shook her head. Ally was an easy baby. Sure, she got fussy, but Megan was coming to know her different cries well so she could see to Ally's needs quickly. She adored that job. "Just tired, I guess."

Feeling Laurie's scrutiny, Megan sat up and took a sip of her drink.

"What *kind* of tired?" Laurie asked.

Megan gave a small smile. "I believe it's of the normal variety. I feel okay, just dragging a little bit today."

"You'd tell me if it was the other kind of tired, right?"

"Yes, mom."

Laurie chuckled and moved about behind the bar, while Megan pondered what she felt like eating. She hadn't made it to the store in the last few days, so there weren't many options at home. The brewery was quiet tonight. The rain was keeping people home.

"If you're feeling up to it," Laurie said, "I could use some help later in the week. One of my waitresses decided to move to Maine with her boyfriend suddenly. I think she's knocked up and afraid to tell her parents."

"Charming," Megan said. "I can help." *And I could use the money,* she thought. She didn't make much money when she worked at the library—and she did better working for the McKenzies now—but she had accumulated some debt. Paying it off was getting difficult. She welcomed the open shifts at Over the Hop.

Laurie served some drinks and came back to Megan. "Chili's good today," she said.

"It's cold enough for it, too," Megan said. "Sounds good. I'll take it loaded with shredded cheddar, onions, and sour cream."

"Onions." Laurie shuddered. "I guess you're not planning on kissing anyone anytime soon, eh?"

"Who am I going to kiss?" Megan challenged. It had been years since she had a date.

"I don't know, Dr. Delicious looks appetizing," Laurie said. "He certainly made my heart go pitter pat."

"I thought you were on a man embargo."

"I am," Laurie said with a shrug. "It doesn't mean I can't window shop. He was looking gorgeous today when I took Nana in. The boys in that family have some damn fine genes."

Frowning, Megan shook her head. "You brought Nana in? Is there something wrong?" Though Laurie was Megan's cousin, Nana wasn't a shared grandmother between them. But Nana was always there growing up, and Megan and her brothers considered her a third grandmother to them. Nana treated them like her own grandchildren.

Laurie relayed the story of Nana's earlier visit, and Megan chuckled and rolled her eyes. That was Nana Kennedy to a T, right down to hitting on Sebastian. The thought of Sebastian and breasts made her face warm up. She pretended to be avidly interested in the baseball game on the TV, so Laurie wouldn't see her blush.

"Is this seat taken?" Turning, Megan smiled at her brother, Gabe. Tall, muscled, and the same hair and eye color as Megan, Gabe was a full-time fireman down in Berlin and took volunteer shifts here in Grayson Falls.

"It's all yours," Megan said. Gabe never nagged her about her health. He left that up to their parents. Megan knew it took a great amount of restraint on his part as he had always been a nurturer.

"There's a handsome guy," Laurie greeted, setting down a pint of beer in front of Gabe. Laurie was born for this kind of life. She knew all her regular customers' preferred orders. Megan didn't drink beer. Alcohol didn't mix well with her medications and her disease, but she could bet, whenever she came in, Laurie would put in front of her either a decaffeinated soda or herbal tea, depending on the time of day.

"I'm hungry, woman!" Gabe bellowed, thumping his chest. "What is my sister eating?"

"Chili loaded."

Gabe pointed a finger at Laurie. "Supersize it."

"Back from your 48-hour shift now?" Megan asked her brother as he took a long pull of his beer. Gabe nodded and set his glass down on the shaved ice strip cut into the bar top to keep his drink cold. "Was it quiet?"

Gabe gave a half-laugh. "A 48-hour shift is never quiet." He shrugged. "Still, not too bad, I suppose."

"You know, I worry about you," she said. Turning on his stool, Gabe looked at her with a raised eyebrow. Rolling her eyes, Megan pulled her plate toward her after Laurie put it down in front of her. She picked up her spoon and mixed up her chili in the bowl that sat on the plate. "I know. It goes both ways. I feel fine. Tired today, but good."

Turning back to the bar, Gabe took another sip of his beer. "I like that you're working for a doctor. I know you're not with the doctor all day, but it does give me piece of mind. She can watch out for you, you know?"

"Maybe if she knew there was a problem," Megan said softly. Gabe's food arrived, but he didn't touch it. Instead, he turned and stared at her. Megan felt the tension around them thicken.

"You haven't told them?" He hissed. "You're watching their kid all day. What if something happens?"

"I'll call 9-1-1 if I need to," she shrugged.

"What if you can't?"

"Well, they both stop in throughout the day to check on the baby. If it were something really awful, they'd find me." And then she'd most definitely be screwed. They'd never trust her with Ally again—assuming she'd live through the hypothetical situation.

"They deserve to know, Megan." Gabe said. "I know you're not required to tell them, but in this case, you need to. They need to understand if they contact you and you don't answer, there could be a very big problem and that the reason isn't just that you can't get to the phone because you're changing the baby."

Gabe placed his hand on hers and Megan looked up into his eyes. She thought she'd see anger there, but it was worse. She saw great concern in his eyes, and she instantly felt contrite when she realized she worried him even more. Gabe was on her team. Maybe he secretly wished she would live with their parents and go through life in a bubble attached to a heart monitor, but he supported her and her need to actually live a life. As long as she was careful in her physical exertion and activities—and he could be sure she was being smart—he stayed her champion.

She also knew that would all change in a heartbeat if he thought for a second that she was doing anything that jeopardized her health.

"What if they fire me?" Megan whispered miserably. She pulled out of his grasp and turned back to her meal. She poked her spoon in her chili a few times, releasing the pungent smell of spices before finally taking a heaping spoonful.

"That's their decision to make," he said, diving into his own huge bowl. It looked like Gabe may have been served half the vat himself. She shook her head wondering how he could eat as much as he did and still maintain his slim physique. "They seem like decent people, though."

"They are," she nodded.

"Then maybe if you explain it to them, they'll understand," he suggested. "After all, she *is* a doctor."

Megan nodded and poked at her chili some more, swirling her spoon around the bowl, mixing up the cheddar cheese and watching as it melted in the heat. She liked her job. Kids wouldn't ever be an option for her. She wouldn't be able to survive a pregnancy, and no adoption agency would give her a child. Spending time with Ally filled a void she didn't realize she had until she took that job.

She would never truly be out of a job. Laurie would take her here in a heartbeat. She filled in waitressing, but Megan also knew they were looking for a restaurant manager to oversee the staffing, inventory, advertising, merchandising, and the like. They wanted to expand the business and needed help.

Over the Hop was owned by Laurie, her brother David, and Megan and Gabe's brother Justin. David was the brewmaster, and Justin was the chef and ran the kitchen. Laurie was in charge of the restaurant. Over the Hop gained in popularity quickly. They sold beer in growlers, but were starting to talk about canning and bottling for local distribution. People came from other towns to visit the only microbrewery in the area.

She wasn't too proud to take a job here, but Megan wanted to feel like she was making it on her own and not as a charity case. It was important to her to stand on her own two feet and feel like her life was *hers*. She didn't want to exist—she wanted to *live*.

Five

A COLD WHOOSH of air and hard smack on the ass woke Sebastian. He peeked one eye open to see his brother standing in his dark room dressed for a run, the light from the hallway shining in around his body in the doorway. Closing his eye again, Sebastian burrowed back into his pillow.

"Fuck off and give me my blankets back," he muttered.

"Up, doc! If you want to meet Nat at the diner for breakfast, you need to get your lazy ass out of bed now," Zach bellowed.

"Must you yell?" Sebastian groaned. "Aren't you afraid of waking up your fiancée?"

"She's up and in her studio, having already done an hour of yoga. Also, Piper's deaf. Me bellowing at your lazy ass isn't going to bother her." Zach said. "Let's go. Things start early around here."

"Why?" *Dear lord, what was wrong with these people?*

"She likes the morning light for painting," Zach shrugged. "Why would I stay in bed if she's not going to be in it?"

Sebastian could hardly fault that particular logic, however, since he wasn't currently sleeping with a woman regularly, he was just fine staying in his warm bed and sleeping until a much more civilized hour. It was still dark out for the love of Pete. Pulling his pillow over his head, Sebastian closed his eyes.

"You're going to miss Nat if you don't get up."

Huffing, Sebastian flung the pillow off his face. "I see her at work." He would never get back to sleep now. The only recourse was to get up and kick his brother's ass. After that, he'd make finding his own place a priority. He was calling a relator *today*. It was foolish to think his brother wouldn't come bang on his door, but at least Sebastian had the option of not answering—or calling the police to report a disturbance.

Sebastian sat up with a string of curses. Who the hell went running at six in the morning?

"Five minutes!" Zach called as he left the room. Sebastian stuck his middle finger up at his brother's departing back. Sebastian was not a morning person, and so, he pushed himself out of bed with more annoyance and aggression than needed and huffed about, turning on the lamp and slamming drawers open and closed as he pulled out workout gear. It was October in the Great North Woods. It was going to be frigid out there—not as cold as Chicago would be, of course, but cold nonetheless. When temperatures dropped, Sebastian usually moved his workouts indoors. This was inhumane.

He was clearly being punished for something. He wasn't entirely sure Jackie wasn't pulling one over on him with all the nutty patients, but Zach was retired. Why would he get up at five a.m. to do an hour of yoga followed by a run? He could do that at the nice, pleasant hour of nine or ten a.m. There was no reason for this idiocy.

He found his brother in the kitchen, leaning up against the counter and sipping from a coffee mug. "Ready, princess?"

"Fuck off."

"Was there a pea under your mattress? You seem a little cranky."

Lacing up his shoes, Sebastian ignored his brother's jab. When he straightened up, he motioned toward the front door. "Let's get this fuckery over with."

With a chuckle, Zach led Sebastian out of the house, and after a few minutes of stretching for Sebastian, they set out. While they followed Zach's course, Sebastian tried to set a punishing pace. If he was miserable, he was going to make damn sure his brother was, too. After all, wasn't that what siblings were for? Zach didn't say a word—not once did he complain. After a few miles, Sebastian began to wonder if maybe his pace wasn't as punishing for Zach as it was for him. Wouldn't that just fuck all—shallow breaths, burning calves, pouring sweat, and Zach couldn't care less. For crap's sake, he was running an eight-minute mile!

When they reached the diner after three miles, they stretched out their legs before going in. Natalie was already seated in a booth facing the door, sipping her coffee, and reading a newspaper she had spread open in front of her. She arched an eyebrow when she saw Sebastian.

"And how on earth did Zach get you out of bed this early?" She asked as they slid in the booth across from her and Maisy, the diner owner, put down two steaming mugs of coffee and two glasses of water in front of them.

"By being obnoxious," Sebastian grumbled, picking up his coffee. "No one should have to get up this early for exercise."

"Mmm ..." Natalie said, turning the page of the paper. "Ethan had a little trouble this morning. It seems cold air bothers his stump. He was up bright and early though, heading over to feed the animals like he does every morning rain or shine, cold or hot. I swear, I don't what could possibly stop that man."

"Low blow," Sebastian muttered into his mug. This was a day he needed his coffee black. He was going to need to operate on a higher octane if he was expected to make it through the day.

Natalie shook her head slowly and motioned with her mug. "Just an observation," she said, before taking a sip. She carefully put her mug down out of the way and folded up the newspaper she was poring over as she saw Maisy approach with their food.

Natalie had a Belgian waffle placed in front of her with a side of sausage. Zach's plate contained what looked like every breakfast item on the menu. Maisy slid a bowl of oatmeal with fresh berries and cinnamon in front of Sebastian.

Befuddled, he said, "I didn't order this. In fact, I didn't order anything."

"You're a doctor," Maisy said, matter-of-factly. "This is a healthy menu choice."

"Yeah, but that doesn't mean I don't like bacon," Sebastian protested, as Zach dove into his breakfast mountain with gusto. This morning was getting crappier and crappier. Could he not get a break *anywhere*? Maisy arched a slow brow at him, and he instantly felt ungrateful. She had gone through the trouble to bring him a breakfast she thought he would like ... wait a minute ... what happened to getting what you *asked* for in a restaurant!?

"I could bring you a side of bacon if you wish, *doctor*," Maisy said with a long sigh. "If you want your new patients to see you setting such a bad example, then it's not my never mind." Maisy turned on her heel and sailed away.

Sebastian turned to look at his siblings. "What patients? We're the only ones in here."

"You are a crab ass in the morning, aren't you?" Natalie said. "No wonder you asked Jackie for the second shift."

"Yeah, I thought doctors were used to getting less sleep," Zach put in around a mouthful of pancakes.

"We are," Sebastian hissed, leaning toward his brother. "Which is why we don't like getting interrupted when we finally *do* get to sleep!"

Natalie took the little plate her side of sausage came on and slid it at her brother. "Here, eat that. Stat."

Sebastian dropped his head into one hand. "No, no, I like this. It may not be what I was in the mood for this morning, but it's good recovery food after a workout." He looked longingly at Zach's breakfast, which was quickly disappearing. "I didn't sleep well last night, and I'm not typically an early-riser. I'm sorry for being so cranky."

Shrugging, Natalie pulled her plate back.

Trying to muster up some excitement over his breakfast, Sebastian dug in as the door chimed a new customer. He took a sip of coffee just as Zach said, "Hey, there, Megan."

Sputtering his coffee, Sebastian coughed violently. Zach started pounding on his back. *Nothing like giving yourself away, you idiot.*

"Are you okay, Dr. Stuart?" He could hear Megan's voice, and he was mortified by his reaction. He nodded his head and gratefully took the water Natalie offered him as Megan moved to sit at the counter, one wary eye still trained on him. Drinking deeply of the water, Sebastian took a few deep breaths and sputtered a few coughs then wiped his watering eyes. Taking a deep breath, he tried to slow his breathing. Were his palms sweating?

"Went down the wrong pipe, huh?" Zach said.

"When I worked in an ER, we used to say, 'Went down Tuesday pipe and it's only Monday!'" Natalie said. Zach laughed. Sebastian glared.

After clearing his throat, he took another sip of water. Things seemed back to normal in his body. Tipping his head in Megan's direction, Sebastian lowered his voice and asked, "Does she come in here a lot at this time?" *In for a penny, in for a pound and all that.*

Natalie shrugged a shoulder. "Often enough. I know she makes breakfast for Jackie and Danny a lot, so she probably eats there, too. She does like the egg white omelets here though."

Sebastian filed that little bit of information away. He checked the time on his Fitbit. He could probably swing breakfast at the diner a few mornings a week at this time, but he'd be damned if he was going to get up and go for a run first. That was just uncivilized.

Stealing glances at Megan, Sebastian finished his breakfast slowly. She intrigued him. Dressed in yoga pants, sneakers, and a hoodie, Sebastian assumed that was her uniform for spending the day with a baby. She intrigued him. No more skin than necessary showed from her clothes. Did she order the egg white omelet? She had ear buds in. What was she listening to? A morning radio show, a podcast?

By the time Megan finished her breakfast and left, Sebastian's oatmeal had long gone cold. His brother and sister were lingering over coffee, seemingly amused by his complete inattention to them. He could expect some good-natured ribbing about that in the future.

The apartment Sebastian wandered through that afternoon was the entire second floor in an old Victorian. Large-planked hardwood floors complemented high ceilings and custom crown molding. The living room had a brick fireplace and hand-carved mantle. A large picture window gave him a beautiful view of the town and the changing leaves. The kitchen was an adequate size for one person, and the apartment had two bedrooms. There was no dining room, but the kitchen was big enough to fit a small table and really, how much room did one guy need to eat? There was a deck outside the kitchen large enough for a grill and table and chairs. It was a few blocks away from the hospital, so he could walk to anything he needed in good weather.

Sebastian stopped in the living room and turned slowly around, giving it all one more look-over. It really was a charming place and not anything like his slick, modern apartment in Chicago. In fact, it was the polar opposite.

He loved it.

"When is it available?" He asked.

"Today, if you want it," the Realtor said. "As you can see, it's empty. The lease is month to month and the security deposit is two months' rent."

Nodding in response, Sebastian looked around and tried to envision the room with furniture in it. He had sold most of his stuff before moving from Chicago. It all had the modern city feel to it, and he knew he would be looking for things that were more cozy and homey here. He was envisioning large, overstuffed leather furniture for the living room. The smaller bedroom would make a good office. He had kept his queen-sized bedroom set, but he would find new bedding. He also kept his office furniture.

And a cat. He wanted a cat. His work hours weren't conducive for a dog, but a cat wouldn't care. Yes, a cat would make a great roommate.

He and the realtor walked into the kitchen, and using the countertop, Sebastian signed the lease, briefly wondering what the chances were of the owner selling him the whole house. It might make a good investment property. He handed over a check, the Realtor handed him his keys, and that was it. She even gave him a recommendation for movers, and after contacting them and finding out they were available today to move what little he had over, he grew excited about spending his first night in his own place in Grayson Falls. He would hit up the grocery store and Sophie's general store while the movers worked. On his next day off, he would find a cat.

MEGAN GLARED AT the ceiling of her living room. She had been listening to jazz music all evening float through the floor. A new tenant—or possibly tenants, as she heard more than one person moving around up there—had moved in upstairs, and it sounded like they were getting ready to put in a late-night unpacking. She sincerely hoped they turned the music down soon. She usually turned in early and would never be able to sleep with all that noise.

Taking a deep breath, she slowly let it out. No, that wasn't neighborly. She doubted whoever had moved in would always be this loud. And really, it was only the music. It wasn't as if they were stomping around. They were just walking. The upstairs apartment had gone unrented for so long that she had gotten used to the quiet and being the only one in the house. She had the option of taking the upstairs apartment when she moved in, but she thought it best not to have to do the stairs all the time. While she only had one bedroom in her apartment, she had a dining room. She didn't use it to eat in—preferring tray tables in the living room to save space—so she had set up her computer in there and an overstuffed chair that had a pullout bed inside.

Not that she ever really had overnight guests—but her brothers did stay over with her during an especially hellish snowstorm. They wanted to be sure she got cleared out—and that she didn't do it herself. They masked the fact that they were worried about her alone in a bad storm with board games and movies. One brother sacked out on the couch; the other on the pullout. And while she knew what they were up to, they really did have a great time.

When Megan was young, she was diagnosed with hypertrophic cardiomyopathy, a disease that made her heart enlarged. There was treatment for it. In fact, some people went their entire life without ever even knowing they had it, but Megan's heart was continuing to grow. She was going to have some hard decisions ahead of her. She had medical insurance—thank goodness—through her parents' dental practice, which Megan gave them money for. Technically speaking, that would be another place she could work, but she wasn't keen on being under the close watch of her parents.

Megan began her wind-down evening routine. She set her kettle on the stove to heat up for her evening chamomile tea and walked into her bedroom to get into her pajamas. Pulling out her flannel pants and long-sleeved Over the Hop tee, she then went into the bathroom to wash her face and put her hair up and change. The music followed her everywhere. It was so loud. It shook the ceiling.

Once changed, she made her way back to the kitchen to prepare her tea bag. Again, the smooth sound of jazz followed. The beginning of a headache started to push around inside her head. Sighing, she dropped her head and clutched the countertop. It just wasn't working like this. Her first interaction with her upstairs neighbor was going to be to complain. They would definitely not be getting off on the right foot.

She shut the kettle off and spun on her fuzzy cow slipper clad heel. She would never be able to relax and unwind with the music so loud. Stepping out into the hallway, she shivered a bit against the chill. The hallway and stairwell upstairs were heated, but not very well. Dirt and leaves were scattered around the foyer and up the stairs. Whoever had done the moving hadn't bothered to clean up behind themselves. She'd wait a couple days to see if the upstairs tenant took care of it. Normally, the landlord hired a cleaning person to come in and keep the common hallway clean, but they only came in once a month. And as one person, Megan just hadn't made that much of a mess, and she never had any reason to go upstairs.

She made her way up the wood staircase, feeling like an old harpy, even to herself. She would be nice about asking them to turn the music down and explain her work schedule and how early she needed to be up.

Once she reached the upstairs apartment, she knocked on the door and waited. And waited. She knocked again and waited. And waited. Finally, she pounded.

Just as the door swung open, Megan heard a male voice yell out, "They probably want you to turn down this crappy music, dickhead!"

Stunned, she stood there staring at Sebastian. *He* was her new neighbor? The man she had been actively trying to avoid for the very reason she was now experiencing. Her hands became clammy and her heartrate sped up. Her tongue felt as if it was tied in knots.

Attempting to speak around the lump in her throat, she said, "I'm sorry to bother you."

Sebastian cocked his head to the side watching her. He seemed as surprised to see her as she was to see him. When he realized he couldn't hear what she said, he turned behind him and gestured. The music shut off and Sebastian opened the door wider and stepped back. Behind him, Megan could see his brother Ryan sitting on the floor with various electronic components spread out. A large flat screen TV was set up on what appeared to be an old dresser repurposed as a television console in the corner near the fireplace. She was surprised it wasn't hung between the windows or on the opposite wall, but who was she to question how men liked their electronics set up? Her brothers took their home theatre systems very seriously.

Sebastian turned back to her and eyed her carefully. Instinctively, Megan patted her hair, which she knew probably looked like a mess. She didn't dress to impress in her own home—well, she didn't typically dress to impress anyway. She hadn't been looking to attract the male eye in years.

"Is there something wrong? Are you okay?" Sebastian asked, concern covering his features.

Megan blinked and realized he had no idea what she was doing here. "I'm your downstairs neighbor." Her words stumbled out quickly. Surprise registered on his face before a slow smile spread across it. Sebastian had a face that turned heads, but when he smiled, damn, the guy could stop traffic.

Or a heart.

He stepped back and motioned her in. She hadn't been in the upstairs apartment, but she'd seen pictures online when she was apartment hunting. The living room had a vaulted ceiling that gave the space a much more open feel.

"Sorry about the music," Ryan apologized for Sebastian. "And sorry it was shitty jazz. The doctor here is musically out of touch."

Sebastian scowled. "I apologize," he said. "I don't listen to music loudly, but we were testing out the speakers. I had planned on making sure it was down to normal levels by ten p.m., just like the lease says."

"Oh," Megan said, twisting her hands. "I turn in early. I have to be at Danny and Jackie's by seven-thirty, so I'm usually in bed by nine." And oh, how that just made her sound so unexciting.

She paused. And why did she care whether or not he found her exciting? He was a doctor, and that was already a strike against him.

Not only was she not looking for a boyfriend, but she definitely wasn't looking for a doctor.

"Okay," Sebastian said. "Well, then you should know, I usually sleep in a bit. I'm on the second shift at the hospital and get home later. I'm planning to buy plenty of area rugs for in here, so maybe it won't sound like I'm clomping around up here in ski boots."

"There's a resort just outside town, do you ski?"

"I do," Sebastian said. "I'm looking forward to trying out the resort nearby this winter. How about you?"

Megan's face fell. She used to ski when she was younger. She loved the feeling of whipping down the slopes, but that all ended when she got her diagnosis. Everything ended then. It all became about monitoring her heart rate and keeping it down. There were times when she felt like a bloody medical experiment.

"Um, no, not anymore." She began to head for the door. "Anyway, thanks for turning the music down. I really appreciate it, and sorry to have bothered you."

"The apology is all mine," Sebastian said, walking her to the door.

Stepping out into the hallway, she closed the door behind her then dropped her forehead into her hand. She shook her head and let out a breath. "You are so stupid," she berated herself. Dropping her hands to her sides, she took a deep breath in and let it slowly out. Then she marched downstairs to continue her boring evening routine.

Six

SEBASTIAN WENT TO the diner every morning since the day he saw Megan there and had breakfast with Zach and Natalie—though he had taken to getting his run in during the lunch hour. He thought he could justify his stalkerish activities because he was having breakfast with his brother and sister, and he truly did like that routine. Maisy even started letting him order his own food, which Sebastian considered huge progress.

Due to their opposite schedules, he and Megan didn't bump into each other at home the way he had hoped. And he now knew the diner wasn't part of her normal routine.

Unless she was avoiding him, which he felt was entirely possible.

She was skittish, and he didn't know how to reassure her that disaster wouldn't befall her if she decided to have dinner with him—or at this point, even a conversation that lasted more than five minutes. He couldn't change his profession—or more aptly wouldn't—so he needed to get around it in some way. He needed to show her all the good things about him that had nothing to do with being a doctor.

He'd do that just as soon as he figured out what those good things were.

Being married to his job for most of his adult life, Sebastian wasn't entirely sure who he was when he wasn't working. He liked music—and had an impressive vinyl collection, if he did say so himself. He liked to read, run, and he liked to be with his siblings.

Christ, was he really that boring? What on earth could he claim to have in common with her?

Maybe she wasn't the girl for him. If they didn't have anything in common, maybe he should just let it go. But he couldn't get her out of his head, and he knew down to his soul that they would enjoy each other's company if she would just give him a chance.

"Am I boring?" He asked his siblings.

"Good god, no," Zach said around a mountain of French toast. "You're entertaining as all hell."

Not knowing if that was sarcasm, Sebastian cocked his head to Natalie for an answer.

"I guess not," she said with a shrug.

"You *guess* not?" He asked. He leaned forward on his elbows and looked at her. "Like, I can be boring? This is important. I need to know if there is anything about me that's interesting."

Natalie twirled her finger in his direction and took a sip of her coffee with her free hand. "This little nutty you're having is interesting."

Sebastian sat back against the booth seat and poked at his food. This conversation wasn't encouraging. Zach and Natalie would be biased. But his brothers and sisters were the only people he knew in Grayson Falls, other than Megan—and he certainly couldn't ask her.

"What's interesting about me that a woman would like?" He asked.

"Dude, you're a doctor," Zach said. "Girls' moms always want them to marry a rich doctor or lawyer."

Rolling her eyes at Zach, Natalie said, "That's a stereotype. Mothers in this day and age don't want marrying rich to be their daughter's crowning achievement—at least not in the real world. I don't know what rich mothers want for their daughters."

"Well, I'm not rich," Sebastian said, picking up his coffee mug and taking a sip. "My father paid for my education, so I'm not hampered down by loans, but I went from a big city surgeon to a small practice and hospital in rural New Hampshire. Doctors don't take those jobs for the money. I need activities or something. Maybe I need to volunteer somewhere."

"Just don't force yourself to be something you're not," Natalie said. "You do have a lot going for you, Sebastian. You're a nice guy, with a stable career. You're funny, good looking, compassionate, and loyal. That's what women look for, not whether or not you kayak or collect stamps or whatever else people do."

"Collect stamps? Really, Nat?" Zach teased.

"I don't know. I don't date," she said with a careless shrug. "But it's the person you are that's attractive, and Sebastian, you *are* a good person. The right woman will see that."

"But it sounds like there's only one person he *wants* to see that." Zach said. "A certain nanny maybe?"

"Perhaps," Sebastian admitted.

Picking at his eggs, Sebastian thought about what Natalie said. He didn't really know Megan. He just knew he was physically attracted to her. But his end goal wasn't to get her into bed. He could get women into bed. He never had a problem with that. His goal was to get to know her better, to explore what this overwhelming pull was she had on him.

He hadn't heard the door chime, but heard Maisy's greeting of the new customer.

"Well, good morning, Ms. Miller," Maisy said jovially. Sebastian's head snapped up to attention. The clink of a ceramic mug on the counter told him that Megan was sitting at the bar. He didn't hear any other greetings, so it sounded like she was alone. "I didn't think I'd see you this week. Would you like your usual egg white omelet?"

"Yes, please," Megan said. He closed his eyes a little longer than a blink at the sound of her voice. It was a sweet-sounding voice, like he thought an angel might sound or a mermaid. Whimsical.

Dear god, he sounded ridiculous, even in his head.

Ignoring Zach and Natalie's chuckles, Sebastian grabbed his mug and moved to the breakfast bar. Standing next to Megan, he gestured to the red vinyl covered stool next to her. "Is this seat taken?"

Eyes wide, she turned. There was panic in them. He made her nervous still. That was okay. He could work with that.

Licking her lips, she broke eye contact, glanced down at the stool, and turned to face forward. "Doesn't appear to be."

Well, that wasn't the most enthusiastic invitation he had ever received.

He sat down anyway.

People were beginning to trickle in and regulars took their normal spots. Maisy came by and refilled Sebastian's coffee and set a small, silver water pitcher and tea bags down in front of Megan. So she was a tea drinker. That was good to know.

"How are you today?" He asked.

"Good." She poured the hot water into the mug, chose her herbal tea, and set the bag in the mug to steep. He glanced down to see if he could see what brand it was, but her hands covered the packet and she put the empty wrapper on the other side of the mug. Picking up the lemon wedge, she squeezed the juice into the mug. He noted she didn't take milk or sugar, but did sweeten it with a little honey then began dunking her tea bag to mix it all up and release the flavor. Taking a moment to commit the process to memory, he then looked back up at her and smiled.

"The changing leaves looked pretty spectacular this morning," he noted. "Are you excited for colder weather?"

Nodding, Megan took a sip of her tea. "I do like colder weather. I'm not wild about all the extra traffic the ski resort brings through town when it's open in the winter, but it definitely makes the businesses in town happy. It's a double-edged sword I guess, because the resort decorates beautifully for Christmas and they do a holiday dinner with carolers dressed up. It's really nice."

"That does sound good," he said. And it did. Maybe he could get her to be his date. "I don't mind winter. I do like the warmer months though. It's nicer to run in than the freezing temperatures and slushy roads that come with winter. Even with toe warmers, my feet end up two blocks of ice."

"Her food arrived, and she picked up her fork to eat her omelet. Sebastian wasn't sure if that was a cue to leave her alone or not. She didn't seem annoyed by his presence.

Zach and Natalie stood up and put their coats on. Zach came over and slapped Sebastian on the back, while Natalie said hello to Megan. They began a short conversation about their next book club meeting and the book they were reading. Zach stopped to speak with someone at the end of the counter on his way out.

So, now he had more information than when he started. Megan liked the colder months and enjoyed reading. Sebastian retrieved his coat from the booth and laid it on the stool next to him at the bar. He didn't want to overstay his welcome, but neither did he want to leave just yet.

Besides, he had just gotten a refill on his coffee. He didn't want to waste it.

"So, you're a reader," he said, as he sat down. Megan nodded while she continued eating her breakfast. "I'm not sure I would enjoy being in a book club. I don't get too much reading time. I'm not sure I would like someone telling me what to read."

Sipping her tea, Megan looked over at him. "It's usually not so bad. If you didn't like the book, you can skip the next meeting so you don't have to pretend you liked it or offend someone who really loved it. I usually slog through them. I like cozy mysteries, romance, women's fiction. I'm not really one for the sci-fi or fantasy, and I have a real hard time getting through non-fiction."

"I can do sci-fi," Sebastian said. "It's not my favorite. I like true crime books and thrillers. Something I can really immerse myself in. I'm not reading anything now. Guess it's time to head over to the library and check some stuff out."

"I covet my quiet time. I'm an introverted person. I only go to the book club because I love reading so much. Some months, I skip it because I'm just not in the mood for a crowd. Does that sound snobby?"

"No, it sounds like something an introverted person would do." Sebastian himself was a more social person. In that way, Chicago *did* appeal to him. But he would need to keep her need for quiet in mind if he were ever successful in actually getting her to go on a date with him.

After draining his mug, he reached for his jacket and shoved his arms in. She looked surprised to see him leaving. Good. That's exactly what he was hoping for. Get her comfortable around him and then leave just when she was enjoying his company. He didn't want to leave when she was still wishing she were sitting alone.

"Well, I've got some things to do before my shift starts," he said. "It was nice bumping into you."

He couldn't resist looking through the diner window as he walked by. She was still blinking and gaping after he left the diner.

THE NEXT DAY MEGAN WALKED ALONG Main Street, which had been shut down for the annual Pumpkin Festival. She loved this time of year in New Hampshire. Mother Nature provided a beautiful backdrop of greens, golds, yellows, oranges, and browns. Dried leaves crunched under her boots, and she burrowed down into her sweater, loving the feeling of coziness.

Everywhere she looked families were enjoying the day. Children went from face-painting to hay rides to bobbing for apples to pig races to the puppet show. Ethan Donahue had set up a stand near the hospital to sell vegetables, hay bales, corn stalks, jams and jellies, and other things he created on the farm. He was also giving horse rides on a gentle brown mare that was tied behind him. Megan had bought a jar of apple butter and a hot apple cider from him and was warming her hands on the cup and taking sips.

Nothing said small town like a pumpkin festival. She wandered over to take a look at the pumpkins entered into the contest. There was one contest for carving and another for painting. Every year, Piper took Jed DeLuca's biggest pumpkin and painted it for display. This year's pumpkin was as large as Megan's television at home. She wrote down her votes for each contest and put the little slips of paper in the appropriate glass fish bowls.

"I don't know. I think number thirty-three is going to take it."

Megan turned to her side and stepped back to face Sebastian. "There's a rumor going around that the new surgeon in town has entered a pumpkin in the contest this year and that it's quite intricately carved."

Sebastian held up his hands. "These hands can make people better, save lives, *and* make amazing pumpkin art."

"I think perhaps yours should be taken out of the contest and put next to Piper's. Professionals shouldn't be allowed to enter."

Sebastian pretended indignation. "You don't even know which one is mine!"

"Pretty sure I do." She smiled and began walking again. Unsurprisingly, he followed her. She just wasn't sure about him. He was interested in her—that was obvious—but did she really want to get involved with a doctor? He was handsome, charming, amusing.

And a doctor.

She had to admit that since he moved to town, she really hadn't felt like he was evaluating her. Either he was doing his best not to show it, or he really wasn't doing any kind of physical assessment of her when he saw her.

And truth be told, why would he? He didn't know of her condition, and she highly doubted he'd be able to diagnose her without the benefit of testing. It was time to admit her prejudice against doctors was irrational.

At her last book club meeting, all the ladies not related to Sebastian keep talking about Dr. Delicious, and wasn't it convenient for the single ladies of Grayson Falls that the new doctor in town was romantically unattached? Jackie, Piper, and Sophie had kept to themselves about the topic of Sebastian, humoring the other women making fools of themselves and discussing him as if he were a car they were thinking about buying. Did that kind of thing bother men as much as it bothered women? She'd have to ask her brothers.

Megan stopped walking at a booth for the local orchard and bought a basket of apples. Snatching one out of her basket, Sebastian bit into it. "I didn't know you were such an apple fan."

"Well, you know what they say. 'An apple a day keeps the doctor away.'"

He was mid-bite when he paused and looked over at her. She couldn't help but giggle as he looked down and studied her basket.

"Damn," he said. "There's a lot of apples in there. At that rate, I won't be able to ask you out until next year."

Blushing, Megan diverted her attention. He had turned her joke around on her and she wasn't prepared. Why couldn't she flirt like a normal woman?

Wait a minute. Did she *want* to flirt with the handsome doctor? Shocked, she realized she did. She was severely out of practice and just now realizing she was probably going to have to ask her cousin for dating advice.

Reaching down, Sebastian plucked the basket of apples out of her hand. "Hey, those are mine!"

"Relax," he said. "I'm just carrying them for you. They get heavy and it's the gentlemanly thing to do."

"And here I thought you were planning on dumping them somewhere and removing your roadblocks." Well, look at that. She *could* flirt.

Throwing back his head, Sebastian laughed. He was beautiful like this—uninhibited, full of mirth, not a care in the world. His laugh drew attention and eyebrows raised at seeing conservative, unassuming Megan walking with the sexy new doctor. She expected

Norrie, the police dispatcher, to have a picture of them up on Facebook by the end of the day.

And really, was that a bad thing?

As they made their way toward the food vendors, she spotted Piper with an easel set up. She was doing sketches for families. Zach was nearby, of course, and he had a crowd of boys and girls around him. They had set up a pitch-back and he was giving free baseball tips to the kids. Megan loved events like these in town as the community came out and really solidified itself.

"Hello there, Dr. Delicious!" Nana Kennedy was walking with Megan's aunt Stephanie, Laurie's mother. Megan groaned at Nana's use of Laurie's nickname for Sebastian.

"It's good to see you, Nana," Sebastian said as they strolled over. Megan leaned forward to greet them with a kiss and a hug. "How are things?" Sebastian asked.

"If by 'things' you mean, my girls, you cutie, they're healing up nicely."

"Mom!" Stephanie groaned. "We're in public."

"Oh, stop," Nana chided. "The man's a doctor."

Looking over at Sebastian, Megan saw that he was actually blushing a bit. He had his head down, but she saw his pink-tipped ears. Rubbing the back of his neck, he looked back up again with an embarrassed smile.

"I'm glad to hear it," he said. "Keep doing what I told you, and you'll be much more comfortable."

"Maybe I need a house call."

"Nana!" This time both Megan and Stephanie chorused.

"You're embarrassing him, Nana," Megan said.

"Oh, poo," Nana replied. "He's a grown man." Nana poked Megan. "And I hear he's single, Meggie. Doc, did you know my Megan here is single, too? Such a sweet girl and a hard worker. She could really use a guy like you."

"Nana," Megan said through clenched teeth. Nana was dangerously close to exposing Megan's secret. If she did, Sebastian might tell his sister and brother-in-law, and Megan might lose her job. She couldn't have that. She had the perfect setup now. She was able to rest and take it easy when the baby napped. While she did do some light housework for the McKenzies to occupy her time when she felt up to it, they didn't expect her to. So, if she needed to rest, she did that instead. She wouldn't have those breaks in any other job. She certainly didn't have that time at the library.

Cocking his head to the side, Sebastian studied her reaction. Her face flamed. While she loved Nana fiercely, right then she could have cheerfully stuck a gag in the old woman's mouth.

"What a coincidence," Sebastian said, facing her. "Megan, I don't believe we've gotten some of those cider donuts yet, and they smell amazing. Shall we?"

"Yes," Megan said quickly—anything to leave meddling Nana's company. They said goodbye and wandered off again.

"She's a hoot," Sebastian said, stuffing his free hand in his pocket.

"That she is," Megan sighed.

After picking up some donuts, they began to head back toward their shared house, which was only a few blocks away. Though Megan loved the festival, she had definitely had enough of it today.

"So, why small-town medicine?" Megan asked, as children with pumpkin painted faces wearing superhero costumes ran by them. "Why leave all the prestige and resources of a big city? I'd imagine a young doctor like yourself would make a lot more money there."

Sebastian looked ahead while they walked. "It's not about the money for me. My brothers and sister were gathering here, and I was the only one that was still far away. We didn't know each other growing up. We're related through our mother, but she had given us all up. She's sick, unfortunately. I've never even met her, but that's a story for another day. Danny's friend, Eric Davis, had tracked us all down and we all just sort of migrated to this area. There's something about this town, you know? It fits me better than I expected." Sebastian waved to someone that had waved to him and called out a hello. "I like knowing my patients and being invested in their lives. Jackie and I are going to start house calls. It's mostly a dead practice, but in this town, I think it will be manageable. Jackie is looking at hiring one more doctor."

Megan really wanted to ask him about his mother, but Sebastian didn't seem to want to talk about her now. She'd wait until he was ready to share that story—if he was ever inclined to share something that private with her. She shouldn't assume that just because she had shown interest, he would be willing to share all aspects of his life with her.

"You have a great family," Megan said. "You all seem very close to each other."

"We're getting there," Sebastian shrugged. He took three apples out of the basket and began to juggle them while he walked and talked. *He juggled. How adorable was that?* "I didn't realize how desperate I was for them until I met them. We started out as friends, and I think that helped a lot. We've grown protective of each other. There's nothing I would do or give up for them."

"It's like that with me and my brothers, too," Megan said. "They can be overprotective of me, sure, but we've always been close. They're like my best friends. I grew up here. Most of the people I went to school with have moved away. A few are still around, and we're friendly. Plus, I have the book club. But it's still mainly my family I look to when I need something or want to go somewhere and don't want to go alone. My brothers or my cousins are always up for anything."

"It's strange, isn't it?" He said, returning the apples to the basket as they approached their building and she took out her key to open the front door. "I have lifelong friends. When we talk or get together, it feels like just yesterday that we last saw each other, but it all comes down to family."

Pushing open the front door, Megan stepped toward her apartment to let him in behind her. "Not so strange." She took the basket of apples from him. "Family always has your back. They know all your dirty little secrets and love you anyway."

"True," Sebastian said. He crossed his arms and leaned up against the banister for the stairway. "Does that mean you have a dirty little secret, Megan?"

Dammit, she'd said too much. Turning, she unlocked the door to her apartment. "Aren't we all hiding something?"

Brow furrowed, he studied her. "I suppose."

Now he was scrutinizing her, and she was painfully reminded of his profession. She backed into her apartment, thanked him for his company, and abruptly closed her door.

And that didn't look suspicious at all.

SEBASTIAN RETURNED TO the Pumpkin Festival a man on a very important mission. He needed to engage Megan more. She did better with him when there was some kind of joint activity involved. She appeared to have no problem sharing things about herself with him as they strolled along back to the house they shared or ate at the diner. Any nervousness she had around him also seemed to disappear when her attention could focus on something else, as well.

Therefore, he needed pumpkins.

There was an old folding table and chairs in the basement that he dragged up to the wrap around porch. He would get the two most perfect pumpkins and invite her to a pumpkin carving date. Easy, casual, no crowds involved.

Not wanting to get sucked into conversations and become diverted from his mission, he moved swiftly through the festival, trying not to make eye contact with anyone. If he hadn't glanced up to check his bearings in relation to the pumpkin patch, he would have missed the man taking a picture of him a few booths up.

What the hell?

As he walked around the festival earlier, he had the feeling of being watched. But it was a small town, he was a new resident that people were still getting to know, and he was walking around with Megan all by themselves. He just assumed it was fodder for the gossip mill.

Looking behind him, Sebastian ensured there was nothing noteworthy that the man could have been taking a picture of instead and there was nobody else around him. He had the distinct impression that the man had taken a picture specifically of him. When Sebastian looked back up, the man was gone.

Maybe it was a photographer for the carnival taking promotional pictures. That was probably it. Or it could have been someone taking pictures for Norrie to put up on the Facebook page. Small town life was an adjustment and Grayson Falls was about the community. Everyone knew everyone and he had to keep reminding himself of that fact.

Bolstered by this theory, Sebastian made it to the pumpkin patch and picked the two roundest, most perfect-looking pumpkins, along with a package of tools to carve them with. Walking back to his car, he realized he could have gotten slightly smaller pumpkins as these two were heavy and awkward. The end result would justify the current difficulty in getting the fruit to his car. Once the pumpkins were safely on his front seat, Sebastian shook out his hands and forearms, which were sore from having to balance the pumpkins.

That spooky feeling that he was under surveillance came over him again and he looked around him. Not seeing anyone, Sebastian did a slower scan like he imagined Danny or Eric might do, trying to notice anything or anyone out of place. Nothing seemed amiss.

Getting in the driver seat, Sebastian started his car and checked his rearview mirror. No one was behind him. He continued to glance behind him during the very short drive back to the house and no one followed him.

Shaking the feeling, he hopped out of his car and bounded up onto the porch, setting the pumpkins on the rickety old table. He briefly considered sweeping the deck of the dried and crunchy leaves, but then decided they added atmosphere. Walking over to the recycling bin around the corner, Sebastian grabbed some newspaper and spread it out on the table.

The front door opened and Megan poked her head out. "What's all this?"

Straightening up, Sebastian answered, "I thought you might want to carve some pumpkins with me for the front stoop."

Glancing over at the front steps, Megan said, "I guess it doesn't look very festive. We do get trick or treaters here, but I don't usually do much to decorate for any of the holidays. I suppose I've been a slacker there."

"Well, I don't want to go crazy or anything," Sebastian said. "But a couple of pumpkins are easy enough."

"Okay." Megan said. "Let me grab my tea and I'll be right out."

While Megan was inside, Sebastian opened up the package of carving tools he bought at the pumpkin patch. Inside were different stencils that could be used as a guide to carve. He *had* done a pretty intricate design on his pumpkin at the festival. It was just the words Happy Halloween with some leaves, but all the letters were connected and the leaves looked like they were sweeping through in the wind. It was pretty good work, if he did say so himself.

Megan came out with a huge, steaming mug and shuffled to the table. Setting the mug down, she placed her hands on her hips and assessed her stencil options. "I think my skills are only good enough for this standard 'Boo.' I don't know that I can do any of these others. I'm no surgeon."

She was poking fun at him and he was charmed. Her comfort level with him was growing. He could do this. He could move at this slower pace if he needed to. Making her comfortable with him was what was important. Everything that came later would be that much more worth it if they moved at her pace.

This, of course, was assuming anything came later. Right now, they were just becoming friends. He didn't know that she was interested in anything else with him and if she wasn't, well, then that's the ballgame as they say. He'd be disappointed, but he'd rather have her in his life as a friend then not at all. She picked her Boo and he picked a haunted house and they got to work. Before long, they were elbow deep in pumpkin innards and laughing.

"You're a very messy surgeon," Megan said, gesturing to where Sebastian was scooping out the sticky, seedy, orangey mess with his hand.

"Well, sure," he replied. "I don't have my nurses with me to assist. Doctors can't be trusted with a surgery such as this on their own, you know. In the OR, we work as a team."

Chuckling, she used a plastic scoop to clean out her pumpkin. Much more dignified than his down and dirty method. "Do you miss it? Being in the OR? I know you haven't been here long, but probably long enough to miss it."

"I do miss it a little bit," Sebastian said. "With scheduled surgeries, you know what your day is going to be like and who you'll be working with. There's comfort in that routine and steadiness. I've actually applied for rights to the University Hospital not too far away to be on their general surgical staff. Even though that won't be my main focus area, I still want to keep my skills fresh." Dropping the gloppy mess in his hand into a bowl, Sebastian picked up another plastic scoop and dove back in. "The hospital here is predictable and yet, not at the same time. I don't know if that makes sense. Anything that's actually life-threatening we can stabilize, but we're going to move it out. Especially if surgery is required. There's an OR there and I can do emergent cases, but again, it's just to stabilize the patient for transport to a bigger facility that can better meet the patient's needs."

"What about the city itself?" Megan asked.

"Now *that*, I don't miss. Adjusting to small town life takes time, but the air is fresh, I can see stars at night, and I'm not so concerned about getting mugged if I'm walking around in the dark. What about you? Did you ever want to leave Grayson Falls?"

Megan paused in her pumpkin gutting as if she were deciding what to say. "I went away to college, not too far, but I did get out of town for that time, and it was nice. It was a relatively large university. But I like Grayson Falls. Cities are too busy for me."

Sebastian was about to respond when he glanced up and saw the same man from the festival lowering his camera. "What the hell?" He muttered, shaking his hands out over the pumpkin. "Hey!" He called out to the man, but the man took off.

"What's going on?" Megan asked as Sebastian ran by her. Not answering, Sebastian ran to the sidewalk in front of the house and looked in the direction the man ran in, but he saw no one.

Walking back to porch, Sebastian rubbed the back of his neck in thought. He wasn't being paranoid. Someone was taking pictures of him. But who and why? He didn't think the guy was a detective. Police knew how to run surveillance without being detected. It must have something to do with his father's campaign, but why would anyone want to bother with him? Unless it was for opposition research.

Sebastian took a deep breath to let go of his anger and tension. He wouldn't let whatever his father was up to mar this beautiful day he was fortunate enough to spend with Megan. Later, he would analyze the situation more fully. For now, he had a pumpkin to carve.

Seven

MEGAN TIED HER waitress apron on around her waist in the office at Over the Hop, ready to start her shift. She was feeling pretty tired this morning, but she figured she'd perk up a bit as she went through her day. Sometimes a body just didn't want to get out of bed. Her brother, Justin, grumbled when he saw her in the kitchen dressed to work. If Megan was working here then she wasn't taking enough time off during the week, to his way of thinking, and was overdoing it. He told her to stay in the back and help prep plates and take care of the salads and bread baskets and other tasks that didn't require her hauling heavy trays and walking around the better part of the day.

Laurie sat behind the desk in the small office hunched over a laptop. The office only held one desk that Laurie, her brother, and Justin all competed for throughout the day. There were two rusty metal cabinets in the corner with piles of paper on top of them, and two chairs crammed in between the desk and the door.

"My Neanderthal brother says I can't work on the restaurant floor today," Megan announced.

Looking up, Laurie arched a brow at her. "Do you feel up to working in the restaurant today?"

Megan shrugged. "Yeah, I feel fine." That wasn't entirely true, but she didn't feel like she couldn't handle it.

"Then I think that matter is settled." Laurie looked back down to the computer and squinted. Laurie needed glasses and was refusing to get them. She said they'd make her look nerdy, and she didn't want to have to touch her eyes to put in contacts.

Continuing to squint at the screen, Laurie began to type. Megan stood and watched. After checking over her shoulder to see if anyone was around, Megan pushed the door shut, staying inside the office, and waited.

Blinking, Laurie looked up at her and noted the closed door. "What's up?"

"Would you date me?" Megan blurted.

"Well, that will shake the family up," Laurie muttered. She pushed back from the desk and put her feet up. Sitting down in one of the chairs, Megan wrung her hands in her lap.

"I mean if you were a guy," Megan said.

"Well, I already know you're a great person with a lot to offer a man, so I'd have to say yes. If I was a dude, I'd totally date you."

Clasping her hands tight, Megan brought them to her forehead and bounced them against her skull a few times. "What am I doing? I'm so stupid," she muttered.

Laurie dropped her feet and pulled herself back to the desk, laying her elbows on top. "What's going on? What are you doing?"

"It's what I'm *not* doing," Megan sighed, looked back up at her cousin. "I'm *not* flirting with Sebastian like I should be. He's interested in me, I know he is, but it's been years since I've been out with a guy. I'm not good at it. I'm boring, and I'm not exciting in bed. I'm so afraid of raising my heart rate that I hardly do *anything* in bed. Who wants a woman that just lays there?"

Waving her hands around, Laurie tried to understand what was going on. "Whoa, whoa, whoa. We're talking about sex? With Dr. Delicious? You want to have sex with Dr. Delicious? I mean what warm-blooded woman doesn't, but I mean, like, seriously?"

"Sex might be getting ahead of myself," Megan conceded. "I'm not the kind of girl that just jumps into bed with a guy. I have to know that it's right. It's not just an enjoyable activity that two people who are attracted to each other do."

"It's not?" Laurie shook her head.

"Not to me," Megan said earnestly. "To me it's about two people who love each other wanting to express that love in a beautiful and private way. It's not just about scratching an itch."

"Your brothers have pumped you full of wild shit over the years. We're the same age. We were raised together. I also have two brothers. And you and I turned out very differently. There's nothing wrong with having sex because it's an enjoyable activity that two people—I don't even know what you said." Standing up, Laurie came out from behind the desk and looked down at Megan, crossing her arms. "Having sex with someone just for the sake of having sex with them isn't taboo anymore, Meg. I've had sex with people I don't care about. It's called lust."

"I get that," Megan said. "And I'm not judging you or anyone else. It's just something different for me, and it has nothing to do with any influence my brothers might have tried to assert over the years. I don't have to be in love with my partner, but I do have to feel an emotional connection to them."

"And are you saying you feel an emotional connection to Dr. Delicious?"

Letting out a frustrated breath, Megan rolled her eyes. "Can we call him by his name, please? At least while we're talking about something like this? That ridiculous nickname makes him sound like some kind of reality show celebrity. Sebastian is real. He's charming, and I'm attracted to him. I'm not talking about jumping into bed with him, but I don't know what to do next. How do I act? What do I say?"

"You say, 'Sebastian, why don't we hang out some time and get to know each other better.'"

"That's kind of forward, isn't it?" She even sounded old-fashioned and out-of-touch to herself.

"No." Laurie dropped her hands to her hips. "You're a strong, independent woman, Megan. Take charge if you want him. God knows half the women in this town are trying to figure out how to score him. If he's interested in you—and you're not wrong there because

I've seen the way he looks at you—then just go for it. You have nothing to lose."

But she did have something to lose—her pride, her dignity, her comfortable, quiet world that maybe she wasn't ready to share with someone.

Laurie squeezed Megan's arm before walking back behind the desk, and sat down to squint at the computer some more. Megan stood up and left the office, rolling over Laurie's advice in her head. She *was* different from Laurie. Her cousin had always been the wild one growing up, going to the parties, hanging out with the popular crowd, living life loud and free. Megan was a wallflower. She dressed to blend in, not wanting to draw attention to herself. She stayed in on Friday nights with a book.

She had come out of her shell a little bit in college, went to some parties, some pep rallies, some campus events, but in the end, it just wasn't for her. She didn't think like the other girls and wanted different things. Maybe her views led her to a boring life, but at least she lived by her convictions. She could honestly say she never compromised her moral values for any reason.

But she also never met anyone before to give her reason to.

Sebastian wasn't like that though—at least he didn't come across that way. She was reasonably sure he wouldn't ask her to change for him.

SEBASTIAN WALKED INTO Over the Hop for lunch Sunday and scanned the brewery's occupants. He saw his brother, Ethan, at the bar and began to make his way through the crowded room. Various patrons called out a greeting to him. Some he had seen at the hospital, and others were just being friendly to the new doctor in town. He had discovered that despite the short amount of time his siblings had lived in town, they had become quite well-known and well-liked, having taken highly visible positions in town. He smiled as he thought of how Grayson Falls had turned out exactly how he thought it would—how he *hoped* it would.

Friendly faces followed him everywhere he went. His citified senses kept waiting for the other shoe to drop, but so far it hadn't. Surely there was *someone* in this town that was unpleasant? It's not like everyone walked around like they were sucking helium, but he hadn't encountered anyone that didn't like new people.

Of course, everyone needed a doctor, so there was that. And that was likely the reason no one had treated him with any kind of scorn—yet.

Sebastian sat down next to Ethan, who clapped him on the back in greeting. Bravo, the dog Ethan served with in the Marines, was curled around Ethan's bar stool, snoozing quietly and staying out of the way. Ethan was having the chili, and it looked damn delicious.

"I can't get enough of this stuff," Ethan said, shoveling in a huge spoonful. "I don't know what they put in it, but it's crazy good." Ethan held the next spoonful up to Sebastian's mouth. Despite the strange looks they may have gotten as his brother literally fed him, Sebastian wrapped his mouth around the spoon and moaned.

"Right?" Ethan said. "I told you."

The chili was hearty, and the taste assaulted his senses. It had some serious heat, too. Sebastian's eyes teared up as the effects from the peppers swarmed his mouth. The burning in his mouth and the tingling on his lips had him reaching for Ethan's beer, but Laurie pushed a glass of water into his hand instead. "It pairs really well with the Scottish Bastard Red," she said. "How about it?"

Sebastian nodded and wiped the tears from his eyes. "Does it only come in dragon fire heat?" He could feel his sinuses getting cleared out from the singeing temperature. It's possible the membranes around his eyeballs were also burned off.

Laurie laughed. "No, you can get it mild, medium, or the fires of hell."

"I think I'll start with medium," Sebastian said, as Ethan chuckled next to him. It wasn't that Sebastian didn't like spicy food—he did—but he also enjoyed having taste buds.

"How's the hospital going?" Ethan asked.

Sebastian shrugged a shoulder. "The people of Grayson Falls get into some strange mishaps, that's for sure—fishhooks in necks, a nail through a toe. Danny and I spent the morning putting together my desk and rearranging the office so we can still fit the couch in there. There's a steady flow of appointments and walk-ins, but it's at a much more manageable pace than the hospital I worked at in Chicago."

"Where your father was the chief of surgery?"

"Yeah."

"Why did you work there anyway?" Ethan asked, taking a sip of his beer. "I mean, Chicago must have a lot of hospitals, and I'm sure there were plenty to choose from in the surrounding area. Why go to the one where your father was? You said the guy never gave a shit about you. Were you trying to get his attention or something?"

His brother was blunt, but then that was Ethan. He was the quietest of them all. He preferred to stay in the background and watch. But he never beat around the bush on things.

"It was for my grandparents," Sebastian said. "My grandmother has always held out hope that I would mend things with my father, but how do you forgive and forget a lifetime of borderline neglect? Sure, the man supported me financially, but I never received any affection from him. There was never a smile directed my way. I didn't ask to be born, but I've paid the price for it."

His father was also the reason Sebastian was a surgeon. He used to resent the fact that he wanted to go into the same profession as a man that barely admitted his son's existence, but then he met Jackie and Natalie and discovered their shared grandfather had been a World War II doctor in France and England. So instead, Sebastian dared hope the calling came from his mother's side of the family.

To his surprise, Megan appeared from the kitchen with a tray. She walked behind the bar and served him his chili, along with little bowls of shredded cheddar, sour cream, and onions. He had no idea she had a second job. There was a lot he didn't know about her, and he wanted to change that.

"It's best when you load it up," she said. She looked tired and the sparkle that was normally in her eyes was noticeably missing. "Laurie said you also wanted a Scottish Bastard?" She picked up a pint glass and moved to the beer taps. Sebastian watched speechless as Megan poured his beer. Why was he so surprised? Just because he was her neighbor now didn't mean she had to tell him her schedule. She was her own person. It was none of his business how many jobs she worked or why.

But he wanted it to be. He wanted to know everything there was to know about her and that was a new feeling for him. In truth, having any feelings other than lust toward a woman was new to him. In Chicago, he had women he called when he needed a date to some sort of hospital event or charity fundraiser. They were women he was attracted to, but he didn't necessarily want to know what made them tick.

"You work here?" he asked, dumbly. *Welcome to the conversation, Captain Obvious.*

"I help out when they're short staffed," she said. "Laurie is my cousin, and she owns this place with her brother, David, and my brother, Justin. My brother is the chef."

"He makes a hell of a chili," Sebastian said. Ethan grunted his agreement while using a piece of bread to scrape up what was left in his bowl.

"Thanks, I'll let him know," Megan said. He couldn't stop looking at her, and he knew she noticed. She was nervous under his scrutiny. She shifted her weight and wouldn't meet his eyes when she slid the glass in front of him. He remembered she wasn't overly fond of doctors. If she was ever going to show any personal interest in him, he needed to find out the root cause of that and figure out how to overcome it.

He watched her disappear back into the kitchen then continued eating his chili and catching up with Ethan until a man in worn, stained jeans and a black t-shirt came out of the kitchen and scanned the area. When his eyes fell on Sebastian, he strode forward with purposeful steps. Sebastian could see the resemblance to Megan and figured this guy for her brother, the chef and part owner of the brewery. "You Doc Stuart?" he asked. Sebastian nodded once. "Can you come back and take a look at my sister? She's ... unwell."

Sebastian didn't need any further information. He popped off the bar stool and followed the man back into the kitchen. Employees were back there milling around. They looked nervous and unsure, like they didn't know what to do now that there was a disruption in the normal flow of the day—that, and he assumed morbid curiosity kept them waiting around to see what was going on. It *was* a small town, after all.

Megan's brother led him back into the office. Sebastian shooed everyone but Megan's brother out of the room—including Laurie, who had a few choice words for him.

Megan was sitting on the floor in the corner, leaning up against the wall. She was pale, sweating, and taking short breaths. The watch on her wrist beeped continuously, and now that Sebastian had a good look at it, he recognized it to be a heart monitor. It recorded her pulse and an alarm went off when her heart rate got too high.

The doctor in him pushed aside the potential love interest. Megan was having some kind of cardiac event.

"Justin ... you jerk ..." Megan said between quick breaths. "I told you, I'd be fine."

"*This* isn't fine, Meggie," Justin replied tersely. "You promised me you'd stay in the back today. You overdid it."

Sebastian held up one hand for quiet, the other picked up Megan's wrist to check her pulse. "Let the argument wait for a few minutes." He checked her pulse against his watch. It was elevated, but not dangerously high. Still, with her other symptoms it definitely looked like some kind of cardiac event was going on.

"How long has this been going on?" he asked.

"It started ... about an hour ... ago," Megan said. "I took a break... When I came back in from the bar ... it got worse. I just took my meds ... I'll be fine once ... I catch my breath."

"You have a history of this?" Sebastian interrogated.

"Yes," her brother said, over Sebastian's shoulder. "When she was about ten years old, she was diagnosed with hypertrophic cardiomyopathy." *Christ that was bad.* Hypertrophic cardiomyopathy was no minor disease. While there were cases of people going their whole lives without knowing they had the condition, Megan clearly was not one of those people. He was worried about her now. Suspecting this might be the reason for her aversion to doctors, he would need to proceed carefully. He was firmly in that role now, but he was proud of his career and happy to help her now in her time of need—even if it hurt his chances with her romantically.

That was a serious issue. Sebastian had prided himself on never being attracted to a patient before, but he was attracted to *this* patient. Sebastian noted her breaths slowed down as the medication began to work. Color was returning to her face. She glared at her brother. "If this had happened with Gabe, he wouldn't have run right out for a doctor! I don't need one." Though Sebastian may not have been thrilled with her words, he could hear her breathing was returning to normal.

"Well you have one," Sebastian snapped back. Megan looked taken aback, then her face flamed. Sebastian felt a twinge of guilt over his atrocious bedside manner, but really, this was not the time for her odd aversion to his chosen profession.

"Oh, God." She leaned her head back against the wall. "Is that what I sound like?"

"'Fraid so," he said, "but I'll let it slide because I don't want to be unneighborly." Sebastian checked her pulse again. It was coming down. If it continued to stay high over the next few minutes, he would have her brother force her over to the hospital. That would definitely put the final nail in his romantic pursuit coffin.

She looked over his shoulder at her brother. "I feel awful about this. You're already short-handed today."

Kneeling down, Justin pressed a soft kiss to his sister's forehead. "I'm sorry if you think I overreacted. I feel helpless when this shit happens to you—we all do. It doesn't hurt to get checked out."

"You should follow up with your treating physician as soon as you can," Sebastian said, sitting back on his heels.

"I'll take her on Monday," Justin said. Megan sighed.

"I can cover Ally for you," Sebastian offered. That was definitely no hardship for him. He wondered if Danny and Jackie knew of Megan's condition. He thought they might, as each of them stopped home during the day to check in.

"It's not that," Megan said softly, looking down. Sebastian would have asked what the problem was then, but didn't want to push her any more than was absolutely necessary for her current situation. He sat back on his heels and waited to see if she would share. She didn't, so he stood back up instead.

"If you're feeling a little better, Megan, I'll take you home." Justin offered, his voice lowered and more soothing, as he stroked the hair out of her face.

"I can do it," Sebastian said. "I live in the apartment upstairs." And there was no way he was going to be far from her if she was having a problem.

Surprise crossed Justin's face. Sebastian would bet Megan's family would back off a bit now that they knew a doctor lived right upstairs.

He could empathize with her. He knew what it was like to be unable to break free from a controlling situation.

Megan looked up at Sebastian and acknowledged defeat, she nodded her head. Sebastian extended his hand and helped Megan to her feet.

"Would you mind if we left out the back?" she asked him.

"Not at all." He turned to Justin. "My brother Ethan is at the bar. Would you mind letting him know I'm giving someone a lift home and I'll catch up with him later?"

"Can do." Justin said. "You take care of my sibling, and I'll take care of yours."

Megan pulled on her jacket and picked up her bag. Sebastian debated trying to carry it for her, but didn't want to come off as too overbearing. In the end, he opted to just stay as close as he dared without upsetting her.

Eight

MEGAN UNLOCKED THE door to her apartment. She was about to turn around and thank Sebastian for giving her the ride home, but somehow, he slipped right by her into her living room. Hands in his pockets, he turned in a slow circle taking in her space. It was comfortable, tidy, cozy, and smaller than his, but she liked it. She had been there for a few years now and didn't have any real complaints.

"I'm thinking about getting a cat," he announced.

Slipping out of her jacket, Megan hung it on a hook by the door and turned to face him, rubbing her hands on her upper arms. She was thrown a bit by his choice of conversation topic. She thought he would dive right into a hundred questions regarding her illness, treatment plan, history—all the things that interested a doctor.

"A cat's a nice idea," she agreed. "Mine's probably under the bed though. He has embraced stranger danger. He won't come out unless he knows you well."

"See, that's what I'm afraid of with having my own cat," Sebastian said. He walked to the overstuffed chair in her living room, pulled off his coat, draped it over the arm, and sat down. Apparently, he was planning on staying for a bit. "What if I get an asshole? What if I get one that doesn't like me?"

"Many cats are pretty friendly and loving," Megan said. "My cat, Thor, is. He just had several homes before he landed with me, so I think sometimes he's nervous someone is going to try to take him home when people come."

"Thor," Sebastian said thoughtfully. "That's a good cat name. Am I keeping you from something? Some sort of routine you go through when you come home?"

"I was going to make myself a cup of tea. It calms my nerves after these events." She waited to see if he would decide to leave. He just stared back at her from his comfortable spot in the chair. Megan sighed. "I have a single cup coffee maker if you'd like to make yourself a cup."

"Sure." Sebastian popped off the chair and followed her into the kitchen. She pulled down a mug for him and showed him where his coffee choices were. Despite it only being mid-afternoon, Megan chose chamomile for herself. A nap could do wonders for her now. Her brother would never allow her to go back and work anyway. Sighing, Megan rubbed her temples.

"Headache?" Sebastian asked.

"Tired," she replied. "I'll be fine after some tea and a good nap." Sebastian merely nodded his head. "No twenty questions? No lectures or advice?"

"Well, as a physician, I'm well-aware of your condition and what your options are. You're standing in front of me, and I see no apparent distress. It's obvious you're feeling better. And your brother assures me you're going to follow up with your treating physician. So no, no more questions."

Dropping her head, Megan pressed a hand to her forehead. "I'm sorry. There's really no excuse for my behavior. You've done nothing wrong."

"I think it's more that I've done nothing right with you," he replied. Picking his coffee pod, he popped it into the machine and pressed brew. Megan prepared a small mesh bag with fresh herbal tea, filled her mug with water, and set it in the microwave. "I'm glad I was there to check on you today, but now I've been firmly put in a role I didn't want to be in with you. I didn't want you to see me as a doctor."

"But you are a doctor," she said dumbly.

"I can't change that," he shrugged. "And I wouldn't. But I was hoping you'd start to see me as just a guy, your neighbor that you might be interested in having dinner with."

Speechless, Megan gaped at him. Was he saying he wanted to go on a date with her? Her instincts warred inside her. Yes, he now knew about her condition, but he was also standing there and acting as if everything were normal. He didn't ask a hundred questions or try to tell her how he thought she should be managing her disease. That was a refreshing trait. Everyone in her family tried to tell her what to do. Her parents were set against surgery, but that was the only option Megan saw to break free of this once and for all.

"I ... I'm not sure we're compatible," she stammered then immediately moved to the microwave as it signaled her tea was ready. She disposed of the teabag and leaned against the counter. All the while, she felt Sebastian's gaze on her. The truth was she was afraid of him. Not because he was a doctor but because she felt herself falling for him despite that and he had the power to hurt her more than her heart condition ever could. What if she fell in love with him and he decided his life really was in Chicago?

"You spend so much time avoiding doctors, and I get it—I do—but have you ever thought that maybe that's exactly who you should be with? Someone who actually *knows* your limits and how to respond?" Sebastian asked. "You've told yourself I'm all wrong, but never stopped to think about the reasons I'm exactly *right* for you." Picking up his mug, he took a sip, then raised his mug in toast. "I'll let you rest and return the mug later. Thanks for the coffee."

Megan closed her eyes, chastising herself for a fool. She heard the door open and quietly close. Taking her tea into the living room, she eased herself down onto the same overstuffed chair Sebastian just vacated. Damn it, it smelled like him. She stretched her feet out onto the ottoman in front of her, pulled the throw blanket around her, and then proceeded to analyze why she continued to be such a jerk.

The tea must have kicked in during her self-reflection as she woke up later to the sound of a soft knock on her door. Rubbing the sleep out of her eyes, she checked the time on her phone and discovered she had slept for nearly three hours. Rested, if not a little out of it from being jarred out of sleep by the knock, Megan got up to open the door, figuring it was likely her parents checking on her. She wasn't disappointed to see Sebastian standing there.

Holding a black cat.

Reaching out to pet the cat behind the ears, she smiled in greeting. "And who is this?"

"I have decided to name him Java because he's black. I thought Midnight or Shadow, but they're probably predictable names. And I like my coffee black, so, Java." Sebastian announced. Though the look on the cat's face was currently one of displeasure, he leaned into Megan's fingers and purred contently. Megan decided this cat must have a resting bitch face like she had a resting aversion to hot, potentially perfect-for-her men.

"He seems sweet enough."

"His body is tense," Sebastian said. "I think he's freaked out, but happy to be out of the small cage he was in at the animal shelter. He was found outside and no one came forward to claim him."

"Poor guy," Megan cooed. "Why isn't he in a cat carrier?"

"He hated that thing. He left the shelter in one, but he was crying in there and trying to get out. I think maybe he doesn't like closed-in spaces."

"Well, you can't blame the little guy. He's having a tough day. He doesn't know you. He may have had a family that he's missing." Slowly, Megan eased her hands around the cat and brought him over to her, scratching his ears and neck. "Why don't I hold him while you get what you need from the car? I assume you got him food and litter, a box, toys?"

"I did," Sebastian confirmed. "Sophie and Brooke robbed me blind. Would you mind taking him upstairs?"

"Not at all," Megan said, rubbing her cheek on the cat's head.

Pausing, Sebastian cocked his head to the side. "Your color looks better. Feeling okay now?"

Megan tried not to tense up. She had resolved to do better. He was asking a question anyone would ask a person knowing they were sick. "Yes, much, thank you." Stepping out into the hall, Megan ensured that her apartment wasn't locked before closing the door behind her.

"Here's my keys," he said, handing over his key ring. "Go on up with him. I'll be right behind you."

She let herself into his apartment and looked around. It looked like he was unpacked, and the place was meticulous. That must be the surgeon in him and the need for a sterile environment. Still scratching around the cat's ears, she sat down on the plush leather couch and nearly moaned. She could be very comfortable wasting away a snowy afternoon watching Netflix sucked into this couch—and it just so happened snow was coming that week. Sizing it up, she determined it could easily fit two people very comfortably. She was blushing furiously when Sebastian walked in juggling bags and a lidded cat litter box.

"I'll get the carrier later." Kicking the door shut, Sebastian unloaded everything in his arms onto the overstuffed loveseat. "You didn't put him down yet?"

Shrugging, Megan met his eyes. "I thought you might want to be here for his first impression."

Sebastian lowered himself down to the other end of the couch and spread his arm out. "Go for it."

Megan put the cat down on the floor between them. The cat stayed there for a minute, looked around, and then turned and wiggled under the couch. Sebastian threw up his hands and laughed. "Dear God, I *did* get an asshole."

Laughing, Megan placed her hand on his arm. "He'll come out. It's a new place, and you're a new person. This is a pretty scary day for a pet. It may take him a little while, but eventually his stomach and his bladder will force him out."

Sebastian looked down at where her hand lay on his arm then back up at her with a raised brow. Blushing, Megan snapped her hand back again as if it were on fire.

"I liked it there," Sebastian said softly. Inside, Megan melted. "Listen," he continued. "I'm attracted to you. I like what I know of you so far, and I want to get to know you better. I don't know how to get around this block you have against doctors."

Megan looked down at her hands. She liked him. Her heart raced when she was around him and not in a bad way. She put her hand back on his arm and tentatively looked back up at him. "Do you have Netflix?"

"Of course," he said.

"Got time off this week?"

"Wednesday."

"It's supposed to snow on Wednesday." This was an excellent co-incidence, she thought, as she eyed the couch.

"This early?"

"It doesn't happen often, but it does on occasion," she said with a shrug. "I was just thinking this would be a great couch for watching Netflix while getting snowed in. Plus, I don't have to worry about be-ing out in bad weather."

"And the covering practice is on duty Wednesday, so Jackie has the day off and you're not on baby duty." He smiled, and she drew her breath in a bit. His face was handsome enough, but when he smiled like that she was useless. She nodded her head.

"They're calling for that much snow?" Reaching over, he linked their fingers together, and Megan felt a jolt. Her gaze snapped back up to his, and she knew he felt it, too.

"Even if they're not, let's pretend they are," she said quietly.

"Sounds like a plan to me." Sebastian flipped their hands over, raised them, and pressed a kiss to the inside of her wrist. An electric current shot up to her elbow. "Did you feel that?" He asked quietly, placing a second kiss to the same spot. Wordlessly, she nodded. "That's why we need to explore this. This could be something amazing."

"It scares me," Megan whispered.

He nodded his head. "It's not something I've ever experienced either. We'll figure it out together, okay?" She nodded in return then rose from the couch.

"I think I'm ready to call it a night," she said. He stood, as well.

"Sleep and rest are always good medicine," he said then winced at his own words.

Smiling lightly, she stepped forward and kissed his cheek. "Thanks for caring." While he stood there dumbfounded, she quickly left the apartment and scurried downstairs. Once in her apartment, she dropped down on her couch, pulled a blanket over her, and grabbed her tablet from the table next to the couch intending on reading until she was ready to sleep.

She had a setback today with the event at the brewery, but she took an important step forward with Sebastian. She had told him she was scared, but the truth was, she was terrified.

Nine

MEGAN SAT ACROSS from Dr. Wilson on Monday morning as he delivered the news she always knew would be coming one day.

"I'm sorry, Megan," Dr. Wilson said. Megan clutched her brother's hand and drew in a ragged breath. "I've been treating you for this for a while now, and I truly think it's time to think about surgery. The echocardiogram shows a significant growth of the heart muscles. You are a prime candidate for a septal myectomy."

Justin squeezed her hand in support. "That's the surgery that can alleviate all the symptoms, right?" he asked.

"Most patients experience no further symptoms after the surgery, correct." The doctor folded his hands and looked from brother to sister. Megan could feel Justin's intense gaze on him. Their family had gone around and around on this issue. Their parents weren't convinced surgery of this kind was necessary. Megan knew otherwise.

In that moment, things were crystal clear to her. The dark wood of Dr. Wilson's desk and shelves, the diploma's and professional organization memberships along the wall, the trickle of water from a small fountain on his credenza, and the bright sun shining through the blinds on her. The quiet ticking of a clock reverberated off the walls like a church bell's deep gong. This was a life altering moment and she would remember it forever.

"Do you think I could maybe do it over the Thanksgiving holiday?" she asked. "If it's safe, I'd like to give my employers enough notice to make other arrangements while I'm recovering."

"I'm reluctant to wait that long," Dr. Wilson said. "But I understand you'd like to have some control over how this fits in your life and when is best. If the symptoms don't worsen between now and then, or the episodes do not get more frequent, I'm willing to put the surgery off until then. But you need to be very diligent with your health. Absolutely *do not* push yourself."

"Meggie, don't you think we should discuss this with mom and dad?" Justin murmured.

Megan spared a sidelong glance for him then returned her attention to her doctor. "No," she told her brother. As far as Megan was concerned, this was not a group decision. It was *her* decision. Nodding her head to the doctor, she said, "That is the route I would like to go. I agree with your advice. I've known this was eventually down the road. I'd like to get it done while I'm still young."

"Wait," Justin said, holding up his hand. "You may have had all these conversations with your doctor, Megan, but your family hasn't, and I have some questions. I'd like to better understand what's going on here."

Dr. Wilson looked to Megan for guidance. Technically speaking, the doctor was under no obligation to discuss Megan's health with anyone other than herself, but he was asking her if she would allow him to discuss it with Justin. She didn't want to let it happen. What she really wanted was to keep complete control over the situation and leave the office. But she wouldn't do that to her brother. She was going to need an ally when she spoke to their parents, so it was best if Justin got his questions answered.

"It's fine," Megan said quietly.

"What questions do you have, Justin?" Dr. Wilson asked.

"What is the alternative to the surgery?" Justin asked, scooting to the edge of his chair and laying a hand flat on the desk. These were all things Megan had discussed with her doctor at length, but none of her family had been present. Though it may look different to Justin, Megan spent ample time thinking over all her options and their accompanying risks. This was the best option available and the one that gave her the best chance at a normal life.

"In some cases, implantation of a cardioverter-defibrillator can prevent cardiac death. But that is putting a Band-aide on a wound." Dr. Wilson said, folding his hands on his desk. Justin was listening with rapt attention. "The septal myectomy can actually cure the disease. Another option is what's called an alcohol septal ablation. What happens then is alcohol is injected into the septum of the ventricles to kill heart muscle cells, but that has a risk of causing problems with the heart's rhythm."

"The ventricles are the bottom part of the heart?" Justin asked.

"Correct," said Dr. Wilson. "The lower two chambers. Another benefit to the myectomy is that we can check for sure that the mitral valve is clear.

"And what are the risks associated with the surgery?" Keeping his attention on the doctor, Justin reached over and grabbed his sister's hand. His hand was sweaty, giving away his nervousness and stress over the conversation. She gave him an encouraging squeeze in response.

"As I'm sure you know," Dr. Wilson said. "There are risks associated with any kind of surgery. That being said, the risks or complications associated with a septal myectomy are relatively low. There could be infection, bleeding, clotting that could cause a stroke or heart attack. There could be poor blood flow during the surgery, which could make it difficult for the heart to pump. These are all risk factors we'll be watching for."

Justin was quiet and the only noise in the office was the ticking of the clock and the water trickling in the fountain. He sat back in his chair and nodded.

"I anticipate a successful surgery," Dr. Wilson continued. "Due to Megan's age and lack of other medical conditions, she is a prime candidate for the myectomy. Once she recovers, she'll be able to maintain a healthy and active lifestyle. She'll even be able to have children."

Justin looked up at Megan. "I guess I didn't think of that."

"Dr. Wilson and I have been discussing this for several months now, Justin," Megan said quietly. "I'm not jumping to this decision."

"She's right," Dr. Wilson said. "Megan and I have carefully gone over her options and also brought in another physician to consult."

Sitting back in his chair, Justin nodded. "Okay." He looked a little shell-shocked. It was never easy to hear the risk factors involved in the surgery. She should know. It was why she took so long in making her decision.

The doctor rose from his chair, and so did Megan and her brother.

Shaking her hand, Dr. Wilson said, "My office will be in touch with you to set up the pre-surgical bloodwork and set the date. If you have any questions, of course, I'm always here to answer them."

"I appreciate that, Dr. Wilson," Megan said. "I will keep that in mind."

Megan said nothing to her brother as they left the doctor's office and walked to his car in the parking lot. She could feel the tension rolling off him, but for the first time in longer than she could remember, she felt at peace. *Finally*, something was going to be done. She felt lighter, hopeful.

Once they were in the car, however, her bother turned to her. "Don't you think you should discuss this with mom and dad? Surgery's a big deal."

Megan stared ahead. "No." She was resolved in her decision, despite being terrified by the potential outcomes. She was mostly afraid she'd be in that small percentage for whom surgery doesn't make a difference for—or worse, dies from a complication.

"Meggie..."

"No, Justin." Megan turned to look at her brother. "*I'm* the one living with this. Me. Not the whole family. I'm an adult now, and I need to be free of this. There's an anvil hanging over my head, and I want to be out from underneath it. I want to go skiing again. And as soon as the doctor says I'm fully recovered, do you know what I'm going to do? I'm going to sign up for a marathon and start training.

I'll break the news to mom and dad this weekend at dinner. You are not to say a word about it before then. Promise me."

"Megan."

"*Promise me*," she said. "I need you with me on this, Justin. I need everyone with me on it." She couldn't do this without her family. She simply couldn't. She couldn't worry about the surgery and family troubles too.

Justin reached across the console and gave her a one-armed hug. Megan sank into him as much as she could. "I'm with you," he whispered. "Always."

Nodding, she pulled back and wiped a few stray tears from her eyes. "Thank you. Please drop me off at the Grayson Falls Hospital. I'll get a ride home from there."

Pausing as if he wanted to say more, Justin finally started the car, put it in gear, and pulled out of the spot. The ride back to town was silent. Megan understood her brother had things he wanted to say, but she had heard them all before. There were risks associated with the surgery, and she knew what they were. She had weighed them heavily and when it came down to it, the chance of living a normal life and being free of this disease was worth any risk.

Megan kissed her brother on the cheek when they arrived at the hospital. She went in through the side door. As the nanny to one of the doctors, Megan had been given certain privileges at the hospital to come and go as she pleased, so if she needed Jackie, she could find her quickly. Of course, Megan would never go so far as to interrupt Jackie when she was with a patient, but it was nice not to have to walk through reception if she didn't need to. The nurse there would make her wait her turn.

She walked up the side stairs and thought about what she was going to tell Jackie and Danny. How could she word it so it didn't sound like she intentionally deceived them? There was no way. Maybe if Sebastian were there to help her, but would that pit brother against sister? She didn't want to do that either. Then again, Sebastian might not be interested in coming down on Megan's side with regard to this. For all Megan knew, he would be upset with her that she withheld pertinent information from his sister and put his niece in potential danger.

Worrying her lip, Megan opened the door to the hospital and stepped into the familiar environment. Why couldn't she have the surgery here instead? This didn't feel so much like a hospital. This building was welcoming and not nearly as scary as the University Hospital where the surgery would take place.

Megan walked straight for the office. When she stood in the doorway, she was relieved that Jackie wasn't within it. Megan hadn't realized that it was Sebastian she was looking for and *not* Jackie. While she knew that she was going to have to talk to her as soon as possible about her disease and the upcoming surgery, it was her boss's brother she most wanted to see now.

Sebastian stood in the center of the office reviewing something on a tablet. Megan's mouth watered as she saw just how good Sebastian looked with glasses perched on the end of his nose and a serious expression.

Sensing her presence, he looked up, a smile spreading across his handsome face.

"Hey! Come look at this." He waved her over. "I tried to cover for you this morning with the baby, but Danny apparently has no faith in my ability to keep an infant alive, so he took Ally to work with him. As a result, Grayson Falls' women were gifted with this image."

Despite her nerves, Megan smiled when she saw that what Sebastian was so studiously looking at was a Facebook book feed. There was a picture with the caption, "Chief Hottie on Daddy duty." The accompanying picture was of Danny with Ally strapped to his chest, looking down at a file and clearly not knowing Norrie, the dispatcher, had taken a picture. The comments below the picture were shameless.

Setting the tablet back on the desk, Sebastian gave her his full attention. "Are you looking for Jackie?"

"Um, no," Megan said. "I was looking for you."

"Oh, okay." Sebastian moved behind her and pushed the office door shut. "What's up?"

"Have you told your sister about my medical condition?"

Sebastian paused. "Jackie? Of course not," he said. "I may not be your treating physician, but you didn't give me permission to disclose your condition to anyone. Though, honestly, you really do need to the tell them."

Megan nodded quickly. "I will. I plan on telling them tomorrow. Would you be there with me?"

Sebastian looked stupefied. He opened his mouth, closed it, opened it, closed it. "Yeah, sure, if you want me to be, of course."

Megan took a deep breath. "I decided on surgery," she said, looking down at her hands. Nervousness ran through her. What if he told her it was a bad idea? When she looked back up, he was watching her closely.

He took off his glasses and tossed them on his desk. Megan was sorry to see them go. "Your doctor explained all the risks?"

Megan nodded her head.

"Do you have any questions?"

Shaking her head, she whispered, "I'm really scared though." She thought that she could confess this to him. He was someone that understood everything about the surgery, knew the procedure, knew every step in the process. He would be objective and not ruled by emotions. He was right. She had never given thought to having a doctor as a friend or significant other, but here she was coming to him immediately after the decision was made. It was his arms she came to for comfort.

She was not disappointed as he drew her in close, burying one hand in her hair and kissing the top of her head. "I'll be here for you," he said, with his lips still pressed to her hair. "Every step of the way."

Ten

IT WAS RIDICULOUS, Sebastian thought. He barely knew her, and he knew everything there was to know about the procedure—he had even assisted in it once. Yet as he stood here holding her trembling body in his arms, he was terrified for her. He cared about her more than he realized, and it was hitting him all at once.

"Is it the septal myectomy?" He asked. She nodded into his shoulder. He suspected so. Based on what she had told him so far, the septal ablation would likely be ineffective. Most often, the myectomy was a cure. When he felt the tears hit his chest, he began to rub her back and pressed his cheek to her head. The scent of her shampoo assaulted his senses. Her silk-like hair slid through his fingers. She needed to work through it and process it all, and he was wildly happy she had chosen to come to him.

"I'm sorry," she said, pulling back a bit and rubbing her face.

Sebastian cupped her cheeks and looked into her eyes. "There's nothing to be sorry about. I'm happy you came to me. I'll help you through it. I know it's scary, but just remember after the surgery, you'll have your life back. You'll have control again."

Nodding, she stepped back farther, wiping the tears from her cheeks. "I'm going to run a marathon."

"Well," he said, "that's certainly ambitious. I'll train with you. Zach and I run most nice mornings. We'll drag his sorry ass into it, too."

She took a deep breath and let it out again. Sebastian marveled in the strength of the woman before him. Maybe she had a medical condition that set her back physically, but she was a fighter. He took a second to assess her. She looked tired. She had grit and was a refreshing change from the hollow, shallow, fashion plates he had dated in Chicago—women who saw a surgeon's salary and the son of a senate candidate and didn't care about anything else.

It was true that he didn't know her favorite color, favorite movie, or where she wanted to travel to. He thought he was coming to know who she was—and she was definitely worth getting to know better.

"All right," she said. "I'll go see if I can relieve Danny of his daughter. Thanks for listening."

"Thanks for coming to me," he said. He watched as she opened the door and bumped into Jackie. Jackie looked between them and arched a brow at him. Sebastian kept his expression neutral.

"Hey, Megan," she said, pasting a smile on her face. "Everything go okay this morning?"

"Yes," Megan replied. "I need to talk to you and Danny though. Can I come by earlier in the morning or maybe tonight?"

"Tonight is good," Jackie said, a look of concern coming over her face. "Is everything all right?"

Megan nodded unconvincingly. "It's just important that I to talk to you."

"Okay." Jackie said. Megan slipped by her before Jackie could ask any more questions, but Sebastian knew he wasn't going to be so lucky. Jackie pushed the door shut and rounded on him. "Do you know what's going on?"

"I do," he confessed.

"What?"

"It's not my news to tell," Sebastian refused. It wasn't easy to say no to his sister. He had a hard time refusing her or Natalie anything, but he would not break Megan's confidence. His sister may be frustrated with him, but it would only be for a few hours. If he broke Megan's trust when they were just starting to be friends, it would cause lasting—perhaps permanent—damage.

"I get the sense I'm not going to like whatever it is," Jackie sighed. "At least tell me this, is she quitting?"

"No," Sebastian said. "At least, not that I know of."

"Well, that wasn't encouraging."

"I'd love nothing more than to ease your worries, Jacks, but I can't betray a confidence."

"Ryan would have," she muttered. The sides of Sebastian's lips lifted up. It was true. Sebastian had a soft spot for his sisters, but Ryan was an easy mark altogether, especially when it came to Jackie. He literally did whatever she wanted. Sebastian needed to stand firm.

Walking forward, Sebastian tapped her nose with the tip of his finger. Jackie scowled. "That's because he's a wuss. I can resist my sister's charms."

"Maybe he just loves me more."

"Nice try."

Sebastian tried to walk past her to leave, but she stepped back in front of him. Squinting her eyes and cocking her head to the side, she asked, "What's going on with you and my nanny?"

"Didn't I tell you that she lives in the apartment below me?"

"Yes," Jackie said. "But I didn't realize you had gotten close."

"We haven't," Sebastian said. "Yet."

Jackie sat down on the couch, looking up at him. "We have no patients now," she said. "Tell me about this."

Turning around one of the visitor's chairs, Sebastian sat down and propped one ankle on the opposite knee. "I like her a lot. There's something about her that draws me in, and I want to find out what that is. I met her briefly when she worked at the library. She wasn't very friendly. She hasn't been an easy person to get to know. She protects herself. I've had to tread carefully with her, but we had a breakthrough recently, which is encouraging. It's been so long since I've had a girlfriend, you know? And I can't call her that now—we're friends and neighbors—but I'd like her to be one day. In Chicago, I never really had a girlfriend. I have women I could call if I needed a date for an event—or other reasons."

"Spare me those details." Jackie held her hands up.

"I think my last serious girlfriend was in college."

94 A.M. MAHLER

"I understand how that goes," Jackie said. "After Danny, I never had a serious boyfriend. I never even tried. I went out on a lot of first dates, but never let anything develop past that. I often wonder now if it was because deep down I knew we'd find our way to each other again."

"We're hanging out Wednesday since the covering practice will be on duty and we're both off," Sebastian said, standing back up. "She wants to watch Netflix all day and get snowed in."

Jackie grinned. "*Does* she? If your power goes out, you'll have to keep each other warm."

"That would be a damn shame," Sebastian said. Opening the door, he left the office with Jackie behind him. He hadn't looked forward to a snow day so much since he was a kid.

MEGAN SAT ACROSS from Danny and Jackie in their living room, holding her breath and waiting for the explosion—or job termination. Sebastian was next to her, just as he promised. He placed a hand on her knee and squeezed. Butterflies flew in her stomach. She was so nervous she didn't even care if Jackie and Danny got the wrong idea about them.

Jackie and Danny looked at each other—silent communication passing between them—Danny subtly nodded his head to his wife. Megan watched in awe. They knew each other so well. The way they interacted with each other made Megan long for a relationship like that. Danny turned back to Megan. "How are you feeling?"

Letting the breath out, she slid her hand over where Sebastian's was on her leg and squeezed tight. "I feel okay now. I have medication. I didn't do too great over the weekend, but things are okay now. And Sebastian was there to help." Looking over at him, she gave him a small, tear-filled smile and he smiled encouragingly back.

Her body was tensed. She would not relax until she knew whether or not she still had a job. While she knew she would always have employment with her family if she needed it, she wanted *this* job. She loved little Ally. She liked Jackie and Danny as employers, and she couldn't stand the idea that they may be disappointed in her or think of her poorly.

She also liked the freedom of the job. If she needed to run an errand, she could take the baby and do that. She often did other things for Danny and Jackie, as well.

"Which surgery did you decide on?" Jackie asked.

"The septal myectomy," Megan said. "I just...I don't want my life to be guided by this anymore, you know? The surgery is going to be scheduled over Thanksgiving, but it will be a long recovery time."

"You've given us plenty of notice," Danny said. "We can call on any number of people to help out while you're recovering. Don't worry about that."

Tears sprang into Megan's eyes, and her breath caught with hope. "You're not going to fire me?"

"Why would we do that?" Jackie asked. "We adore you."

"But I didn't tell you I had this condition." Megan shook her head. *How could this be going this easy?*

"Are you trying to talk us into firing you now?" Danny asked.

"No!"

"Okay, good." He said. "We like you. You take great care of our daughter and us—even though that's not your job. You're also not obligated to tell your employer about a medical condition. Okay? So, you just tell us what you need and when you need it, and we'll be there for you. That's how this family works, and you're part of this family."

A tear slid down Megan's cheek, and she quickly brushed it away. "That means so much, thank you. I truly love this job, and I was afraid you would be mad."

"Then you didn't give us enough credit," Danny said, gently.

"I'm sorry about that, too."

Jackie slapped her palms on her thighs. "All right. That's settled. You've given us plenty of time, so we'll come up with a plan for care for Ally *and* you." Megan opened her mouth to object, but Jackie held up a hand. "I won't have it any other way."

"I can't be a burden," Megan began. "It's already an inconvenience—"

"Nothing is an inconvenience for family," Jackie refused, standing up. Megan rose, as well, and Jackie moved in for a hug. "Can we interest you in staying for dinner?"

Sebastian stood and stepped in, running a hand up to Megan's shoulder. "I think another time. We already have plans tonight." Jackie arched a brow and looked between them. Megan's face heated, wondering what Jackie thought of her brother and her nanny together, and just what his plans were as this was the first time she had heard anything about it.

Not that she and Sebastian were together—not by a long shot. But they felt like more than friends—something more intimate without being physical. It was different than any other relationship she had ever had before.

Disappointment seemed to cross Jackie's face. Megan knew that Jackie was the mother hen of the family and thrived on taking care of her siblings in any way she could, even if it just meant feeding them. Megan imagined since Sebastian had only recently moved to Grayson Falls the novelty of him hadn't worn off yet, despite working with him day to day.

"Mind if I catch a ride with you?" Sebastian said as they walked outside. "I walked to the hospital and rode over here with Jackie."

"Sure." Megan unlocked the car. Once they were inside, she said, "So what are our plans this evening?"

"Oh, nothing," he said. "It just looked like you could use the out. I know that was emotional for you, and Jackie can get overwhelming in her constant need to take care of people. She means well, but doesn't always realize how pushy she can get."

"If there's one thing we have in common," she said as she backed the car up to turn around, "It's a pushy family." Pointing the car in the right direction, she began to slowly make her way down the dirt road that led from Jackie's and Ryan's respective houses to the hospital.

"I don't know," Sebastian said. "I think we'll find we have a little bit more in common than that."

Glancing sideways at him, her lips curved. "Maybe a little bit."

Eleven

MEGAN WALKED AROUND her apartment tidying up with her phone pressed to her ear. She was trying to get upstairs for their Snowmageddon day, but Laurie had called a few minutes ago and Megan didn't want to go upstairs still on the phone.

"Are your brothers coming over today?" she asked.

"No," Megan said. "I told them not to bother. I'm going upstairs to Sebastian's. He has a huge leather couch and a fireplace. We're going to binge watch Netflix and chill."

Silence greeted her on the other end of the phone. What? Did she say something wrong?

"You know that's hipster code for having sex, right?"

Megan straightened up full height, eyes widened, mouth agape, adrenaline running through her veins. "What? No."

"'Fraid so, my friend." Laurie laughed. In fact, she cackled. Megan had no idea that was euphemism. How could she? She didn't hang out with anyone except her brothers and cousins.

Wait a minute. *Did Sebastian think that?* Was he planning on a totally different afternoon than she was? What was she going to do? She couldn't have sex. She could die during it!

"This is a nightmare," Megan groaned into the phone. "Do you think he knows that's what it means?"

"Being a hipster guy from a big city," Laurie replied. "I'm going to say that's a big 10-4."

"But that wasn't my plan! I really did want to binge watch shows and hang out. What if he thinks I wanted to have sex and when he finds out that's not the case, he doesn't want to hang out anymore?"

"Then he's a jerk that's not worth a further minute of your time," Laurie replied.

Dropping her head into her hand, Megan couldn't believe what an idiot she was. All this time she'd led a relatively sheltered life in a small town and didn't have any interest in keeping up with the latest culture of people her age. What a country bumpkin she was. Up until this moment, she didn't care if that's what she was. She was happy with her little life in her little town, but now she was going to show Sebastian just how unsophisticated she was.

"All right," Megan said, letting out a breath. "I'm going to go get this mortifying moment in my life over with."

"But let me know the outcome!" Laurie called out as Megan hit end to the call.

SEBASTIAN OPENED HIS door just as flakes were starting to fall outside. Megan stood there in plaid pajama bottoms and a faded gray Southern New Hampshire University sweatshirt, a steaming mug in her hand, and a quilt slung over her shoulder. Her hair was in one of those messy buns his sisters preferred to wear at work. Glancing down at her feet, Sebastian smiled to see her feet ensconced in cow slippers. In a word, she looked adorable.

"Coffee?" he asked, nodding to the mug.

"Hot chocolate," she replied. "Too much caffeine in coffee for me. I brought extra packets. They're the official beverage of snowstorms."

Stepping back to let her in, Sebastian replied, "I'd dispute that. I have two growlers of Over the Hop Great Northern Wheat in the fridge. Beer warms you just as much."

"I'm not much of an alcohol drinker." Moving to the couch, she shrugged the quilt off her shoulder and hunted around for a coaster. Finally finding one under a magazine, she set her mug down on it.

Sebastian shut the door and strolled over. "I would think not with the medication you're on. Alcohol can cause a lot of problems." Dropping down on the couch, Sebastian turned sideways and pulled his knees up. He, too, was dressed in flannel pants and a Mavericks sweatshirt with his brother's name and old number on the back.

Megan found a coaster and reset the mug on the end table next to her then arranged herself under her quilt.

"I do have blankets, you know," Sebastian said.

"This is my favorite movie watching quilt," Megan said. "It's from the general store. It's one of the mysterious Sadie's."

Cocking his head to the side, Sebastian said, "Mysterious Sadie?"

"Stitches by Sadie," Megan said, taking a sip of cocoa. "Every so often, Sophie and Brooke get a shipment of beautiful quilt products from somebody named Sadie, but no one knows who she is. She's only ever provided a post office box to send the money from the sales to. It's all a big mystery. Sophie thinks Sadie isn't the woman's real name. I don't know why she would want to stay anonymous. She does beautiful work and her products rarely stay there long. This quilt could fit on a twin bed, but I use it in my living room. It has wool in it, so it's extra warm without making you all sweaty."

Sebastian didn't immediately respond to that statement. He couldn't. He was too busy thinking of Megan getting sweaty. *Whoa there. Those thoughts will get you nowhere today.* He must have stayed quiet too long because she nudged him with her foot.

"I have something I need to get off my chest," Megan said suddenly. This didn't sound too promising. He wondered what he had done wrong.

"Okay," Sebastian said carefully.

"Did you know that saying 'Let's what Netflix and chill' was a euphemism for having sex?" Okay, so maybe he wasn't in trouble. But he could see how he could easily *get* in trouble here.

"Actually, I did know that." Best to be honest. Megan's eyes widened in shock and a very attractive blush crawled over her face. "But I knew what you meant when you asked. I know you just literally want to binge watch Netflix and chill out. I absolutely was *not* expecting sex today." And that was the absolute truth. With her condition, elevating her heart rate that way could be dangerous.

Of course, thinking about that made him wonder if she had ever had sex before. He thought it was just as likely she did as she didn't. And this line of internal examination wouldn't get him anywhere.

"I feel like such an idiot. I had *no* idea! You must think I'm terribly unsophisticated."

"I don't think that at all," he said. "I think you're amazing just the way you. I don't care that you didn't know what it meant. The only thing that matters is that *I* know what you meant. I have no expectations in that area today."

Megan visibly relaxed. He'd never say it out loud, but her mortification of her gaffe was utterly adorable. She was intelligent and wise, but also very sweet.

"So, what are we watching today?" she asked.

"This is your party. I thought you had a plan."

"No plan." She shook her head. "I just thought this would be a great couch to spend a snow day on."

"Ah, so if I was working today, you'd be on my couch without me?"

"Possibly, but I don't have a key."

"I don't lock the door," he said. "The outside door is always locked, so I don't lock the apartment."

"You should. Grayson Falls may not be a hotbed of crime, but we have had problems. You never know what kids are going to do when they get bored."

He looked at her for a drawn-out moment, hoping what he was about to confess to wouldn't send her running back downstairs. "I leave it unlocked in case you need me."

Her cheeks pinkened, but she didn't break eye contact. He wasn't sure what her embarrassment was for, but he found her blush endearing. It had been awhile since he spent time with a woman who genuinely blushed.

Megan adjusted her position, so her feet were stretched out in front of her on the oversized ottoman and she faced the picture window to watch the snow. Sebastian mirrored her position, but also used it as an opportunity to sit next to her instead of on opposite ends of the couch. He'd get nowhere with her if he couldn't get her used to being near him. Deciding to test the waters further, he pulled part of her blanket over onto himself and huddled down next to her. This was definitely not a bad way to spend the day.

Outside, the snow fell fast. If it kept up this way, they'd get a lot more accumulation than what was forecasted. He shivered with the knowledge of how the wintery chill felt if he went outside. It would be a good day for a fire and sinking into the couch with warm blankets.

As Megan stretched over to pluck her mug from the end table, Sebastian's cat chose that moment to hop up onto her lap.

"Oh, sure," Sebastian chided the cat as the feline kneaded Megan's lap before settling down. "My lap's not good enough, but hers is? Traitor." He reached over and scratched his pet behind his ears, earning a purr. "Still, I guess I can't blame you."

"He seems to be settling in," she said, sipping her drink.

"You know he stole my egg sandwich this morning." Charmed by her laugh, he continued, stroking his hand down the cat's back. "You laugh, but that was my breakfast. I set it on my computer desk at my elbow while I did a little work, and he jumped over my shoulder and made off with it. His stealth would put some special forces soldiers to shame."

Throwing back her head, Megan laughed. It sounded like it was coming from her toes. "You're trying to look annoyed, but your words have no heat. You like him."

"He's got personality, I'll give him that. He seems to be settling in now. The morning after I got him, he finally came out from under the couch to explore."

"He's so sweet. You couldn't have stayed mad at him for long."

"He's also eaten a bagel, an English muffin, and a chocolate cup-cake," Sebastian said. "I think he must have lived outside for a while and doesn't realize yet that he's going to be fed regularly here and he doesn't need to forage for his own food."

"He'll figure it out." She scratched him a little more then took another sip of her drink. "What's your family in Chicago like?"

He paused, trying to decide how honest he wanted to be about them. He figured if he really wanted the two of them to get to know each other better, he was going to have to give her the good, the bad, and the ugly.

"I was raised by my paternal grandparents," he began. "My father and mother had a one-night stand at a party where my father went to college, and here I am. My mother split town from what I was told. I only found out recently that she has schizophrenia and she left all of us behind after we were born except for Zach. My mother, Daisy, is a whole different story, but I wanted to let you know about her. My father married a woman who I'm pretty sure doesn't like any-one. I have two sisters and a brother from them, but I'm not close with those siblings. I was never really afforded the opportunity. They came to family parties, but whatever my father and stepmother had told them about me made them very stand-offish. I was never re-ally able to break down the wall they'd erected, so after a while, I just stopped trying. I was their brother. They were uninterested. And there wasn't really anything else I could do about it." Looking down, Sebastian picked at a string on the quilt.

"My grandparents, on the other hand, were warm and loving. If it weren't for them, I'm sure my father would have given me up af-ter my mother split, but my grandparents couldn't stand the idea of knowing they had a grandchild somewhere out in the world. My fa-ther provided financial support, but that was all. Never called on my birthday or came to any Little League games. I was shocked when he attended my graduations. I think my grandmother shamed him into it." Leaving the string alone, Sebastian crossed his arms over his chest and looked out the picture window at the falling snow.

"I didn't even know about any of my siblings here until Eric Davis showed up investigating. Jackie and Ryan discovered they were related when her father died while they were in high school. They didn't know about the rest of us until Danny asked Eric to investigate our mother. Zach knew about us all, but he didn't have any information on how to find us. He wasn't even sure of all our names. Zach's father is a psychiatrist. He married Daisy, and they had Zach. I guess the man's considered my step-father."

"Wow," Megan said, shifting to her side, she propped an elbow up on the back of the couch and rested her head on her hand. "That's quite the family. So, you don't keep in touch with your Chicago siblings at all?"

"I have tried a few times over the years, but they're unresponsive."

Megan reached out for his hand and linked their fingers. Sebastian took the comfort she offered. He'd long ago come to terms with the fact that his relationship with his father and his family was always going to be non-existent to strained. It had stopped hurting him decades ago. Now, he just found himself resigned and didn't often think of them.

"And your brothers and sister here seem to be the opposite."

"They are polar opposites," he agreed, thinking that included his sister Natalie. "We've gone our whole lives without each other, but when we all got together, I was in awe of the camaraderie that formed so quickly and the love ... I wasn't prepared for the immediate love. They embraced me even after I told them my father had directed me to dig up anything I could on them and report back in. He was concerned my new siblings could be damaging to his senate campaign."

"Sebastian, I'm so sorry for all you had to deal with." Megan reached over and squeezed his hand. "My parents can be overbearing, but they've certainly never used me as a pawn. That must have been devastating as a boy."

Sebastian shrugged. "It was at one time, but it was always the way. I think what was most devastating was when I really questioned why I didn't live with my father. When he would come visit his parents—usually without the rest of his family—he would rarely interact with me beyond asking me about school and if I was being well-behaved. He never played games with me or watched movies with me, never asked about things I liked. I used to beg him to let me live with him when it was time for him to leave. My grandfather finally sat me down and said, 'Sebastian, your father doesn't have enough love in his heart for anyone but himself. We love you too much to let you go.'"

"Your grandparents sound like wonderful people."

"They're the best. I miss them now that they're in Florida, but it feels so good to be out from under my father's thumb. I'm intending to fly down to see them in a few weeks. I don't have any large expenses, so I should be able to afford to pop down once a month or every other month for a weekend to see them."

Waving a hand at the picture window with the snow falling outside, she said, "Florida sounds pretty good right now."

"Well, maybe you'll come with me on one of those visits."

"I've never flown before."

Surprised, Sebastian looked at her, shifting now to mirror her position, but instead of resting his head on his hand, he linked their fingers and stroked her hand with his thumb. The tension between them rose. "Never?"

"I got my diagnosis when I was ten years old, and my parents didn't want me to fly. So, we always went somewhere we could drive. It took us three days to get to Orlando one year and three to get back. My brothers and I fought the entire time in the car. My parents weren't keen on putting us in the car for more than a few hours after that." She shrugged. "It's no big deal. We went to Bar Harbor a lot, Cape Cod, Canada. It's not like I didn't go anywhere, just not by airplane."

"We'll rectify that." He wanted to show her the world.

"I was an active kid and just learning how to ski when I got my diagnosis. I really liked skiing and was devastated to have it taken away."

"I'll take you skiing," Sebastian said.

"I was always told I couldn't do things like that."

"You'll be with me," he said. "I'll keep a close eye on you. Surely your parents can't object to anything that has you under doctor supervision."

"Sneaky. But it's too tempting to pass up. If you think it'll be safe, I'm game."

Her eyes sparkled, and he just couldn't resist her anymore. Letting go of her hand he threaded it up into her hair and pulled her a little closer. Pausing to make sure he was reading her correctly, he leaned forward. When he saw no resistance, fear, or revulsion, he slowly pressed his lips to hers.

Feeling her tense up, Sebastian thought he had made a terrible mistake. Had he moved too fast for her? He had been so careful leading up to this not to come across too strongly.

She relaxed and tugged him closer by his shirt. When she opened her lips for him, he knew he had never tasted anything as sweet or as addicting. Consumed by her, he shifted his body to a more comfortable position. He hoped to be here kissing her for a while. Megan tugged him down with her as she laid out lengthwise on the couch. Encouraged, he stretched out along her body, slid his hand over her waist to her lower back and pulled her into his body. A little moan came from her as they made contact.

When was the last time he had kissed a woman this delicious, this responsive? Sweet Christ, could he spend the day just doing this? Would that be too much to ask for?

Pulling her underneath him, she responded by plunging her fingers into his hair and hooking her leg over his hip. He tipped his forehead against hers, breathing heavy.

Her breath caught when he slid his hand under her sweatshirt and he came in contact with her bare flesh. His fingers tingled and he couldn't remember something like that ever happening to him before. By her intake of breath, he knew she felt it too.

He was just moving to kiss her neck when everything crumbled around them.

Beep. Beep. Beep.

"Dammit," Megan whispered when her heart monitor went off.

Beep. Beep. Beep.

Pressing a kiss to her forehead, Sebastian calmly slid his hand down her arm to her wrist and checked her pulse. It was definitely elevated.

"How do you feel?" He asked softly, pulling her hand up and pressing a kiss inside her wrist.

Blushing, she met his gaze. "Amazing."

Grinning like a fool, he kissed the tip of her nose. "Me too." Reaching over, he grabbed the remote then slid to the inside of the couch and gathered her into his arms. "Let's take a break for a bit—get that heart rate back down."

Megan covered her face with her hand. "I'm so sorry, and I'm *so* embarrassed."

Kissing her forehead again, he tightened his arms around her. "No need to be either. I understand what's going on, and it's good to learn your limits. I'm also ridiculously flattered that I can do that do you."

Slapping his arm, she laughed. "Male ego rears its ugly head!"

Sebastian handed her the remote control and pushed off the couch. "Find something to watch. I'll get a fire going. Ethan loaded me up with firewood, and I've got it out on the back deck under a tarp."

Megan got up to refresh her hot chocolate and make them a snack while Sebastian went about the process of building a fire. He made several trips out to the deck and back in to stack all the wood they would need for a while and set about crumbling newspaper and stacking wood. Megan sliced cheese and apples and arrange them on a platter she found in his cabinets with crackers and grapes.

Struck by the domesticity of the scene, he watched her in his kitchen. This could be her life if she let him in. She looked up at him and blushed. Face flaming, she turned back to her task. He wondered if she was thinking the same thing. Or maybe she was thinking back to that amazing kiss they shared.

After Sebastian had the fire blazing, they decided on their watch schedule—a new superhero movie, a mystery, and a romantic comedy—and settled in with snacks. Two movies in, Sebastian checked the snow accumulation out of the picture window. "Wow," he said. "I think we're going to get more than what they called for. It's really coming down."

He stopped at the window to take in the wintery scene. Everything was blanketed in a thick coat of fluffy white. The road was completely covered and it was obvious a plow had not come through yet. The Grayson Falls road department were skilled at keeping the roads cleared and drivable during snow storms, but this was coming down too fast for even them to keep up. He loved the first snow of the year. He was one of those people that never get enough snow. By the end of the winter, most people he knew were happy to the see the end of winter, but Sebastian loved this time of year.

"Happens." Megan reached over to grab some cheese slices and crackers and burrowed further under the blanket. "It was still warm over the weekend, so I doubt it'll stick around for a long time. I don't think the ground has frozen yet."

"Who's in charge of shoveling the walk?" Sebastian stretched out his back and turned back to her. Damn, she looked good this comfortable in his home.

"My brothers usually come and do it."

"I'll take care of it then," he decided aloud. He liked the idea of being the man around the house—though his back might disagree with him after he was done shoveling. "Text them and let them know they're off the hook. I saw shovels in the laundry room."

"I can help." She flipped back the blanket and started to push herself off the couch.

"*That* I'm pulling doctor on. Snow shoveling is too strenuous an activity, especially this much snow. Save it for the two-inch storms."

Shrugging, Megan wrapped herself back up in the blanket. While Sebastian didn't have to worry about clearing snow living in the high-rise in Chicago, he did make sure he always went over to his grandparents and dug them out. He was used to the work, and it would be good exercise since he missed his run that morning.

"Throw some logs on the fire and get that hot cocoa going. I'm going to need the warmth when I come in."

"That I *can* do," she said, pushing herself off the couch.

At home in his house, she disappeared into the kitchen as Sebastian began to bundle up to make a first pass at clearing the snow, hoping for a snowy winter.

Twelve

WHEN MEGAN AWOKE she was bathed in the sunlight streaming through the picture window into Sebastian's living room. Turning her face toward the warmth for a few minutes, she adjusted her position to cuddle down further into Sebastian's embrace. Though the fire burned low in the hearth, the warmness enveloping them felt like an old friend. She couldn't recall having made the decision to stay over. They must have just drifted off to sleep.

This definitely wasn't a bad way to wake up.

Feeling her movement, Sebastian tightened his embrace, but continued to drift along in sleep and not quite wake. She was glad she had given Sebastian the chance to prove they could be something more than just neighbors.

When her heart monitor went off yesterday, Sebastian didn't get frustrated. He didn't huff and end the date, or look at her like she was a freak. He assessed her situation and calmed her down. Maybe he was right. Maybe he *was* exactly who she should be with. He certainly had more confidence in them than she did.

She didn't have an extensive dating history. She wasn't jaded. She just believed she hadn't met the right guys. She had a boyfriend in high school, but they broke up before they both left for college. Since then, she went out on a lot of first and second dates. But the dating pool in Grayson Falls was shallow, having grown up with most of the eligible bachelors.

Sebastian could hardly be considered a boyfriend. A few make-out sessions didn't constitute a relationship, though they had hung out a few times now and he hadn't flinched in showing his support of her with his sister and brother-in-law. They were getting to know each other, and she liked what she was learning.

"Your thinking woke me up," Sebastian said, pulling the covers up over his shoulder to trap them underneath.

Reaching up, she lightly scratched his trimmed beard. "Just enjoying the morning view."

Opening his eyes, he smiled down at her. "I could get used to this morning view real fast. I'd kiss you, but I have morning breath."

"I hope you weren't under any illusions that I woke up with a full face of makeup and minty-fresh breath because you'll be disappointed."

Dipping his head, he pressed his lips to hers. "You've woken up perfect."

Sighing against his lips, she ran her hands up his back. Determined to keep things easy so she could continue to enjoy her new favorite activity of snuggling with him in the morning, she wouldn't allow the kiss to get out of control like it had the day before. Sebastian must have been of the same mindset because he pulled away and pressed a kiss to her forehead.

"I'll stoke the fire and get breakfast going," he said, pushing himself off the couch.

She immediately missed the warmth of his body. She wanted to burrow back down into their cocoon, but her full bladder had other ideas. Rising off the couch, she shivered against the chill that had settled over the room.

The sunlight on her face had been nice while she was under the blankets and pressed up against Sebastian's body. Wandering over to the window, she checked outside to see how much snow fell.

"Holy shit! There's like a foot of snow out here!" Sebastian yelped from the sliding door to the deck. He was clearly doing the same thing. Pressing her hands to her face, Megan smiled in anticipation. Even for a town accustomed to getting snow, a foot of the fluffy white stuff took a little while to clear. She had a four-wheel drive vehicle, so she would check in with Jackie and Danny about their plans for the day. As chief of police, Danny would definitely be going to work, but Jackie may just respond to the hospital from home.

"Guess I'm not walking into work today," Sebastian said coming in with an armful of wood, as his phone signaled a text. He put the wood on the hearth then reached for his phone. "Oh," he said. "Jackie said the covering doctor said he'd stay today since he was stuck anyway and will handle anything that came in. Guess we have another day off."

"An unexpected snow day," Megan said.

Loading wood into the fireplace, Sebastian spoke over his shoulder. "I say after breakfast, we resume our position under the covers and find a show neither of us has seen to stream." He stood up and turned around. "How about it?"

Touched that he wanted to spend yet another day with her, she nodded. "I'd say that's perfect."

"YOU KNOW YOU DON'T have to walk me to my door, right?"

Sebastian stepped to the bottom of the stairs, his hand running down the scuffed bannister. "I know." He said. "I need to get my mail, too. After two days of burrowing in, I should probably see what the outside world requires of me."

Megan turned to him, her back to her apartment door and Sebastian stepped up to her. He wrapped his arms around his waist and nuzzled into her hair, allowing her scent to wash over him. She always smelled so sweet. Was it her shampoo? Soap? Natural scent? What? These were the things he needed to discover—the mysteries that drove him insane late at night when he was alone in bed.

Megan tilted her head and Sebastian pressed gentle kisses along her neck.

"Is this really happening?" she asked. The wistful tone in her voice caught his attention and he pulled up to look at her.

"I had fun." He said. "We're probably good on snow for a little while, but we made the most of it. I'll miss sleeping with you in my arms tonight. Are you sure you don't want to stay over? I can come down here too."

Now that he had a taste for her—knew what it felt like to hold her all night—he wanted more. She gave him an inch and he wanted a mile.

Pressing a hand to his chest, she smiled to take the sting off the gesture. "I need to be up early in the morning and I don't want any distractions."

Dipping his head again, Sebastian nibbled on her ear. "I like being a distraction."

"I don't function well on lack of sleep." Her tone was apologetic and he lifted his head, suppressing his urge to sigh. She was right, she needed rest, and he certainly didn't want to contribute to her performing at less than her best.

"Okay, then." He stepped back, but not before pressing a kiss to her forehead.

"I'm sorry." She winced.

"For what? Setting boundaries? You don't have to apologize for that. We're playing by your rules. If you want some space, you can have it." Even if it did feel as though after their steps forward the last two days, she was now taking a giant leap back. He wasn't the kind of guy that pushed once a line was drawn. He hated guys that talked about their ability to score a reluctant woman by pushing until she gave in. Guys like that were scum. Sebastian was raised better than that.

"Thank you for understanding. I just need to recharge." Smiling, she went up on her tip toes and pressed a kiss to his lips. "I had a great time. Maybe on our next joint day off we can do something just like it."

"We'll compare schedules." He was already looking forward to the next time he could spend long hours with her in his arms.

"Good night." She disappeared into her apartment and closed her door.

Sebastian walked over to his mailbox and pulled out the accumulated envelopes and magazines. Walking up the stairs, he leafed through it all. Most of it was junk, a couple of bills, a medical journal. Entering his apartment, he dropped all the mail onto a small table by the door holding back one thin manila envelope. The address of a Chicago lawyer was up in the corner. Frowning, he slid his finger along the top, tearing at the seal. Sliding two pieces of paper out, his blood ran cold as he read the contents.

His father was sending him a confidentiality agreement preventing Sebastian from divulging his relationship to his father. Jaw tense, bile rolled around in his stomach. His breathing picked up and anxiety coiled in his chest. This was his father's biggest insult yet. Complete detachment of any relation between them.

It should make Sebastian happy. If he signed this, he could sever all ties with the man and be free. But that was only in theory. In reality, Sebastian wasn't the one winning, his father was. Donovan Stuart continued to have control. To truly be free, Sebastian had to take control.

Pulling out his phone, Sebastian took a picture of the documents and attached them to a new text to his father.

Is this supposed to change the fact that you have a son?

Pressing send, he slid the phone in his pocket and went into the kitchen to pour himself a beer. Taking three long sips, he set the beer down on the counter and stood for a minute, wondering if this had anything to do with the photographer that was sniffing around. Did his father send that man or did his opponent?

Squirming a bit, he drank more of his beer. He felt dirty—in need of a shower. Opposition research. That's what he had been reduced to. He'd bet money he was about to become a scandal for this father. The beer sat sour in his stomach and he pushed it away from him across the counter. Acid churned inside him and he tasted the adrenaline in his mouth. Rushing to the bathroom, he lost the content of his stomach in the toilet.

He stood at the sink and rinsed out his mouth then stared as his reflection. Who was the pale, drawn looking man with a green tinge to his skin looking back at him? He hardly recognized himself.

Sebastian *wasn't* a scandal. He was a human being. He was a little boy scared and not understanding why his father didn't love him. He was a man trying to make his own way in the world out of the overpowering shadow of a man that was never going to be a real father to him.

His phone signaled an incoming text and he fished it out of his pocket.

The sire: Just sign the papers and we'll both be free.

Looking back at himself in the mirror, Sebastian doubted that very much. He would never be free.

Thirteen

SEBASTIAN HAD NEVER been more surprised than when he opened his door and saw his younger half-sister by his father, Shannon, standing there. After opening his mail yesterday and discovering the confidentiality papers from their father, her presence on his doorstep was highly suspicious. Was Shannon their father's closer then? Had she come to make sure Sebastian signed the papers? She was in for surprise. Sebastian would not be bullied by his so-called family.

He supposed she must have contacted their grandparents for his address, and their grandmother, in her joy that one of her other grandchildren had shown an interest in him, was all too happy to oblige. Of course, he wouldn't really know until he spoke.

"What are you doing here?"

Okay. Maybe that wasn't the most welcoming of greetings. But seriously, *what was she doing here?* Had he ever held a conversation with her that lasted more than a couple of minutes? He didn't know anything about her, and he wasn't even sure how old she was. To her credit, she never sneered at him like the other two, but she never went out of her way to speak to him. Come to think of it, she always looked slightly afraid when he was around.

"Hi," she replied shifting her weight from side to side. Nervousness? That he wasn't expecting. Her eyes sparkled with unshed tears, and he wondered if maybe somebody died. Maybe this didn't have anything to do with his father's papers. He dismissed that when he realized he hardly rated an in-person visit to deliver important news.

"I'm a little, well, stunned," he admitted, still holding the door open and not making any moves to step back and allow her to enter.

"I'm sorry about just popping up like this out of the blue, but if I had called or emailed, I was afraid you'd tell me not to come. And I didn't have anywhere else to go. I didn't have anyone to turn to." She said quickly.

He took in her appearance. Tears glistened in her eyes, but she did not allow them to tumble over down her cheeks. Behind the sparkle of tears, her eyes hid fear.

He had a bad feeling about this.

"Nice try." Sebastian said. "You can tell our father that I'm not going to sign his papers. Like it or not, he's got four kids instead of three."

Confusion covered his sister's face and she cocked her head to the side. "What?"

Leaving her in the doorway, Sebastian crossed to his coffee table, grabbed the papers from his father's lawyer and marched back to the door, and shoved them in his sister's face.

"He didn't send you to come get these?"

"I don't know what they are." She shook her head.

"He wants me to sign confidentiality papers agreeing not to tell anyone I'm his son." Sebastian snapped out, refusing to believe there was any other reason his sister, who never paid him any mind, had any other reason for coming to see him. "You're going to tell me he didn't send you to retrieve my signature? This is all some wild coincidence. I'm not going to buy it."

Her face went from confused to angry. "I'm not his courier." She snapped back. The venom in her voice made him pause. He wasn't convinced, but he would hear what she had to say.

Sebastian stepped back to allow her to enter and helped her take off her coat, which he then hung by the door. Gesturing her into the living room, she perched herself at the end of the couch cushion while he remained standing.

"Can I get you something to drink?" She shook her head.

"I don't know what he's done to you now," she said. "But I can promise you, I don't know anything about it. I haven't seen him in weeks—since I packed up and left his house."

"Are you in some kind of trouble?"

"I guess that depends on how you look at it." Her voice broke. "I'm so sorry for showing up unexpected. I just didn't know where else to go. I could go to grandma and grandpa, but I didn't want to burden them with this. I felt like they should enjoy their time now."

Ah, he thought, *that's it.* "How far a long are you?"

She looked surprised he figured it out so quickly. She had certainly given him more than enough clues.

"Almost eight weeks," she said miserably.

"And the father?"

Laughing ruefully, she rose, closed her arms over her chest, and wandered to the picture window. "He denies even knowing me. Unfortunately, I don't have much proof that we did know each other because I was hiding our relationship from everyone—and quite well apparently. All I have are some texts, and none of them talk about a romantic relationship. I could force a DNA test, but he refused to acknowledge it. And if that's the kind of person he is, that's a negative influence on my child I don't want. I know all about undesirable fathers, and I don't want one for my child. It's not like he was a criminal or anything, but Father wouldn't have found him suitable anyway. He was a history major and planned to teach. Our father would never consider that an appropriate profession for his daughter's husband."

No, he wouldn't. Sebastian knew at least that much. Anyone with less than a six-figure salary was definitely ruled out.

"And you thought coming to me was a good idea because...?"

He didn't mean to sound like a heartless bastard, but this was someone that though she may not have been outwardly mean to him, never cared to communicate with him before now. She could be a spy for their father.

She sat back down, and this time, tears did escape her sad eyes. "I haven't been much of a sister to you. Father always told us you hated us and didn't want anything to do with us. He told us awful things he claimed you said about us. You're so much older than me. When I finally figured out that he had lied, I thought the damage had been done and you wouldn't be able to forgive me."

"I think I get to decide who I give forgiveness to," he said, pushing his hands into his pockets and watching her as she dropped back down to the couch and buried her face in hands.

"I don't deserve it. I know I don't! I was complacent and instead of defending you and showing loyalty, I cowered before him like I've done my whole life." Looking back up at him, she brushed the tears from her face. "Do you know he didn't even come to my college graduation? I changed my major from pre-law to creative writing. He doesn't know how much I've written alone in my room—none of them do. He was furious and refused to attend my graduation and even forbade my mother, brother and sister from coming, as well. He didn't even skip *yours*."

"That's because I became a doctor and Grandma and Grandpa made him go. I saw him in the audience, but he didn't stick around." Sebastian shrugged. He had become so accustomed to the artic freeze from his father that it hadn't even stung when he saw his father leaving before the ceremony ended.

"I don't need money," she said hastily. "I've sold a book and got an advance. I just need someplace to stay. I don't want to take money from my trust fund. I guess I will, if I really need to, but, well, you should have seen Father's face when I told him I was pregnant. He told me I was 'just like her,' then he turned his back on me and wouldn't say another word. I don't want anything from him. I don't know why I told him to begin with."

Sebastian thought the confidentiality agreement was the worst insult his father could dish out, but he was wrong. It was this. The *her* he referred to was, of course, Sebastian's biological mother, Daisy, whom he had never even met. The woman who so-called 'saddled' him with an unwanted baby. If what Shannon was saying were true, she could expect her baby to receive the same treatment Sebastian did growing up, and he wouldn't wish that on anyone—not even the siblings who barely acknowledged him.

"He was never a loving father to us either, you know," she said softly. "We lived our life under threats of being cut off financially if we didn't toe his line. Our sister Erica is practically engaged to someone she barely knows. There were many times I envied you living with Grandma and Grandpa. I know you grew up with love and laughter. That was in short supply in our house. He's just not a man that was built for a family. There are times I think he only had us so he would look like a family man when he ran for office."

Sebastian couldn't form an opinion on whether or not that was true, but it sounded plausible and it wouldn't surprise him. The truth of the matter was, Sebastian just didn't know the man well enough to say one way or another what he was capable of—despite having had been Sebastian's boss.

"Do you swear he didn't send you here and your arrival here the day after I receive notice from his lawyer is all just a coincidence?"

"I swear." She nodded and swiped at her eyes. "If you got something like that, I'm sure mine aren't far behind."

Maybe he was an idiot, but Sebastian was going to give her the benefit of the doubt. He had been starved for a relationship with his brother and sisters in Chicago that an overwhelming part of him wanted to latch on to whatever he could get.

Finally, Sebastian sat down and propped his ankle on the opposite knee. "What is the book about?"

Marveling at how his sister finally lit up, he smiled. She had found a passion, and if she could be successful with it, she would be fine whether she had their father's money or not.

"It's a mystery thriller—the start of a series, actually. I've finished the first book and have signed with a New York agent and publisher. I'm working on the next book now. I can do this, Sebastian. I can stand on my own two feet and make my own way. I can be home for my child and raise him or her myself and not leave it to a nanny. I just need someplace to land right now while I figure out where I want be. Please don't turn me away."

Pausing, Sebastian assessed his sister. She really didn't know him well, but maybe they could change that.

"We hardly know each other, but you *are* my sister. Family is important to me. It always has been, which is why growing up was so difficult for me. All I have to offer though is this couch for now. The second bedroom is an office at the moment."

"Oh, Sebastian, thank you so much. I'll try not to be a burden. The couch will be fine," Shannon assured him. "I didn't bring much with me. Just some clothes and my laptop. I was living at home, so I don't have any furniture or anything. I know I don't want to be in a city and definitely not Chicago, but I also don't want to be alone."

"You're welcome to stay as long as you need to," he said. "My sister, Jackie, can do your exams while you look for an obstetrician. I have family here, Shannon, a lot of it from my mother's side. They'll consider you family, as well. I'm the only one of all of us that had any more siblings. My brothers and sister here are very important to me, and it's crucial you not only understand that, but respect it. If you can accept that, then I'm here as long as you need me."

Nodding, Shannon said, "I look forward to meeting them."

"Good." Sebastian rose to his feet. "I work the second shift at the hospital today, so let's get started making some room in that second bedroom. We should be able to free up the closet and fit a dresser in there. If you're here more than a few weeks I'll think about converting it to another bedroom."

Launching herself off the couch, Shannon wrapped her arms around his neck. Stunned, Sebastian paused a minute before enveloping her in his embrace. He wasn't ready for the emotion that washed over him as he held her in his arms for the first time in his life—a loving link to his past when there were so few.

He would help her because she had come to him. And if it put the screws to his father at the same time, well, that was a happy byproduct. He just hoped he made the right decision.

Fourteen

SEBASTIAN FELT THE clap on his back and turned to see Ethan sit down next to him at the bar at Over the Hop. Ethan eased himself slowly down on the bar stool and let out a quiet breath when he finally sat down. His dog, Bravo, settled at his feet and out of the lane of foot traffic.

Sebastian could see his brother's pain but knew better than to ask about it. As a partial amputee, pain came with the territory, and Ethan rarely showed weakness. But as his brother turned to him, Sebastian carefully schooled his reaction to his brother's appearance.

Dark circles were under his eyes. His skin was pale, and his cheeks had a hollowed out look. Ethan's normally clean-shaven face sported scruff that had clearly been there for a few days. And his eyes ... there was a haunting behind them Sebastian had never seen before.

"Fancy seeing you here," Sebastian said, turning back to his beer. He didn't want to stare too long and make his brother uncomfortable.

"I was in the mood for a burger for lunch," Ethan replied. *And perhaps a bit of company*, Sebastian thought. Ethan adjusted his position. Bravo sat up and rested his chin on Ethan's knee. Absently, Ethan scratched behind the German Shepherd's ears.

"So he's with you today," Sebastian noted, reaching down and stroking the dog's head. "I'm so used to seeing him with Nat."

"Been stuck to my side like he's glued there." Ethan waved to grab Laurie's attention and a beer appeared in front of him. He was holding back, Sebastian could tell, but he would not push his brother for something he wasn't ready to share. Ethan had demons—they all knew that. But it was hard to remember when he was always affable. He was quiet by nature, but one rarely found him out of sorts.

Sebastian put a supportive hand on his brother's shoulder, rubbed a bit, and let his hand fall away. He hoped he conveyed that he knew something was troubling Ethan and that Sebastian was here if and when Ethan needed to unload his burden.

"So, my sister showed up on my doorstep pregnant," Sebastian announced.

Choking on his beer, Ethan sputtered. "She just *had* a baby! Is she not going to take any time to enjoy the one she has before she has more?"

"Not that one." Sebastian shook his head, though he enjoyed Ethan's reaction.

Ethan's face got dark, and he stared straight ahead. "I will *kill* Davis. He doesn't own her, and it will be my great pleasure to remind him of that fact."

"What?" Stunned by his brother's sudden vehemence, Sebastian studied Ethan's hardened profile. "Davis? Eric Davis? What are you talking about? *Who* are you talking about?"

Turning back to Sebastian, Ethan's expression cleared somewhat. "Who are you talking about?"

"My sister Shannon from Chicago."

"Oh." Ethan took a sip of his beer. "Interesting that she came to you."

"Did you think I was talking about Nat?" Sebastian lowered his voice to a near whisper as they always did when they spoke about Natalie in public and wanted to make sure not to be overheard. "Something's going on between her and Davis?"

"Not officially," Ethan said. "But they're hot for each other. You could break out in a sweat just being around them. I'm pretty sure nothing's happened, but you just startled me."

"Well, thinking about them now is going to keep me up at night now, thanks."

"Why should I suffer alone?"

Though Sebastian knew Ethan was joking, he looked at him seriously and said, "You never have to." Glancing at his brother out of the side of his eye, Ethan nodded his head once in acknowledgement.

"So why did she come to you?" Ethan asked.

"It sounds like my father has practically disowned her," Sebastian said, turning straight as his meal arrived. Ethan wasn't looking to make eye contact during their conversation, so Sebastian wouldn't put him in the unwanted position.

"On the house," Laurie said. "As far as we're concerned, neither one of you pays here."

Knowing Ethan was uncomfortable with the accolades, Sebastian kept the attention on him. "Why me?"

"You're keeping watch over someone that's very important to us," Laurie said. "We're grateful, and this is how we can show our appreciation."

"Okay," Sebastian said. "But I actually *like* her. In fact, I'm crazy about her. I'm not spending time with her because I'm a doctor, and her family thinks she needs one. I just want my motives to be clear here."

Laurie arched a brow then leaned on her elbows and smiled. "Really? Is Dr. Delicious off the market?"

Frowning at Ethan's chuckle, Sebastian turned back to Laurie. "That's between myself and your cousin and not fodder for Facebook."

Straightening up, Laurie waved him off. "You're up there anyway from the pumpkin festival. You two looked real cute together. Anyway, both our motives are clear then. We're still going to feed you when you come in."

She strolled away to help another customer. "You and the nanny, huh?" Ethan said, finally with a genuine smile across his face. "Danny's going to kick your ass if you mess with his nanny."

Fifteen

MEGAN SAT ON the couch in her parents' living room waiting for the storm to come. She had just told Gabe and her parents about the surgery. Justin stood quietly to the side, leaning against the door jamb. There were tingles in her chest, but not from her condition. If their reaction was anything like Justin's, she was in for a battle. She held her tears at bay. She could not appear weak or in any way impressionable.

Shaking her head, her mother fought the tears in her own eyes. "No. There are too many risks in surgery."

"There are more risks in not getting it," Megan said quietly.

Gabe looked surprised when Justin moved behind Megan and put his hand on her shoulder. She felt his strength, and she was happy to have it. "Whoa. Did not see that alliance coming," Gabe said. She understood his surprise. Justin usually came down on the side of their parents.

"I support her decision," Justin said. "She had a well-informed discussion with her doctor on Monday, and he answered all my questions. I felt just the way you do, but now that I've had time to digest it, and I've heard the pros and cons to all her options, I realize that she's making the right choice. I don't want to see her suffer anymore."

Grateful, Megan reached up and linked her fingers with her brother's. His support was hard won, and he was a valuable ally now. Gabe moved from the chair he was in to the couch next to her. She'd always had his support. She and her brothers now presented a united front. She reminded herself that though she would like her parents' support, she was still going forward with the surgery. She didn't need their approval to do it. They would eventually have to come around, especially after they see she wasn't going to change her mind.

"Is this because of that doctor you've been hanging out with?" her mother demanded. Megan sighed, dropped her head, and rubbed her eyes. "Is this his influence? Is he pressuring you? I do hear he's a surgeon. Maybe he gets some kind of referral fee."

Lifting her head, Megan pushed her palm out. "Mom, stop." Her mother blinked at the firmness in her daughter's voice. "Sebastian never once asked me about my treatment plan. *I* told *him*. And when I did, he only asked if my doctor had explained everything and if I had any questions. He has nothing to do with my decision. He only just got rights to University Hospital. He gets nothing out of this." Anger on Sebastian's behalf rolled through her.

"Don't take that tone with your mother." Her fathered ordered. "You're springing major surgery on us and just expecting us to follow along. When do we get to talk to the doctor? When are we presented with the options? We're your parents. We created you, god dammit."

Silence followed her father's tirade. Justin squeezed her shoulder.

"I'm not springing anything on you, dad." Megan said. "You've always known these options. When I was younger, you decided against any surgical procedures. And maybe that was the right course of action then, but I don't feel that it is now."

"But you could *die*." Her mother sobbed on the last word.

"I'm barely living now." Megan could hear the brewing tears in her own voice. "I can't *do* anything. Sebastian kissed me and just when things were heating up, my heart monitor went off. I can't have a real relationship with a man and I certainly can't have children. I can't ski like I used to. I can't run. I can barely walk at a brisk pace. *This isn't a life.* Everyone handles me with kids' gloves. I can't stand it. I need you to understand now and hear me. *I am unhappy.*"

The tension in the room hung heavy. Nobody dared speak. Even her brothers seemed to hold their breath. What was there to say? She had laid her feelings bare.

Her father put his arm around her mother and squeezed her shoulder. "We're just scared," he admitted. "It hasn't been easy watching you battle this illness all these years, and knowing you're about to undergo a dangerous procedure makes it difficult. We may seem unreasonable sometimes—we may even act that way—but the fear parents have ... there's just nothing to describe it. We worry about all of you every day. Gabe is running into burning buildings. Justin could get caught in a robbery at the restaurant, and you have a weak heart. We'll never not worry about you. Parents are supposed to die before their children. We're prepared for that. But we're not prepared to lose any of you. We never could be."

Taking in their father's words, Megan and her brothers were quiet. Her parents had never explained things like that. They never talked about how they felt and why they sometimes acted the way they did. And of course, she had nothing to compare their fear to. She loved her family and would be devastated if something happened to them, but she also knew she could recover from the loss and go on. She couldn't imagine the pain of losing a child or the fear they spoke about.

"And would you trade any of us to take that fear away?" She asked.

"Never." Her mother said through her tears. "All three of you have been a great joy to us. Our lives are fuller—richer—for having you in it."

"If I don't get that surgery," Megan said. "I won't ever know that joy. My life will never be fuller or richer. It will also be a shell of what it *could* be. *Existing* isn't a life."

Turning to Megan, Gabe said, "What is the recovery time like?"

"I understand it to be about five weeks before I can move around well enough to drive and resume work. We're trying to schedule the surgery for the day after Thanksgiving, so I'll hopefully be mostly recovered by Christmas. The McKenzies are very supportive, and my job will be waiting for me when I've fully recovered. In the beginning, I won't be able to lift so much as a gallon of milk, so I'll need help at home."

"You could stay here," her mother offered. It was good that her mother at least accepted Megan's determination for the surgery. She could only imagine what the woman would be like afterward.

"I appreciate the offer. I think I'd be more comfortable at home, and I have my cat to think about," Megan said. "It would be a great help to me, mom, if you could maybe arrange for people to pop in and check on me?"

Nodding vigorously, her mother said, "I will. And I'll arrange my schedule at work to be with you as much as I can. I'm sure your Aunt Stephanie and Nana will help. We can cook things ahead of time and freeze them so you'll have an easier time in the kitchen."

At least her mother had a purpose now. She had specific things she could focus on, and just maybe she wouldn't worry so much.

Sebastian had also pledged his support, and she would be grateful for it, even if it was only to check on the incision. However, after the snowstorm they spent together, she hoped he would also be able to provide emotional support and comfort. There had been no resolution to their relationship status, but Megan knew whatever it was, they were currently something more than friends, if not necessarily significant others.

Another thought occurred to her. If she and Sebastian were heading toward a romantic relationship, would he be willing to wait until she was recovered from her surgery for sex? Was she being too presumptuous? Just a few weeks ago she wasn't even sure she would ever date him, and now she was worried about their currently nonexistent sex life?

Even if they ever were to get to that stage, she had very little experience. He'd likely lose interest. She was sure he'd dated more sophisticated women than herself in Chicago. In her current job, she usually wore yoga pants. Crawling around on the floor with a baby, lifting her up and down, and sometimes getting spit up on, she certainly didn't dress to the nines for that.

She liked quiet nights in watching movies or reading. When her brothers or cousins wanted her to go out with them, she was still always home by nine p.m. Even the book club ended early. She just wasn't a very exciting person.

As they sat down to dinner, the tension still hung over them. It didn't feel right to be at odds with her parents, but she was an adult and her decision was made. Justin's work and the brewery seemed to be the only safe topic they could discuss. Gabe was a fire fighter and had a dangerous job. They all knew he could run into a building and not come out again, so conversation focused on Justin.

Justin seemed to realize this on his own and did his best to lead the conversation, talking about their new ideas for beer and menu items. Her family made small-talk but Megan's impending surgery hung over the table like a guillotine. She was certain she was making the right decision for herself, but her heart felt heavy knowing her family was hurting because of it.

After Justin dropped her off at home, and before Megan realized what she was doing, she found herself trudging up the stairs to Sebastian's apartment—each step growing lighter than the last. She wasn't sure if he was working that evening or if his shift ended yet, but she wanted to see him. She needed to see the reassurance in his eyes that she was making the right choice.

When the door opened though, it wasn't Sebastian who answered, and she felt like she was running with cement blocks on her feet as she hurried down the stairs.

SEBASTIAN AND SHANNON realized at the same time what Megan thought had happened. Mortified, Sebastian looked over at his sister who had answered the door in a tank top and pajama bottoms that showed off her stomach. Her hair was still dripping from her shower.

This didn't look good at all.

"Oh, gross," Shannon said, just as Sebastian said, "Oh, shit," and tore out the door after Megan.

His heart thumped like the tail of a dog as he came to a stop in front of her door and started banging. "Megan, please open up!" He pleaded and pounded, a lump in his throat. When she didn't answer, he didn't let up. He had heard the slam of her door as he was running down the stairs, so he knew she didn't leave the building. "Please! Megan, please! It's not what you think!"

Whose raw and desperate voice was this? His? Fear clawed at him each second the door stayed closed. They didn't have any kind of exclusive agreement—they didn't even have a definition of what they were to each other, but he was frantic to explain.

Why hadn't he told her that his sister had come to town? Not even a quick text, *'Hey, that stranger in the building is my sister.'* Nothing. He was such an idiot.

"I'm not going to stop until you open this door," he announced. "My brother-in-law is the chief of police. I delivered his baby. I like my chances. Open the door!"

Nearly falling through the opening when the door swung open, Sebastian grabbed onto the door jamb to keep himself from falling on his face. Megan stood before him with glassy eyes and flushed cheeks. She looked like she was ready to fall apart, and though he hadn't technically done anything wrong, he never wanted to be responsible for putting that distraught look on her face.

"My sister Shannon from Chicago is staying with me for a bit while she gets on her feet." His words were rushed, but it was important that he set her mind at ease as soon as possible.

Her hand fell from the door, and she stepped back. "It doesn't really matter," she said with a sigh. Turning, she shuffled her feet to the couch and dropped down where her cat was waiting.

A knot formed in Sebastian's chest as he tentatively walked into the room and closed the door. "Why wouldn't it matter?"

"I don't have any claim on you. We aren't exclusive. I mean, are we anything? You can date whoever you want. I'm just your neighbor you spent Wednesday kissing. People do that all the time, right?" She pulled her favorite quilt over her and wouldn't meet his eyes.

Frowning, Sebastian crossed the room and sat on the coffee table in front of the couch. Her hands were buried under the blanket, so he hooked his finger under her chin and forced her to meet his gaze.

"You're right. We didn't say anything about exclusivity, and we didn't say anything about seeing other people. But that can be changed. I don't play the field. If I'm in a relationship with a woman, I'm only dating her. You are *not* just my neighbor. You're the woman I'm falling for and completely crazy about. I don't know what other people do, but I spent two really great days kissing you and spending time with you, and I want to do a lot more of that. I would love to call you my girlfriend, if you'd let me."

Pressure released from his chest at having all that out there now. What remained to release the rest was for her to tell him everything would be all right. Things had been so tenuous between them. She had already been apprehensive about giving him a chance, and he screwed up already.

"Why?" She asked.

Speechless, Sebastian just blinked at her. "I don't understand." He shook his head. "Why what?"

"Why would you want all that with me? I'm just—"

"The most fascinating woman I've ever met in my life." He cut her off. "Megan, did you not hear the part about me falling for you? I nearly went brainless just now upstairs when I realized you thought Shannon was some kind of love interest of mine. I've never been more drawn to a woman than I am to you. When we first met, it was like I was waiting for you."

"I think I'm falling for you, too," she whispered. "I didn't want to. I'm scared shitless of what's going on inside of me, but I also have never felt more alive." Relief washed over him. It was going to be okay. *They* were going to be okay.

"What happened to make you doubt us?" He pushed a lock of hair behind her ear then trailed his finger down her cheek. "It couldn't have just been Shannon."

"I told my parents about the surgery tonight," she said quietly. "They disagree with my decision, but I think they'll be supportive. I just thought about my condition and the surgery and the recovery time and, I don't know."

"I think you do know," he said, gently. "Tell me what the problem is so we can fix it together."

Looking down and picking at her quilt, she shrugged. "It's a lot to ask someone to take on this early in a relationship. I can't do any ... activities ... that raise my heartrate. I mean, I *have* done it before. I'm not completely inexperienced."

He took in her flushing face and inability to look into his eyes. "Wait. Is this about sex?" He asked. "Do you think I'm going to lose interest because you think you can't have sex until like January?" Nodding, she looked away.

"Wow," he said, sitting back. "I honestly don't know whether to be insulted or relieved that this is such an easy fix." Frowning, she looked up at him. No wonder she immediately jumped to the wrong conclusion when Shannon answered the door. If she had any confidence in herself or them as a couple, she wouldn't have run. She would have confronted them right then and there. How could such a strong woman be so vulnerable?

"You haven't given me enough credit if you think I'm only in this for sex," he said. "I'm getting to know you, and I'm enjoying that. I'm not on a time clock here. I never was. You seem to have formed ideas about what my life in Chicago was like without asking if any of it is true. I'm a physician. I know what's ahead for you, and yet, I dove in with you. That doesn't tell you anything?" He slid back on the coffee table, resting his hands on his knees.

"I'm offended on behalf of both of us, Megan. You're not giving yourself enough credit either if you think you're only worth a few rolls in the hay. I get to decide what's too much for me to handle. And it's not about taking care of you—though, I promise you, I'm going to be the best nurse you've ever had. It's about coming to Grayson Falls and finding my whole life. And you're a part of that, if you want to be."

Looking up at him, she smiled tentatively and whispered, "I do."

"Good," he said. "Now stop talking that way about my girlfriend. You'll find I'm pretty protective of her." Her smile spread across her face as she sat up, displacing the cat, and wrapped her arms around him.

"I'm sorry," she said. "I was vulnerable tonight and I started doubting everything. We're still getting to know each other and some things we haven't explored yet. I should have talked about it instead of freaking out."

"You'll do that next time."

Chuckling, she pulled back. "You're so sure I'm going to screw up again?"

"We both are," he nodded. "But if we promise each other right here and now that we'll communicate with each other and talk it out, we'll be fine."

Nodding, she sat back. "I promise."

"Me too."

Pressing a kiss to her forehead, he stood up. She grabbed his hand and squeezed. "Jackie isn't on tomorrow. You are. Maybe you want to stay down here tonight?"

Giving her hand a tug, he helped her to her feet. He cupped her face and leaned in. She met him half way. Her taste was intoxicating. Her scent seeped into his pores. The smoothness of her skin made him need in a way he never did before. Not interesting enough for him? He was enchanted, bewitched, charmed. For the love of god, she put a whammy on him. After mere weeks, he was positive she was the one.

Breaking the kiss, he tipped his forehead to hers, sliding one hand up into her hair and wrapping the other around her waist to hold her tight.

She was vulnerable?

He was wrecked.

Sixteen

SEBASTIAN WALKED INTO the office at the hospital and felt the tension immediately. Jackie and Ryan faced each other, tension claiming their posture. Ryan leaned back against one of the desks, with his hands gripping the top on either side of him, knuckles white, and Jackie stood before him with her arms crossed.

"What's going on?" Sebastian asked.

Crossing his arms, Ryan glared at their sister. "She's pissed at me."

"What did you do this time?" Sebastian asked.

Instead of trying to deny he'd done anything wrong like he always did, his brother dove right in. "You know how she and I are business partners in Willis Reilly Racing?" Sebastian nodded, but Ryan clearly wasn't expecting Sebastian's participation in this conversation. "Business is doing very well, but we're hitting a plateau. I want our name out there more. To do that, I want to take on a team of drivers and get into the game. We can afford it, and I've had several offers for sponsorship if I ever went down this road."

Arching a brow, Sebastian looked to their sister. Jackie's face could have been carved from stone. "Her father died in a race car," Sebastian said slowly. "Surely you can understand why she isn't jumping at the prospect."

Ryan pushed off the desk. "Her father was *murdered* in a race car."

Instinctively, Sebastian moved in front of Jackie. "Go easy, man," he said to Ryan.

"This is business," Ryan said. "That was a tragedy, but the car didn't kill him. He hadn't done anything wrong. I've spent the last decade designing a safer car, and I continue to make modifications. Hell, Ethan will be testing one at our track this spring with a dashboard clutch that doesn't need its own pedal. She's skittish." He threw out his arm toward Jackie, and Sebastian countered his stance. He'd never thought he would be protecting one of his sisters from one of his brothers, but the instinct in him was too strong to ignore. His body just moved on its own. "This is the next step for us. She *knows* that. *Jimmy* would not want us holding back because of him."

Holding up his hands in peace, Sebastian watched his brother start to pace.

"Ry, maybe you should just head out and let her absorb this. Just give her time."

Stopping, Ryan glared at Sebastian. "She's *had* time," he said. "This isn't the first time I've brought this up. It should be noted that she's got a hell of a car sitting in her garage." Ryan stepped to the side so he could see their sister. "Jacks, I've done everything I could to protect you since day one. I have always been devoted to you and that has never wavered—not once. You know there's nothing I wouldn't do for you, and if you say no, I won't do this. We *both* need this. You bought the track with me, and you went into this business with me. You did that because you believe in me. I'll keep them safe."

When Jackie didn't reply, Ryan shook his head. Leaving the office, he threw over his shoulder, "And Danny's wants to kick your ass over the nanny."

"Her name is Megan!" Sebastian called out to his brother's back then pushed the door shut and turned to look at his sister. Running a hand down her dry face, she blew out a breath.

"You stood up to him," she said, looking up at Sebastian. "For me."

"It wasn't fun," Sebastian replied. "The less I have to be in that position, the better. I hope I didn't do any lasting damage to our relationship. We don't go back as far as you do."

"Which is why I'm confident in saying you didn't damage your relationship. If anything, he respects you more now. He's right though. If I say no, he really won't do it. If I said no, he wouldn't own a track right now, and that place gives him so much joy. I can't deny him his dream. He has a vision for things, and I won't change it."

"So, you're going to take on drivers?" Sebastian asked.

"I just don't know," she sighed. "He's right. I need to do it. I need to take control. I hope you don't think too poorly of him right now. You only saw the breaking point in this push and pull we've had going on about this for a while now. He knows when to push me and when not to, and today it was time to push."

"I don't think poorly of him," Sebastian said. "You, Ryan, and Ethan, even Zach, have had longer to establish a relationship than I have. I'm still getting used to life around here and the dynamics. Which reminds me, my sister Shannon from Chicago is staying with me right now."

"Wow," Jackie said. "I only know what you've told us about your family there, but that's a little surprising, isn't it?"

"Stunning, especially given the fact that I just found out my father wants me to sign a confidentiality statement that I won't disclose my parentage," he agreed, leaning against the desk in the spot Ryan recently vacated. "She's pregnant. It seems our loving father kicked her out, and the father of her baby isn't in the picture."

"No offense, but I don't think your father is going to win his election on the family values platform."

"No," Sebastian laughed. "Definitely not. I've been spending all my nights this week with Megan, but I need to start spending them at home and getting to know my sister better."

"Oh, have you?" Jackie crossed her arms and gave him an expectant look. "Are you defiling my nanny?"

"Not that it's any of your business, but no, I'm not," Sebastian said. "We're taking it slow. She's amazing though."

"Yes, and I'd like to keep her around. So, don't mess it up to the point where she quits because she doesn't want to chance running into you." Jackie pointed a stern finger at him.

"Not going to happen," he assured her. The absolute conviction he felt in his answer was overwhelming. He knew—without the slightest doubt—that if she ran, he'd follow. He would never give her up without a fight. "Listen, since we're slow, I'm going to cut out early and head over to your place. I want to check on Ethan."

"He's been struggling," she nodded. "He'll come out of it, Sebastian. We watch him close—all of us do. He needs some time and space. Bravo does wonders for him during these episodes. Ethan does so much, it's hard to remember how difficult it can be for him. Natalie says he has sleep meds, but he never takes them. She thinks he's scared of not waking up from one of his nightmares."

He pushed off the desk. "You're a good sister."

"You're turning out to be a pretty decent brother," she said. "You can let Megan know that I'll be knocking off in about an hour if all hell doesn't break loose."

Sebastian turned and left the office, heading for the side door of the hospital. As he walked to his car, he went over everything that just transpired. Of course, he wasn't scared Ryan would have physically hurt Jackie, but emotionally, he was saying some pretty harsh things. The need to protect his sister was almost primal. It had just overtaken him. He needed to apply that to his sister Shannon, as well. She had come to him in her hour of need and though they weren't close, she deserved that loyalty from him, as well—if only just to protect her from their father. It couldn't have been easy for her come to him thinking there was a good possibility that he could just slam the door in her face—which he almost did.

Resisting the urge to head right in Jackie and Danny's house to see Megan and the baby, Sebastian walked around to the entrance of Ethan's barn. He knew exactly nothing about farming, so he hoped Ethan would be in the barn and not out in the fields or somewhere else on the property since there was snow on the ground. As it happened, as he entered the front door of the barn, Ethan came in the back door astride the same mare he had at the festival, with Bravo following closely.

Despite his injury, his brother had a commanding build. From pictures Sebastian had seen, Ethan looked like hell's fires in a uniform holding a rifle with a badass dog next to him. On a horse, he looked powerful—a superhero in his layman's disguise. He romanticized his brother's life and he knew he shouldn't. Ethan didn't think of himself as anybody's hero, which to Sebastian made him even more of one.

Ethan cocked his head to the side when he saw his brother. "Danny lock you out of the house?"

"I'm really not concerned about what Danny thinks about Megan being my girlfriend."

"Girlfriend, huh?" Ethan said. Sebastian watched his brother dismount the horse with more ease than he expected. It wasn't a quick dismount, but steady and sure, as he made sure his good leg was secure on the ground before bringing down the prosthetic. As Ethan led the horse into a stall, Sebastian followed. Bravo lay across the stall door.

Raising his hand to stroke the horse's nose, Sebastian eyed his brother while Ethan began to groom the horse. Sebastian knew that Ethan adored this small farm he was creating. In just a few short years, he had animals, crops, and a small business, and he had fixed much of the equipment that had been left behind by the last owner. After what Ethan had been through in the military, the peacefulness and predictability of the work must feel like heaven.

"I'm falling for her," Sebastian said. "Hard."

"I'm not surprised," Ethan said. "There's something in the water around here."

"You'll be next," Sebastian said.

"Not many women around looking for a guy like me."

Ethan didn't seem bitter when he said that, just stated it as a fact. What Ethan didn't realize though was that this town loved him. They had a war hero in their midst, and they were proud of that. It was true that there must have been more residents of Grayson Falls to serve in the military, but the Marines didn't give out purple hearts and medals of valor to just anyone. Ethan's sacrifice—and what he was doing with himself post-discharge—made him beloved.

Whether he wanted to be or not.

"You know, every time I came to visit, I was always amazed at how much you were able to achieve while I was gone," Sebastian marveled. Picking up another grooming brush, Sebastian slowly approached the horse. He had no experience with them and their size alone was intimidating. He mimicked Ethan's movements on the other side of the horse. He didn't know if he was doing it right, but it was definitely relaxing. The appeal in spending time with these quiet, proud animals was becoming obvious.

"Just farming," Ethan shrugged.

"Don't play it off," Sebastian said. "It's a labor of love. We both work with our hands, just in different ways."

"I don't save lives."

Looking up, Sebastian gestured around them with his brush hand. "Don't you? These are all rescue animals. You're even going to let the pigs live."

When Ethan met his brother's eyes, Sebastian took the time to do a visual assessment. He looked better, more rested, and his eyes didn't look as troubled. Ethan's gaze softened when Sebastian took too long in his study and he realized what his brother was doing.

"I'm feeling better," Ethan said, before returning his attention back to the horse. "Nightmares happen, bad days happen, pain happens. It's just my reality now. I deal with it. I'm not going to eat my gun or blow away half the people in the diner. I have medications I can take when things get real bad, but I'm not interested in living my life sedated either. I'm certainly not the only former soldier experiencing this, and some are far worse off than me. These episodes just need to run their course. I went to the brewery the other day hoping I was past it, but I wasn't. I don't usually hang out around people when it happens. People notice and they look at me with pity. I'm not a hero. I had a nine to five job, and I had a bad day at work."

"Well, we're alike in that way," Sebastian said, brushing the horse. "People die when I have a bad day at work, too. I know you don't think of yourself as a hero, and I get that. But you are *my* hero. You show me what strength and humanity are—what compassion and patience can do. It has nothing to do with what happened to you over there. That's just who you are. And one day, that's what the right woman will see."

Chuckling, Ethan took Sebastian's brush and put them both away before pulling out a blanket for the horse. "Well, I thank you for the love advice, big brother, and I thank you for looking out for me." After the horse was covered, Ethan slapped Sebastian on the back in a classic man hug. "Call off the rest of the pack, if you would." Sebastian raised a brow. Like that was going to happen. "Well, it was worth a try," Ethan laughed.

Bravo stuck close to Ethan as they walked out of the barn. Even the dog looked better than he had the other day. It was incredible how in sync man and beast were. Sebastian thought about his cat and how he was still trying to get the little devil just to come out when he was home, let alone provide comfort when he was troubled.

"I suppose you'll be going in to see your *girlfriend* now," Ethan said. Sebastian looked up at the house where he imagined Megan inside with baby Ally. She loved that baby so much, and after her surgery, children could be possible. Would she want her own or would she be content taking care of Jackie's kids? Sebastian had always wanted children of his own. They weren't a deal breaker in relationship to him, but he did long to give a child better than he got from his own parents.

"Yes," Sebastian said. "I'm going to see my girlfriend now. And I'm going to kiss her. It's one of the perks of having your own woman. You should try it sometime."

Opening his truck door, Ethan whistled for Bravo, who bounded up and into the passenger seat with ease. Ethan climbed in after him and turned to his brother. "Who says I don't have one?" Laughing, Ethan slammed the door shut, started the truck and drove away, leaving Sebastian standing there.

Seventeen

THE GRAYSON FALLS Literary Society, as they called themselves, gathered monthly in the cozy upstairs space over the General Store. What used to be an apartment had been transformed into a retail and gathering place showcasing New Hampshire writers, musicians, and artists. The relaxed setting had comfortable couches and a stunning stone fireplace. With its creaky wood floors and painted knotty pine walls, it had a distinct old New England feel that Megan adored.

The General Store was a popular morning meeting place, as well, since the back patio had been refinished with café tables and rocking chairs were added to the deep front porch. There was a breakfast counter that did a brisk morning business serving good coffee, teas, cocoa, pastries, and breakfast sandwiches. Sophie and Brooke owned the store together and were a strong team. They tried very hard to cater to everyone and keep people shopping in town instead of driving to the closest big box store, which was nearly an hour away.

As Megan settled into her favorite chair and footstool, she pressed two fingers to her forehead. A low-grade headache had been pestering her all day. To make sure it wasn't dehydration, she drank plenty of water throughout the day, but despite taking medication, the pesky throbbing persisted. She had almost gone home instead of to the book club meeting, but she enjoyed the social interaction, and Sebastian had said he was going to have dinner with his sister.

He had been staying with her every night, but he wanted to spend a little more time with Shannon and get to know her. Megan couldn't comprehend having siblings she wasn't close to—ones she barely even spoke to. If she didn't have her pesky brothers, she didn't know what she would do. They may live for annoying her, but they were her best friends.

Feeling warm, she took a sip from her water bottle as she thought of the nights she was sharing with Sebastian. There was no sex involved—lots of kissing, lots of exploring each other's bodies, and lots of conversation. It was intimate. She was falling for him—hard. She began to make plans for her future after the surgery, which she never did before. Megan had never really invested herself in anything other than her family because she didn't know what the future had in store for her and her disease. But both her physician and Sebastian were optimistic about the outcome and her chances for a normal life afterward.

Sebastian had gone so far as to look for marathons scheduled in the following fall and smaller races in late spring and summer, plotting out training schedules to start after her recovery period. He talked about visiting national parks for hiking, biking, and kayaking—all the things he wanted to explore with her.

And at night, he held her while she slept. All through the night, she felt his arms around her and felt at peace. Whatever life threw at her, she had this time with him and cherished it.

Stifling a yawn, Megan pulled out this month's book selection. Norrie, the police dispatcher, had them working their way through a time travel series when it was her turn to pick, and Megan wasn't a fan. The books were long and, to Megan's mind, not very engaging. It could have been that the characters didn't go to any time periods that Megan wanted to learn about. Then again, there was a lot of swearing and sex, and that wasn't really what she liked to read.

Still, everyone in the club got a chance to pick, and Megan's turn was coming up. There was a mystery she had her eye on that she was thinking about choosing. A classic who-done-it would be perfect entertainment during her long recovery post-surgery.

Slowly, the other women began to join them—Brooke, Natalie, Laurie, Norrie, and Jackie had assembled. Tonight, they seemed to be missing a few other women from town. She suspected those who didn't make it probably didn't like the book. Megan should have tried that tactic.

The room felt warm, but the girls hadn't made a fire this evening. Sweat trickled down between her shoulder blades. She thought maybe she should just head home, but with Sebastian out with his sister, she would be all alone. Megan had a feeling she probably shouldn't be by herself right now. She couldn't shake the feeling of impending doom that was sweeping over her.

Taking a deep breath, she tried to focus on the cover of the book, but it was blurry. The discussion had already began, but it was as if she was listening through ear muffs. A dull pain centralized in her chest. *Dammit, not now, not in front of all these people.* Her breathing was shallow and, vaguely, she knew she should take her medicine right away, but she couldn't seem to reach down into her purse to get it.

Beep. Beep. Beep.

And that's the ballgame.

"Okay, Meggie. Let's get your meds out." Calmly, Laurie came to her side and reached for Megan's purse. Now, Laurie sounded like she was in a tunnel. Megan was loosely aware of her appearing on her other side.

Beep. Beep. Beep.

"Let's give her some space." Megan thought that was Jackie's voice, but she couldn't tell. And her vision was failing. The pressure in her chest increased with the searing pain. Breathing was near impossible.

Beep. Beep. Beep.

Then with crystal clarity, she heard Jackie say, "We're about to lose her," right before everything went black.

The last thing she heard was the *beep beep beep* of her watch.

A TEXT FROM PIPER SENT Sebastian bursting into the upstairs room of the General Store, where Jackie and Natalie were already working on Megan. Chaos hammered in his chest as he saw Megan lying unresponsive, pale and small under Jackie's hands.

Falling to his knees at Natalie's side, he reached for Megan's hand, but Natalie gently pushed him back.

"You're too close to this, Sebastian," Natalie said, briefly putting her hands on his upper arms and easing him back. "It's better if you stay back."

Stay back? *But he was a fucking doctor!* "We have to ... we have to ..." What? They had to do what? Damned if he knew. He did his best to recall the steps that needed to happen right now, but panic won out.

Beep. Beep. Beep.

The continuous alarm on Megan's watch echoed around his head. The monotonous tone rang out over the otherwise silent room. Jackie and Natalie didn't even need to speak to each other, such was the rhythm they had honed over the last few years.

Beep. Beep. Beep.

"Take that fucking thing off her!" He couldn't stand to hear one more god-awful beep. He knew she was dying. He didn't need a god-damn watch to keep reminding him. Carefully as to not get in Jackie's way, Laurie reached for Megan's wrist, removed the watch, shut it off, and put it in her purse before backing off again.

Checking Megan's pulse, Jackie moved swiftly. "We lost her." Natalie immediately moved back as Jackie began CPR.

We lost her. We lost her. We lost her... The words echoed around Sebastian's head. Words he himself had said many times in an operating room.

With heightened senses, he was aware of absolutely everything that was happening in the room. The heavy breathing of the others, the silent tears, Laurie and Brooke clutching at each other, Piper's furious texting. Everyone staring through grief while Jackie worked to bring Megan back.

He looked up at his sister. Trails of sweat were running down her face as she worked. He knew what was going on inside Megan's body now as Jackie worked furiously to restart Megan's heart and keep oxygen moving to her brain.

Shaking his head, Sebastian's mind finally started moving. "We can stabilize her in the hospital," he said. "Her heart has expanded too much. It's getting crushed by her ribs and sternum. There's too much pressure."

"The helicopter is on its way," Jackie said. "The trip to University will be fast."

"We don't have that much time."

The paramedics pushed into the room and everyone moved out of their way except Jackie and Sebastian.

"We can take it from here," one said.

"The fuck you will," Sebastian growled. "Dr. McKenzie will continue her care and you will assist."

Arching a brow, the medic turned away from Sebastian. They dropped their bags down and surrounded Megan, as Jackie began giving orders about what to bring out. The defibrillator came out, and Natalie moved in to prepare the pads while the medics cut away Megan's shirt to expose her chest.

Jackie sat back on her heels as Natalie applied the pads to Megan's chest and pushed the button on the defibrillator. The automated voice filled the room as everyone waited.

"Assessing the patient ... please stand back ... no pulse found ... deliver shock ..."

Natalie pressed the button for the machine to give Megan her first shock. Then they waited. Time slowed to a stop. These moments for a doctor while they waited to see if they saved a life or lost one were interminable. Each death took away a little piece of you.

This one would take everything.

"Assessing the patient ... please stand back ... no pulse found ... deliver shock ..." The lifeless voice of the machine as it evaluated the lifeless body of his whole world left him hollow.

Again, Natalie pressed the button delivering another shock. Sebastian imagined the electrical current running through Megan's body, looking for another one to jolt Megan's heart back to life. Seconds strung out.

"Assessing the patient ... please stand back ..."

And they waited. Frozen in place as the machine searched for signs of life inside the woman he'd come to love. There on the floor, his future lay dying. Technically, his future was already dead. He couldn't breathe. Everything in his body stopped as he waited to see if his own heart would start again.

"Pulse detected ... do not shock ..."

Sebastian thought they must have been the most beautiful words in the English language—even if they were delivered by a machine. Everyone in the room let out a collective breath at once. Through the blur of his tears, Sebastian watched Jackie and Natalie get back to work, the paramedics handing them what they needed. The stretcher was brought into the room, and Megan was moved swiftly to it. Jackie followed the medics out the door.

Natalie hit Sebastian in the chest, and he looked down to see he was now holding Jackie's purse. Looking up at his sister, he saw she was swinging her own over her shoulder and grabbing her coat, as well as Megan's things. "I'll drive you," Natalie said. "You can't drive yourself." Sebastian merely nodded, handed her his keys, and followed his sister out of the room.

They walked out of the store into the spinning red lights of the emergency vehicles against the darkness. Numbness overcame him and his body went through the mechanics of moving, but only because he was being led by Natalie. His knees felt like jelly, and he wanted to lay on the ground and cry until someone woke him up from this nightmare.

Danny stood there with another officer, while another one waited in his car to give a police escort to the ambulance over to the baseball field where Danny's radio told them the helicopter now waited for Megan.

Stopping Sebastian with a gentle hand on his forearm, Danny looked at him with compassion. "Jackie saved my life," he said quietly. "She'll save Megan. She knows what she means to you. Jackie won't let her go." Sebastian nodded. Leaning in, Danny gave Sebastian a quick hug and a pat on the back, then Natalie led him over to his car.

The drive to University Hospital would take forty-five minutes, but the helicopter wouldn't even use a third of that time. Sebastian thought of nothing and everything on the way—somebody would need to feed the cats, the pumpkins were now rotting on the front steps and needed to be thrown away. Reaching over, Natalie took his hand with her free one. He didn't let go, and they drove in silence.

He thought about what an amazing team his sisters were when they worked together. They hadn't spoken to each other once. They simply did what needed to be done. Was it because they were related or just that they worked together so frequently? The three of them answered the calling they shared with the grandfather they never met. But looking at his sisters and seeing their devotion to their work, he knew the man must have been amazing.

Squeezing his sister's hand, he whispered, "I'm glad you're here. You and Jackie were brilliant."

Natalie smiled and squeezed his hand in return. "I'm glad I could be there to help." Nothing more needed to be said. The silent acknowledgement that Natalie was happy to have found her siblings and to be a part of their lives was the closest they'd likely come to admitting their relationship to each other. Sebastian didn't need any more. Natalie came with him because he was her brother, and he needed her support.

"How did you know to come there?" Natalie asked.

"Piper texted me," Sebastian said quietly. "I don't even remember getting there. How could she have gotten under my skin so fast, Nat? I came here to break free from my father's grasp, and it was like she was waiting for me. Is that arrogant? I don't know. It wasn't easy to convince her to go out with me in the first place. But now that we're together, I feel like I've been searching for her my whole life—the other half of me. Have you ever felt that way?"

"In a way," Natalie said. "I think I found a part of me that had been missing when I came here. I didn't know there was ... more to me."

"Ah, Ethan," he said. "Makes sense."

"Ethan and I are *not* a couple," Natalie said in frustration. "I'm so tired of saying that!"

"Oh, I know," Sebastian said. He was too tired, too raw, and too open to pretend she was something other than his sister, Ethan's twin. It was just the two of them, on a quiet ride in the dark. It was the worst kept secret among them, and Sebastian just didn't have the energy to play the game. "I've always been jealous of the bond you two have. I could never have it with my other siblings."

"Sebastian ..." Natalie trailed off.

"I can't do it tonight, Nat," he whispered, his head resting against the seat and facing her. "We all know, and we all know that we know. I get why you keep up the pretense—I do—and I respect it. But I just can't tonight. It's just us."

Squeezing his hand, she said, "I'm always here for you, Sebastian. It doesn't change."

"Likewise."

They settled back into silence then. Despite Natalie driving over the speed limit, the ride dragged on. He thought about Megan and all the things he wanted to do with her—the marathon, hiking, skiing, kayaking—anything to get the adrenaline going and make her feel alive.

God, please let her still be alive.

Eighteen

SEBASTIAN BARRELED THROUGH the emergency room doors with Natalie right behind him. He had barely remembered to grab his identification from the car for the hospital and clip it to his shirt. Now he could almost go wherever he wanted.

The familiar scents of bleach and adrenaline, the sounds of a baby crying, the constant ringing phone, and the drone of a television assaulted his senses and comforted him at the same time. The emergency room was a controlled chaos with nurses moving around them, opening curtains and disappearing behind them. Exhausted doctors reviewed charts and moved from patient to patient trying to provide the best care they could in the small amount of time they had. Police officers were fixtures in large emergency rooms as they waited for certain patients to be released so they could be taken to jail.

Now he was somewhere he understood. Now he was in an environment he thrived in. For the first time that evening, his confidence in himself returned.

Jackie stood at the nurse's station filling out her report of everything that happened from the time Megan collapsed until the time they rolled through the door. Jackie also had rights to this hospital, so she could see any of her patients that were admitted. Sebastian knew it wasn't often that she was up here as she only really tended to come for any pediatric patients of hers.

Breathlessly, Sebastian grabbed Jackie's hand. "Where is she? *How* is she? I've been going out of my mind."

"She's being prepped for surgery," Jackie said gently. "Her cardiologist just got here a few minutes ago."

Desperate, Sebastian clung to her hand. "I need to be in the operating room, Jacks. You need to help me do this. *I can save her!* I need to save her."

Putting down her pen, Jackie grabbed Sebastian's wrist and pulled up. "This hand is trembling, Sebastian," she said. "These hands can't work with precision, and you are not a cardiologist. You are a trauma surgeon. You are too close to this, and you *know* that. Get ahold of yourself."

Natalie put an arm around Sebastian's shoulders and squeezed. He shook his head at Jackie, ready to argue more, despite knowing his sister had no authority to allow it. "I need to be with her."

"You can observe," a voice behind them said. They turned and saw an older man, tall, graying, and well-groomed. The man stuck his hand out. "I'm Jeff Anderson. I'll be assisting in the surgery. I can't have you in the room, for obvious reasons, but you can watch through the glass." Dr. Anderson nodded to Jackie.

Squeezing his shoulder, Natalie rubbed up and down Sebastian's arm. "I'll stay here and wait for Megan's family," she said. "I'll give them her things and wait with them. Jackie can go with you and bring us updates. Okay?"

Numb, Sebastian nodded and took a deep but shuddered breath. It was the best he was going to get. He couldn't go into the OR. Jackie was right. He was in no shape to either assist in the surgery or be that close. But at least he could watch. He could see Megan's face. He could be there with her—not that she would know it, but *he* would.

Pulling his shoulders back, Sebastian straightened to his full height. He nodded to Dr. Anderson. "I appreciate that."

"I can see what she means to you," Dr. Anderson said. "Know that we won't give less than our very best for her."

Nodding again, Sebastian felt Natalie's hand fall away. Jackie handed her report off to the nurse behind the desk and together, she and Sebastian followed Dr. Anderson through the doors leading from the ER to the sterile corridors behind them. The squeaks of their shoes on the linoleum floors echoed in the vacant halls. The fluorescent lights gave the halls an eerie, institutionalized look Sebastian had never noticed before. Is this what families saw as they came to visit a loved one?

People lived and died in the hallowed walls of this building, and Sebastian was gaining a new appreciation for what loved ones felt within them. The hospitals had always been a temple to him—one he hoped he served well. But now it felt confining. He was not a god tonight, here to beat death and slay illness. He was a man struggling to feel again, to fill the emptiness inside him in any way he could.

He didn't know he could feel this soul-crushing despair. Never having lost anyone he loved before, he had been lucky. His grandparents had their mishaps, but they were healthy enough. Growing up, he had heard about his brother and sisters in Chicago having various things wrong with them—appendicitis, tubes put in their ears, the occasional broken bone—but nothing was serious. There was that time Sophie was in a car accident and the time Ryan got winged by a bullet, but he had only just met them and wasn't emotionally invested yet.

He had never imagined a scenario where he would be useless as a doctor when it was most important. Debilitated by his need for Megan to be all right, he wasn't able to function in a way that could save her. Jackie had though, and she saved Megan.

Dr. Anderson showed them into the observation room connected to the empty operating room where Megan would be brought soon. Inside, Sebastian saw the medical team. An anesthesiologist was there setting up. A nurse counted instruments. Another set up monitors. Sebastian didn't often see this part as he was scrubbing in, just like Dr. Anderson was now, along with Megan's cardiologist. He didn't even know that guy's name.

Standing at the window, Sebastian wrapped one arm around his stomach and rested his other elbow on top of it. His free hand came to his jaw. In the reflection of the glass, he saw Jackie take a seat and pull out her phone, no doubt texting Danny and the others to give them an update.

"Danny said you saved his life," Sebastian said, his voice hoarse. "I didn't know what he meant."

Jackie put the phone down and looked up into the OR. They both stared as the surgical team entered and surrounded the table Megan was on.

"I guess that never really came up before when you were around," Jackie said. "Danny and I met at school. We started seeing each other. He understood me at a time I felt like no one else did. Ryan was there with me, of course. He experienced my father's death literally right alongside me. God, I don't know what I would have done if I didn't have him. That's when it came out that we were related. Our fathers, in their infinite wisdom, had decided not to tell us unless, one, we tried to date, or two, something happened to one of them. I forgave them for their idiocy a long time ago."

Sebastian watched as Megan was attached to the heart and lung machine that would pump oxygen to her blood and keep it moving throughout the surgery. Everything was double checked before the procedure would begin.

"Danny was amazing. I tried to avoid him at first, but you know Danny. Nobody avoids him for long. Eventually, he weaseled his way into being my friend then it became more. He was my first boyfriend. My first love—as it turned out, my *only* love. When his father pulled him from school on prom night, I was devastated. We found out later that his father intercepted all the letters we had written each other, and we fell out of touch through no fault of our own."

The head surgeon began the procedure. They would start with an incision down the center of Megan's chest before using a small saw to cut through her sternum.

"One day, I was working in the ER in New York, and Danny, a cop there too, came in on a stretcher with a gunshot wound. I should have stepped aside when I realized it was him. I know that. I knew that then, but I just couldn't. I couldn't leave his side for a single second. I *had* to be the one to save him. I couldn't accept it any other way. And I did it. I stabilized him in the ER. After his surgery, I brought him New Hampshire to recover. He had come to New York to find me again because he heard from Sophie that I was there." She let out a half laugh. "Leave it to Danny to know just how to get a busy girl's attention."

The sides of Sebastian's lips curled in a half smile. In the time Sebastian had known him, Danny wasn't one to do anything half-way. "How did you do it?"

"I don't know," she said softly. "I don't even know if I was conscious at the time that I was doing it. I just did. It's a blur to me now. I felt trapped inside myself while he was in surgery. It wasn't until I saw him in his room afterward that I really was able to breathe fully again. That I realized that I had always loved him."

Sebastian pressed his hands to the glass and leaned forward like he would be able to magically fall through it and be in the room with Megan. He longed to touch her, to hold her hand, to whisper to her that he was here and she would be okay.

He stood rooted to the spot during the hours-long surgery. Jackie went in and out, presumably to update the others, stretch her legs. She brought back coffee and water for them. But Sebastian wouldn't—couldn't—leave.

He stayed at the glass and drew his finger along it, tracing Megan's face, stroking her hair—anything to feel closer to her—to feel like he was doing *something*.

Suddenly, there was a flurry of activity, nurses removed instruments, the surgical team repositioned itself, acid churned in his stomach and his head felt light as Sebastian realized with dread that they had lost her again.

"NO!" He shouted, pounding his fists on the glass. "Breathe, god dammit! Fight!" He continued his pounding. Jackie tried to put herself between him and the glass, but he refused to budge. Tears ran down his face as he screamed again. It took a matter of minutes for the surgical team to get Megan back, but it felt eternal to him. When things were running smoothly again, he tipped his forehead to the glass and pressed his palm up next to him. He was exhausted. He couldn't take much more.

Backing away from the glass, he collapsed into a chair behind him. He had been standing there for god knows how long. For the first time since he had gotten the text from Piper earlier that evening, he pulled out his phone. Scrolling to his text string with Megan, he started a new text and typed.

I just lost you for the second time tonight. I need you to pull through, Megan. I need you to do it because my heart can't take it if you don't. I'm watching the procedure and dying a little more each minute that goes by. I need you to live because I need to tell you that I've fallen in love with you and that I'm waiting for you. I will be by your side every step of the way. Just live so I can breathe again.

He hit send without even thinking about if she should learn that he loved her through a text message. He needed to feel close to her and that was the only way he knew how. As he watched the surgery and the hours dragged on, he thought of nothing. He had zoned out and thoughts were no longer staying in his head. He had tried to occupy his mind by following along with the procedure in his head, but he couldn't keep up. He had started to think about all the things they wanted to do when Megan was better, but he ended up just staring into the operating theatre. He had been awake for more than twenty-four hours and was beyond exhausted.

When they lost Megan again, he had nothing left to give. He dropped his face into his hands and wept.

Nineteen

WHEN MEGAN FIRST swam up from the abyss, all she saw were bright lights. She couldn't move her arms or legs. Her mouth felt like she had swallowed cotton and her chest ached. She was cold, so very cold. Through blurry eyes, the bright lights and white was all she could see. Was she dead? Voices swam around her, weeping, begging, something that sounded like someone banging on a window. Was this the tunnel people talked about, or was she going to have an out-of-body experience? She wasn't looking down on herself, so she thought she might still be in her own body. But the cold ... people got cold when they died. The pain could mean she was alive.

The struggle to stay awake was too exhausting, with heavy eyes she gave in to the anchor weighing her down.

When next she awoke, there were muffled voices around her. It was dark, and she was warmer. The voices called to her. Distorted faces appeared in front of her, but her vision swam. She felt her hands squeezed. Waiting for her eyes to adjust, she tried to figure out where she was and what had happened. She thought perhaps she had the surgery, but for the life of her, she couldn't remember celebrating Thanksgiving. Had the holiday come and gone?

Things began to come into focus. Her mother's face was before her, tears streaming steadily down her cheeks. Megan didn't have the energy to do anything but look at her and hope her own eyes conveyed the question she needed answers to. Her father's face also came into her vision, and he leaned down and kissed her forehead.

"One of the valves to your heart was blocked, baby," her mother said. "You had a heart attack at your book club meeting. They lost you three times." Her mother covered her mouth, her voice breaking on the last few words. She stepped away. Her father's face appeared.

"Laurie said that Dr. McKenzie and one of her nurses brought you back." He continued where her mother left off. "Dr. McKenzie went in the helicopter with you. I've hugged her so many times that

I might have made her uncomfortable. I don't know how I'll ever repay her for saving my baby. Free dentistry for her and her family for life, I suppose."

Megan tried to smile, but didn't have the strength to lift the corners of her mouth. Her chest felt like it was being pulled together.

"The doctor did the myectomy as you two had planned, and they cleaned out all your valves. Everything looks good." He said. "You made the right decision, honey. You took charge and did what was right for you. I'm so proud of you, princess, and so happy you're still with us."

Fighting sleep, Megan tried to nod, but drifted back off.

When she next woke, she felt stronger and more alert. Nobody had appeared before her this time, but she was able to move her head to look around the room. When she looked to her right, she saw a dark-haired head laying on the bed, turned away from her. She knew that head of hair, but she wasn't sure what he was doing here. Running her fingers through his hair, she laughed lightly—until she was reminded of her incision and tears sprang to her eyes. *Note to self, absolutely no laughing.* When his head popped up, his anxious eyes met hers.

"Thank god," Sebastian said softly as he switched positions, moving to sit on the side of the bed. Leaning down, he pressed a kiss to her forehead. When he pulled back, she saw his eyes were glassy and he desperately needed to trim his beard.

"It's okay now," she whispered, reaching up to cup his cheek. It was all she had the strength for.

Rubbing at his eyes, Sebastian gave her a small smile. "I lost my shit," he said with a small laugh. "If it weren't for my sister, I don't know what I would have done. I've never felt so powerless in my life."

Nodding slightly, Megan considered what he'd said. She imagined he'd be worried about her, knowing he cared about her. But he was a doctor. He would have known everything that was happening.

She would have thought that would have given him some comfort. He was pale with dark circles under his bloodshot eyes. His clothes were rumbled and his normally well-trimmed beard looked a little shaggier.

"I'm sorry I worried you," she whispered before a coughing fit overtook her. The pain in her chest was excruciating. She felt it stabbing her in her back like knives from a fire. Trying not to cough only made it worse. Tears poured down her face and sobs escaped.

Rubbing her back, Sebastian said in her ear, "You have to let it out. I know it hurts, baby, but the coughing will help in the long run. We'll get you up and walking around later or tomorrow maybe. That will help you, too. Squeeze my hand. Let me help you with the pain."

Crushing his fingers, she endured the agony. Her body shook violently with the fit. All she wanted in the world was for it to pass. Her brain felt like it was shaking around in her head, and her ribs ached. When it passed, she was sore, but she did feel better. Sebastian eased back against the pillows and kept a hold of her hand as she attempted to take deep breaths to calm herself and her heart down.

Stroking her hair, Sebastian sat back down next to her on the bed still holding her hand. The look in his eyes couldn't be mistaken as anything other than love. It hit her right in her repaired heart. Her chest felt a different kind of pressure—a welcomed one. Could this wonderful man really love her? Boring, conservative her? It seemed impossible but it was written all over his face.

Before the heart attack, she knew she cared about him—even that she was falling for him. But her one thought as she drifted in and out of consciousness—as she slept and slept—was that she would never see him again, and that terrified her more than what she was going through. He snuck up on her. She wasn't looking for, nor did she want, a relationship. But he showed her what it could be like between them and it turned into literally what she lived for.

A lone tear ran down his cheek. Leaning forward, he pressed his forehead to hers. Closing her eyes, she savored his nearness.

"You scared the fucking shit out of me, baby," he said. "I saw you on the floor with Jackie and Natalie working over you, and I froze to the spot. I couldn't do anything. I didn't even know what to do. All my training, all my years of school were utterly useless." Cupping his cheeks and holding his head in place, she let him get it all out. "The only thing I knew with crystal clarity was that I couldn't live without you. When I was faced with that possibility, I snapped. You're inside me, Megan, filling all my empty parts."

She ran her fingers through his hair, gently scratching his scalp until she grew too tired to continue. When her hands fell away, he sat up and stared intently at her.

"I'll take care of you now," he promised. "Anything and everything you need during your recovery, it's yours. I'll be by your side."

That sounded pretty good to her. In fact, it sounded perfect. When her eyes grew heavy, she saw him pull the chair near the bed closer. With his hand in hers, he sat down by her side as she drifted off to sleep. Just like he promised.

SEBASTIAN COULD FINALLY breathe again. Megan really had made it through. She spoke to him, looked at him, touched him. Finally, he could release himself from this odd suspended animation he had been in since the surgery concluded. This endless waiting.

Until she woke up, Megan's parents were his companions. They didn't ask what his intentions were toward their daughter. Her brothers—when they were sitting there—didn't interrogate him or pass out threats about what would happen to him if he hurt their sister. They all just stayed quiet, supporting each other, leaning on each other when needed. Sebastian had begun to feel as if he were part of their family.

Occasionally, one of Megan's family members would ask questions about what to expect during the recovery period and what they should look out for going forward. Relieved to finally be of some use, Sebastian answered each and every question they had. Mostly, they got to know each other. He enjoyed hearing stories of when Megan was younger, funny family antics that he had been denied growing up. He could have that now. He could give that to his future children.

If Megan wanted children.

If someone told him a year ago he would be contemplating marriage and in love with a conservative girl from New Hampshire, he would have laughed. He had lost himself for a while in the fast-paced life of Chicago. He had become someone he barely recognized.

When he came home one night to find Eric Davis waiting for him, everything changed. Originally, Sebastian had thought the visit had something to do with his father's campaign. Eric had interrogated him about his family and upbringing before telling him he had siblings. Given Sebastian's background, he had naturally demanded a DNA test first. A few weeks later the results came in the mail, and Sebastian's world had tilted on its axis. Suddenly, there were possibilities he could only ever dream of—a family that he could start over with, one that had something so major in common with him. His stomach had turned when his father had ordered him to find out if they had any skeletons in their closet. They did, of course, everyone did, but it was nothing he would tell his father about.

The strong family bond that had developed over time—the one he craved his entire life—drove him to make life changes. He had everything he needed here. This town, his siblings, and most of all, the woman lying in the bed all held his heart.

He was nearly successful in breaking free of all ties to Chicago until Shannon showed up. True to her word, she parked herself on his couch each day and worked feverously on her laptop. He had interrupted calls with her publisher or agent about deadlines and release dates. She helped keep the kitchen stocked, and the household chores ... well, she did her best. Shannon never had to clean anything in her life, so she often pulled up videos on You Tube to learn simple things like how to do laundry, clean a kitchen floor or a shower. She wasn't the greatest, but she tried.

Sebastian, on the other hand, grew up with weekly chores. His grandparents were diligent in teaching him basic life skills, and as he grew older, those chores and skills became more age appropriate. Thanks to his grandparents he could balance a checkbook, perform basic auto repair—though now he had Ryan and was happy to pass that one off to his brother—chop wood, clean the house, sew buttons on a shirt. It was his grandparents who taught him the value of hard work.

Megan's brother Gabe entered the room then, shutting off the overhead lights and leaving a small glow. Had evening come? Sebastian didn't know.

"Go home, Doc." Taking up residence in the opposite chair, Gabe looked over at Sebastian. "Seriously, you've been here since she was brought in. Sleep in a real bed, take a shower, and eat real food."

Shaking his head, Sebastian leaned back in his chair, propping a foot on the opposite knee, signaling he was settling in. "I told her I would stay by her side."

Gabe sat forward and rested his elbows on his knees. "She'll understand, especially when we tell her just how long you've been here. These chairs were designed to make you leave. You of all people should know that. One cannot survive on hospital coffee alone."

"Believe me, one can," Sebastian assured him. *Leave?* To a certain extent, Sebastian knew what Gabe was saying, and in a different scenario, it would have made sense, but Sebastian had made a promise.

"Look, you're in love with my sister. It's obvious, and I get that, even respect it. But her family would like time with her—my parents want time with her. Go home, sleep in a real bed, take a shower, eat real food, and come back."

Running a hand down his face, Sebastian looked back at Megan's brother through dry eyes. "I've been selfish."

Gabe waved him off. "Nah, you've been having the feels, as Laurie says. We appreciate everything you've done for Meggie and everything I'm sure you'll do to help during her recovery. You've been a source of comfort to her and my family, knowing you were close. She doesn't have a lot of experience with men. Those that stuck around once she revealed her illness and the limitations because of it were usually run off by her over-protective brothers."

"I'm glad to have made the cut," Sebastian said on a half laugh. "Sorry if I've overstepped. I've never been in this situation. I've never been in love before."

Sitting back in his chair, Gabe looked over to his sister. Sebastian was thankful to be able to recognize the look of love, of unwavering loyalty Gabe gave Megan.

Admitting defeat, Sebastian stood up and stretched out his back. He bent down and pressed a kiss to Megan's forehead. She never stirred. He let his eyes roam over her perfect face, despite having already committing her to memory. "Tell her I'll be back?" Sebastian asked Gabe. After seeing Gabe nod his agreement, Sebastian turned and stepped out of the room. He could feel a tether pulling him back, but he kept going—his feet moving as if they were walking through thick mud, so reluctant was he to leave.

He had to admit Gabe was right. When it came down to it, just because Sebastian was in love with Megan, didn't mean he had any authority over her. Her family trumped him, as they should. That's how families were supposed to work.

And the harsh reality was, he and Megan had only connected a little over a month or so ago. So, not only could he not expect her to be in the same place he was emotionally, he certainly couldn't expect her family to know. To them, it wasn't about what she meant to him, but what *he* meant to *her*. And though he knew she cared about him, he didn't have confirmation of anything more.

It was a position he'd never thought he'd find himself in. He had assumed he'd be married to his career—that was until he walked into his sister's house one morning and saw Megan again. Everything in his body stopped at the first sight of her and then all together took notice of the nanny with the messy bun and yoga pants, at home in Danny and Jackie's kitchen as if she were supermom. A warmth had surrounded him as he stood there and tried not to drool over her. There in his sister's kitchen, he had seen visions of a life he had never put much thought into, but with the sun shining in the window on her, it became a life he suddenly desperately wanted.

Instead of going home, he went to work. He could use the support of *his* family now. The parking lot didn't look very busy, and he knew Jackie was on today. Walking through the side door of the small hospital, his suspicions were confirmed when Jackie stood in the hallway, leaning up against a storage cabinet drinking coffee.

"Well now," she said. "Look what the cat dragged in. I see Gabe was successful."

Moving to the coffee maker, Sebastian took his mug down from the shelf, and chose his coffee pod. "You told him to boot me out, didn't you?" He was too tired to be mad about it. His back hurt from spending all those hours in the uncomfortable hospital chairs. And he smelled. He couldn't have been pleasant to be around.

"I did," she confessed. She turned her body and leaned her hip on the cabinet, taking a sip. "I knew you would resist every reason given but for her family wanting time with her—which they do. Sebastian, you're of no help to her if you're not rested and at your best. You know this."

Pouring creamer into his mug, Sebastian nodded his head. "You've been bringing the tough love lately."

"You've needed it," she shrugged. "I know firsthand what it's like to *need* to be at that bedside, but the distance is also necessary so you don't fall down the rabbit hole. It's important that you remember not to smother her."

"I know that in my head," he said. "I know all of that. I've said it to patients' families dozens of times, but I never realized it was so hard to do."

Willing himself to perk up, he drank deeply of the coffee, letting it roll down his throat and warm him inside. Jackie was across from him sending a text. When a reply was received, she nodded and pushed herself off the cabinet she was leaning on.

"Zach is coming to get you," she said. "He's going to take you for a run. You need it. You need to get all your pent-up frustrations out in a healthy way. Otherwise, it would have been a late night at the bar, and that's not what you need right now. Then you're going home to sleep."

Sebastian stepped forward and drew his sister into a hug and pressed a kiss to her forehead. "What would we do without you?" he said with a sigh.

Shimmying in his arms, Jackie pulled back. "Good god, you smell awful."

Twenty

MEGAN HAD BEEN home a week, and Sebastian was spending time with Shannon. They were dismantling the office in Sebastian's apartment to turn into a bedroom for her. Sebastian had been spending most of his time downstairs with Megan, and Shannon had started sleeping in Sebastian's bed since he slept down with Megan at night. If things kept progressing with Megan in the direction they were headed—in the direction he wanted them to go—Shannon would be able to keep this apartment and he'd move entirely downstairs. This room would make a perfect nursery for Shannon's baby.

Sebastian wasn't so old-fashioned that he thought Shannon needed a man to raise her child, but it irked him that the father had fled the picture. He never understood how men could do that—how his own father did that. Sebastian could never walk away from a child of his—whether he had planned to have said child or not. He had a responsibility to them and would never just be a name on a check.

But he wanted children. He wanted to teach them to ski, play catch, ride a bike, throw a punch, to hold a door open for a lady. He wanted to nurse them through every sniffle, sickness, and injury, be the one that taught them to drive, and celebrated with them when they got accepted to their first choice college. He didn't have that growing up, and he wanted that for his kids—he wanted that for Shannon's kid.

Looking over to where Shannon was boxing up books, Sebastian studied her. According to Jackie and the ultrasound, Shannon was healthy as a horse and so was her baby. They would be able to find out what sex the baby was with the next ultrasound.

Picking up his drill, Sebastian ducked under the desk to continue disassembling it. "Have you heard anything from the baby's father?" He had more confidence to broach the subject when he wasn't looking her directly in the eye. They were getting to know each other, but they didn't enjoy the same relationship he had with his other sisters—yet.

"I was thinking about splitting my time between a place like this in the mountains and a beach house, maybe something on Cape Cod."

Aha, we're deflecting the topic.

Pushing himself out from underneath the desk, Sebastian waited until she looked up at him. "So that's a no?"

Looking back down to the books she was stacking in the box, she said, "He's not interested. I texted him and gave him this address, and there was no response. I don't need him. I thought we were more serious than it seems we were, but that's on me. It wasn't his decision to keep the baby, it was mine. He wasn't ready to be a father."

"If anyone understands having a father who wasn't ready, it's me," Sebastian said with a sigh. Putting the drill down, he rested his elbows on his bent knees.

"He never wanted to be a father," Shannon said quietly, looking back up at him. "You were a mistake, and we were for political reasons. He just wanted to look like a family man. I don't want someone like that in my life, Sebastian. I'd rather this baby have no father than have one like ours. One day, I'll meet someone, and he'll love both of us."

Sebastian put his hand on her knee. "I'm sorry for pushing you. No brother likes to see his sister in this position."

Brushing at a stray tear that had escape, Shannon grinned at him wryly. "So *now* you're going to be the protective and over-bearing big brother. I could have used you at other moments in my life."

He knew she meant it to be light-hearted, but his heart felt heavy when he thought about everything they were denied. "I could have used you in my life, too. But the past doesn't matter anymore. We can't let it. We have now, and going forward, we'll be there for each other the way we wished we could be growing up. No more looking back, only forward."

Nodding, Shannon smiled. "Deal." Shannon went back to stacking books in the box and Sebastian started pulling the pieces of the desk apart. He would store it in the basement for now, since that was left for the tenant's use. They worked in companionable silence for a bit. Sebastian would bring a box to the living room and Shannon would start on another. When there was a knock on the door, Sebastian moved quickly to answer it thinking it may have been someone from downstairs needing him for Megan. He was surprised when he opened the door to his brother.

"Ethan." Looking down, Sebastian saw that Ethan was, of course, accompanied by Bravo, who was leaning up against Ethan's leg.

In greeting, Ethan held up his hand, wrapped in a bloody towel. "Jackie is out of the town for the day with Danny."

Sighing, Sebastian waved him in. Ethan was always doing something to himself—usually cutting himself on some old piece of farm equipment he was trying to save. Sebastian knew Ethan pushed himself hard. His brother was determined not to let a prosthesis get in his way.

After bringing him over to the sink, Sebastian gingerly unwrapped the towel. Though the material had stuck to the wound, Ethan didn't wince when it was pulled away. His brother was tough as nails. Losing the lower part of his leg in a roadside bomb explosion gave him a higher tolerance for pain.

The gash was deep and wide. It would take a number of stitches to close it up. "How did this happen?" Sebastian asked while he inspected the wound.

"I cut it on the glass in the cab of the tractor," Ethan said, eyes on the wound.

Pausing, Sebastian took in what his brother reported. "Did you put your hand through the glass, Ethan?"

Still not meeting Sebastian's eyes, Ethan whispered, "I'm honestly not sure."

Nodding, Sebastian stepped back. "Let me get my stuff." Sebastian left Ethan's side and moved to the hallway closet to retrieve his medical supplies so he could properly clean and close Ethan's wound. If Ethan was unsure if he put his hand through the glass cabin, Sebastian wondered if he had blacked out. Perhaps Ethan was struggling a little more than they thought.

He would need to tread carefully with his brother.

Returning to the kitchen, Sebastian set his things on the counter. Ethan still stood there with his bleeding hand hanging over the sink. Sebastian took a moment to study his brother's face. The haunted look had returned to Ethan's eyes. He looked sad and troubled. Sebastian's heart went out to his brother. He fought demons Sebastian could only imagine. Glancing down at the dog that leaned up against Ethan's leg and looked up lovingly at his brother, Sebastian realized that his brother and the dog had the same demons.

Before Sebastian could interrogate Ethan further, Shannon entered the kitchen. Ethan and Shannon looked at each other in interest, looking each up and down from head to toe, each with an appreciative glean in their eye.

"So, this is kind of surreal," Sebastian said, as he began to work on Ethan's injury. "Ethan, meet my sister, Shannon. Shannon, meet my brother, Ethan."

"Yeah, that was weird," Ethan agreed. "Nice to meet you."

"How do you do?" Ethan looked surprised by Shannon's formality, but she was raised to be the utmost polite. Shannon did show emotion. Eyes fixated on Ethan's bloody hand, his sister looked like she was going to vomit.

"Are you squeamish around blood, Shan?" Sebastian asked.

Shannon took a couple steps back. "A bit."

"Ethan is a farmer," Sebastian explained. "He grew up in Iowa where his adopted parents lived. After he got out of the military, he came here to Grayson Falls and has brought Jackie's small farm back to life. This isn't the first time that the farm equipment has won."

"Not hardly," Ethan agreed.

Shannon nodded her head to Ethan. "Thank you for your service." Ethan shrugged the praise off like he normally did. "What branch of the military did you serve in?"

"The Marines," Ethan said. "I was a working dog handler. I worked with Bravo here."

Sebastian applied a local anesthetic to Ethan's skin in preparation of closing the wound.

Looking down at the dog in question, Shannon said, "He served with you? He seems so docile. Were you in combat?"

"We were," Ethan said simply. He didn't elaborate, and Sebastian was glad when Shannon instinctively knew not to ask.

"Can I pet your dog?" She asked. "Does he not do that? The videos on the internet always show the dogs as mean."

Sebastian made his stitches small. As he worked, he tuned his brother and sister's conversation out. He was vaguely aware of Ethan introducing Shannon to Bravo as his "friend." It was how Bravo differentiated between good people and bad people. Not everybody got to be Bravo's "friend."

Sebastian ran through different scenarios in his head on how best to handle Ethan's struggles. Did his siblings really not realize the episodes were as bad as they were, or was Sebastian making more of them? Blacking out while driving heavy machinery was a problem. Was Ethan trying to hurt himself, or was it an accident that happened during the black out? Ethan had assured Sebastian he was getting better, but this might have been a setback.

Sebastian would start with talking to Ryan and Zach and then speak with Natalie for any insight on what was happening at home.

Maybe it would turn out that everything was okay with Ethan, but Sebastian had his suspicions there was more to the story. He couldn't help but think that Ethan had come to him for help.

MEGAN GENTLY SHIFTED her position on the couch and propped her feet up on the coffee table. They had discovered her trusty chair and a half with ottoman was too difficult for Megan to get out of on her own, so she had set herself up on a corner of her couch with everything she needed within easy reach. As soon as she settled in with her favorite quilt, the cats jumped up and positioned themselves around her. Sebastian had brought his cat down while she was in the hospital and it happened that Thor and Java became good friends.

"I'm not sure they should be so close to you," her mother said, frowning at the cats.

"They're fine," Megan said. "They give me comfort. I'm not so weak that I can't move them off of me if they get to be too much."

At Sebastian's direction, Megan took short walks around the yard a few times a day. It was cold out, but the fresh air and moving around felt good. Her back was sore, and she still couldn't lift anything more than five pounds, but there was always someone around to lift something for her. She was never alone, and it was starting to grate on her. But when she was frustrated, she did her best to slow down and remind herself everyone only wanted to help and that she did still need it.

She could maneuver the shower by herself, and she felt stronger every day. However, she never realized how often she used her shoulders and arms until she couldn't anymore. She could bring her dishes to the sink, but washing them tired her out. Until she was cleared to pick up more than thirty pounds, she couldn't start her job again as she wouldn't be able to pick up the baby. Her mother had suggested Nana could help her, but Megan rejected that idea. Nana was old and lifting probably wasn't the best idea for her either.

It had only been a week, and she knew that the recovery time would take at least five weeks. She just needed to work on her patience.

Meeting Sebastian had shaken up her introverted tendencies, but in a good way. He only wanted to be with her, so he didn't ask her to venture to overly crowded places on a date. She had thought that it was because of her medical condition, but then wondered if he just understood her that well.

Her mother brought her over her favorite herbal tea, and Megan sipped reverently of it. Closing her eyes, she looked forward to getting her quiet moments with her tea back. She could admit that she needed assistance, but certainly didn't need full-time help. But seeing her mother lose it after Megan had woken up after surgery had pretty much solidified to Megan that her mother could do whatever she wanted. Megan having a heart attack was her mother's worst nightmare. That they had lost Megan three times before she finally pulled through must have been debilitating when her parents found out.

Megan didn't remember anything about the whole event, but she did recall her dreams—snippets of children and a life with Sebastian. Little League games, dance recitals, skiing, crossing the finish line of a running race, all things that were possible for her now. He was the one she wanted to share it with.

"Your young man will be coming back soon to check on you," her mother said, sitting down in Megan's beloved chair and a half with her own cup of tea. "I'm surprised he stays away as long as he does."

"He does need to get back to work," Megan said.

"He loves you, you know, that boy." Sliding Megan a knowing look, Janet sipped her own tea.

Megan couldn't argue with her mother. After reading the text Sebastian had sent her in the hospital, she had been moved to tears. He had said he was falling in love with her, but was he just distraught?

Or now that Megan had pulled through, did he feel differently? He hadn't mentioned his text to her at all. Was he ignoring it? Did he even remember sending it? Regardless, Megan wouldn't be the one to lay her feelings bare first. She didn't have that kind of courage.

"I know he cares about me," Megan said, sipping her own tea and stroking Thor, who had snuggled down by her side, while Java made himself comfortable on the back of the couch behind her head. "We haven't known each other that long, Mom. In the end, we might not want the same things."

"He wants you, and a mother can see that plain as day."

Her mother picked up her magazine, signaling she wasn't going to share anything else on the conversation, which wasn't like her. Her mother was a bit of a family gossip needing to know everything about her kids. Megan had noticed that her mother hadn't tried to pry answers from her about her brothers' love lives, and Megan was shocked to realize she didn't know. She was out of touch with her brothers for possibly the first time ever. It had been some time since before her heart attack that they had hung out just the three of them. Megan would need to change that. Sebastian was working this weekend, and she would summon her brothers then.

Megan hadn't realized she was tired enough to sleep until she woke up stretched out on the couch. Her mother was saying goodbye to Sebastian and was giving him instructions on heating up the dinner she had left for them in the refrigerator. Had he been upstairs all day? She appreciated that he was giving her space when she seemed to need it and back by her side when she needed that.

Hearing the door shut, Megan lifted her head. Smiling at her, he squatted down in front of her, pushing hair off her face. It was then she could see the smile wasn't reaching his eyes.

"How are you feeling?" He asked.

She gave a little shrug and pushed herself up to sit on the couch, wincing. Sometimes she forgot her sternum was wired shut. Where her family instantly tried to lift under her arms and do all the work, Sebastian sat back a bit ready to help only if needed.

"You look upset," she said, cupping his cheek.

"Baby, I'm never upset when I'm with you."

"Sebastian ..."

"It's just family stuff," he waved off. "I'm not sure I should really say anything until I talk to my brothers and sister about it. It's nothing you have to worry about. One of my siblings is struggling, and it hurts to see it. It's easy to give advice over the phone from a few states away—harder when you're in the thick of it."

Leaning forward, she pressed her lips to his. Shifting to his knees, he pushed back a bit and ran his hand into her hair. She was suddenly aware of how long it had been since she washed it and hoped it didn't feel too greasy. At the very least, she was aware that she had brushed her teeth that day and so she felt confident deepening the kiss. His hand came up to her face, and he tipped his head.

Damn, but she loved the way this man kissed. She could do this all day. He could be sweet and thorough or hot and needy. Before him, she couldn't remember the last time she had been well and truly kissed. It was an exchanging of souls that she had never felt before. She knew with absolute certainty that when they did get around to making love, it would be nothing short of spectacular. No one who was this thorough of a kisser could be anything less than a thorough lover. She suspected Sebastian wasn't one to rush the main event.

Gentle as butterfly wings, he rained kisses around her face, leaving a tingling warm trail behind them. Megan allowed herself to sit and enjoy the attention. She clutched his shirt and failed to keep her breathing steady.

Thank goodness she didn't have to wear that heart monitor anymore because it most certainly would give her away now.

Tipping her head back when he moved to her neck, she let out a little moan. Could this sweet moment get any more perfect? Was it possible to get better than this?

Pulling back, Sebastian tipped his forehead against hers. "Megan, I'm in love with you."

Wow, the moment could *get better.*

"I hope I'm not rushing you by saying this or freaking you out, but I am completely in love with you. I lost a piece of myself each time when I thought that I lost you before I could tell you how I felt. I was crushed. I wouldn't have even recognized myself if I had the ability to look at me from the outside. Your brother literally had to kick me out of your room to get me to go home and take a shower. I was afraid of what would happen if I so much as stepped out into the hallway. I know you may not feel the same way about me just yet, but I couldn't let more time go by before telling you. I should have told you as soon as you woke up."

Framing his face with her hands, she kissed his forehead, his cheeks, and his lips. "I do feel the same way. I love you more than I thought I could, and I was also afraid of moving too fast. Once I let you in, you were everywhere inside me. I could dream of a future again. Dreams of a husband and children that I gave up when I was but a child myself finally seemed like they could be a reality again. With you, there were possibilities. I don't remember having the heart attack, but I remember fighting to stay alive for you. I wanted that life, and I fought for it with all my heart and soul."

With a smile on his face, Sebastian kissed her again and pulled back, looking into her eyes. The sadness that was there a few minutes ago when he came back was gone, replaced by a face that was luminescent in its love for her. "Well," he smirked. "You put up a hell of a fight."

"I have a lot to live for."

Instead of wrapping her in his arms like she thought he would, he instead pushed up to his feet and held a hand out to her. "Come on," he said. "It's time to check the incision and change the bandage."

"Wow," she said, taking his hand. "That wasn't just a bucket of water you just threw on me. It was an entire arctic lake."

"I know," he said, tugging on her hand and helping her stand. Wincing at the pain in her back, she finally stood straight. "I needed it, too. Not being able to consummate our declarations with a rousing romp in bed is unfair, but it is what it is."

"A rousing romp, huh?" Smiling, she followed slowly behind him to the bathroom off the bedroom.

"Don't change the subject, Ms. Miller," he said, as he entered the bathroom and patted the counter. "Up onto my exam table. Time for your check up."

The doctor was back for his house call.

Twenty-One

ZACH OPENED THE door to his house and clasped Sebastian's hand in a cross between an arm-wrestle and handshake. Ryan was already sitting on the sofa before a roaring fire with a beer. Piper was nowhere to be seen. Sebastian didn't want to meet in public, and he was afraid Ryan's house was too close to the farm if Ethan decided to head over to see his brother when he was finished with work for the day.

Curled up in front of the fire was Ryan's mutt, Wilson. Zach disappeared into the kitchen, presumably to get Sebastian a beer.

Ryan waved a hand toward his dog. "Sophie is painting the bedroom today, and Wilson stepped in the paint and tracked it all over the place twice. So, he's here for a play date with their dog, which neither dog is interested in. You ought to get yourself a lazy dog, too. It'll round out our pack nicely."

"I have a cat who I think hates me. The little asshole stole bread right out of the toaster this morning."

Zach returned to the room and handed Sebastian a beer. "I'd have let you pick your own beer from the fridge, but Piper is in her studio working. If you interrupted her, she'd take the bottle, crack it in half, and slice your jugular. Trust me, I know of what I speak. My fiancée on a deadline for a show is fucking scary," Zach said.

Lowering himself down to a chair near the fire, Sebastian sat across from his brothers. They were so different from each other—Zach, a baseball legend, and Ryan, stock car racing's darling engineer—but they were united in their love for their family.

"I'm assuming whatever you wanted to talk about has to do with Ethan," Ryan said, "since you said he wouldn't be coming."

"I'm pretty sure Ethan has post-traumatic stress disorder," Sebastian opened. "I don't think that comes as a surprise to anyone."

"He gets nightmares," Ryan said. "Sometimes they're bad, and he carries them around with him for a few days. But then he'll pull out of it and be fine."

"I know I haven't been here to witness them like you both have—but I'm here now and this one keeps pulling him under," Sebastian said.

Pursing his lips, Ryan looked over at Zach, who shook his head and looked down at his beer. It was a tough conversation. Sebastian knew that. They each felt like it was a betrayal of Ethan to talk about him like this when he wasn't here, but Sebastian would not confront Ethan without all the facts. He needed to know first if he was overreacting or if there was real cause to worry.

"Has he ever tried to hurt himself before?" Sebastian asked.

"What the fuck?" Ryan jumped up to pace, hands on hips. Typical Ryan, going from zero to sixty in point five seconds.

Zach was a little more careful in his reactions, schooled into him from years of dealing with the press. He asked, "What do you mean hurt himself? He's never hurt himself that we know of."

Sebastian ran through what happened at his apartment and what Ethan had said. "He once told me about the explosion. He had to punch out the glass window in the Humvee so Bravo could crawl out and then pull him out of the wreckage. Bravo was still pulling him away when the Humvee had exploded again. If Ethan hadn't punched out the window, they both would have died."

"That doesn't mean he's running around punching windows." Holding out his hand, Ryan stopped pacing. "We go to him with this, and we're off base, it's going to take a long time to build up his trust again."

Leaning his elbows on his knees, Sebastian scrubbed his fingers through his hair and then looked up at Ryan. "I'm not afraid of having to have the conversation, Ryan," he said. "And I'm not afraid of having to build up his trust again. But I need to know how bad it is before I go there. He came to me because I told him he could. He knows he cut his hand on the glass, but for the life of him, he can't remember how it happened. He doesn't remember having a flashback, but it's the only thing that makes sense. He admits that."

Sitting back down, Ryan let out a heavy sigh. "I'm sorry about my reaction," he said. "Ethan and I are tight. He can do anything. Sophie said he was a bad ass when someone broke into his and Natalie's house to get to Sophie. She said he was cool as ice as his dog dragged the dude away. She said there was a look in his eye that she'd never seen on someone before. When I asked Ethan about the whole thing, he just shrugged and said there was a time when that was just a typical day at the office for him. I don't know everything he went through over there, but I know he didn't come back unscathed."

"He's usually such an affable guy," Zach said. "In a good mood, pleasant to be around, jokes with you. He's pretty quiet, but Ryan and I aren't, so it's probably hard to get a word in."

Nodding, Sebastian sat back against the chair, hooked his foot up on his opposite knee, and took a long pull from his beer. There were a couple of possibilities here. First was that things really were manageable for Ethan. Secondly, his brothers were in denial that their hero was human and stumbled upon occasion. Or third, they were just too wrapped up in their lives to pay close attention to what was going on in Ethan's life. As long as Ethan appeared his normal self, there was no reason to delve any deeper.

Sebastian's money was on option two. Sooner or later, Atlas shrugged.

MEGAN EASED ONTO a stool at the bar at Over the Hop just before the lunch rush. Wait staff were preparing for one of the two busiest times of day, wrapping silverware and filling ketchup bottles and water pitchers. There were a few occupied tables scattered around, but nobody she recognized. At this hour, the televisions were turned to news stations and sports networks. Signs of winter and the coming holidays scattered about. A wood pile was stacked next to the fireplace, and some evergreen bunting was being wound around the windows. An artificial tree stood by the fireplace waiting to be decorated.

"Well, look what the cat dragged in," Laurie said, coming out from behind the bar to hug her cousin. "You didn't walk here, did you?"

"I did," Megan said. "I needed the exercise. My doctor said I could give it a try. I may have someone drive me back though. It depends how long I stay and how much energy I have when I'm done."

"I'm surprised your sexy doctor isn't with you." Laurie returned to her spot behind the bar and moved around filling drink orders and stocking what she needed for the lunch shift. Megan knew the routine as she had filled in behind the bar plenty of times.

Tipping her face up to the sun shining through the bar window, she paused to appreciate its warmth. She hadn't been stuck inside her apartment for long, but it still felt nice to be out of there.

"He's working," Megan said. "He mostly helps now at night and in the mornings. I'm already leaving Jackie without a nanny. I couldn't also leave her without her second doctor." Though she wished she could. Having Sebastian around made her feel so much better. Who would have thought this man that nearly begged her to hang out with him would be so essential to her existence?

"And how are things going there with the doctor whose yumminess I shall not name?" Megan rolled her eyes while Laurie leered suggestively at her.

"I'm not sure I've ever really been in love before. Sure, I thought I was in high school, but that was young, puppy love. This is something so different. Everything with Sebastian is so vivid, so much more. Am I nuts?"

Slinging a towel over her shoulder, Laurie leaned against the bar behind her and crossed her arms. "So, we've gone from, 'I like him and I don't know what to do,' to 'I'm in love with him and I don't know what to do?'" Pushing off the bar, Laurie stepped in front of Megan and leaned on her elbows. "When I say that man is crazy for you, I mean he's certifiable. He lost his ever-fucking mind when he saw them doing CPR on you. I've never seen anything like it. You don't need my advice. Just keep doing you because it's all working, honey."

Resting her chin on her fist, Megan sighed. "My doctor told me yesterday that if I keep progressing the way I am, I can be cleared for physical activity in two weeks at my next appointment."

Picking up a glass, Laurie shoved it in the ice freezer in front of her then sprayed cold unsweetened tea in it. "You always were an overachiever. And that's great. You'll be able to walk here and back." Placing the glass in front of Megan, understanding finally dawned on Laurie's face. "Oh, you mean *physical activity*." Nodding, Megan picked up her glass and drank. She needed to cool down. Just thinking of being intimate with Sebastian was making her flushed. "And without the limitations of not getting your heart rate up." Megan nodded again. "Girl, you're going to be swinging from the ceiling fan!"

Flushing, Megan dropped her head and put her hand up to hide her face from the other customers. Maybe she didn't know them, but that didn't mean she wouldn't end up on Norrie's Facebook page all the same.

"We have to get you some props!" Laurie continued, laughing at Megan's reaction.

"Would you please stop," Megan hissed in a hushed tone, face on fire. She looked around to see if anyone was paying attention to their conversation. Thankfully, the scattering of people in the pub were minding their own business. "I'm still me. And maybe I can be more active a participant now, but I'm not kinky or anything."

"Okay, so maybe you're not ready for toys," Laurie said, holding her hands palms out. "But we should at least get you something amazing to wear. This is a big deal. Not only will it be your first time with him, but your first time really being able to let go and enjoy it."

"You make me sound like a medieval virgin heading off to her marriage bed." Megan rolled her eyes. Laurie handed her a tablet so Megan could put in a food order. After punching in her turkey club, she handed it back to Laurie.

Setting aside the tablet, Laurie shrugged. "In a lot of ways, you are. I know you're conservative, shy, and not entirely comfortable in your body. That's just you. But this will open things up to you. *Sebastian* will open things up for you. He'll show you how beautiful you are—how sensual your body can be. You can explore together and find your new comfort zone. I'm excited for you. I guarantee you Dr. Delicious is amazing in bed. I refuse to believe he can be anything else."

"I think you're more excited than I am."

Justin popped out of the kitchen, looked at his sister, and then looked around her. His timing couldn't be any worse. Thank god he hadn't come out during their conversation about sex. "Who dropped you off?"

"No one," Megan shrugged. "The doctor said to give walking a try."

Justin's eyes narrowed, and he joined Laurie at the bar. "He said to do that by yourself?"

"He didn't really specify." Megan looked down at her glass and stabbed the ice with her straw. Anything to avoid looking her brother in the eye. Her doctor really didn't say either way, and she assumed that if he wanted her to have someone with her, he would have told her. She took advantage of it because she needed to gain some freedom back.

She braced for the lecture she was going to get about pushing herself and being more aware of her safety. She scared the hell out of her family. She knew that, and so, she would let him lecture.

Instead, he surprised her. His facial features softened. Walking over to her, he said, "It's hard, Meggie. It's really hard to let you spread your wings because I'm so scared. But it's time, I know that. I'll probably still be an asshole about it." Chuckling, despite her eyes tearing up, Megan hugged him. "Looks like somebody else has realized you're out of your prison, too."

Pulling away, Megan checked the restaurant behind her to see who her brother was talking about. Sure enough, Sebastian was heading her way. Swooping right in, he kissed her—a kiss that wasn't quite appropriate for a public place, and given her brother's reaction of, "Seriously, Dude?" he agreed. Blushing, she pulled back.

"I was going to go home for lunch, but after Norrie's Facebook post about how nice it is to see you out and about, of course, I came here." Sebastian was not at all embarrassed or apologetic about his ostentatious public display of affection.

"She walked here all by herself," Justin said. "What do you think about that?"

Turning back to her, Sebastian raised his eyebrows. "I think it's excellent progress."

Justin scowled. Megan assumed her brother might have been hoping Sebastian would also be reluctant to let her spread her wings, but he would be disappointed. Sebastian didn't hinder her; he empowered her.

"Do you feel up to the walk back, or do you want me to give you a lift?" he asked, taking the stool next to her.

"Let's see how I feel after lunch," she said. Sebastian put in his non-alcoholic drink order—he did have to go back to work after all—and a large food order. He must have been instructed to bring back lunch for everyone.

Justin returned to the kitchen, and Laurie, after tossing Megan a saucy grin, moved down the bar to help new customers. Turning on his stool, Sebastian faced her. The look of excitement on his face was too happy to deny, and she leaned forward and gave him a much more chaste kiss than the one he planted on her.

Looking down, she picked at imaginary lint on her leggings. *Take charge*, her cousin once told her. She took a deep breath and let it back out again. "So, my doctor told me yesterday that if I keep progressing the way I am, I'll be cleared for physical activity at my next appointment." She couldn't believe she was starting this conversation in the pub, but if this was when she had her courage, she'd roll with it.

Leaning in, Sebastian tipped his head down and lowered his voice. "To be clear, we're talking about sex, right?"

Heat bloomed up her neck and face. She knew her skin must have looked as red as a tomato. Nodding quickly, she kept her eyes downcast. Gently, he hooked a thumb under her chin and raised her head so he could look her in the eye.

"We're a long way from making love if you can't look me in the eye when we talk about it," he said softly. She nodded and unknowingly licked her lips. "So," he continued. "Shall we go somewhere? I could find us a nice, romantic bed and breakfast. We could make a whole weekend out of it. Maybe in New York City."

Her eyes widened. Shaking her head, she waved her hand in a stop motion. "It's not that big of a deal." He raised a brow at her. "Well, I mean, it *is*, but I don't want to make a production out of it." Pressing the palm of her hand against her forehead, she squeezed her eyes closed. "That's not right either. I'm so bad at this."

Cupping her face in his hands, Sebastian pressed a gentle kiss to her forehead. "You're perfect at this. And the first time we make love is also going to be perfect because it won't be scheduled or planned out. We're going to let it come naturally, okay?" Nodding, Megan fell just a little more in love with him then. "Did you think I was going to slam you up against the wall and tear your clothes off the minute you got the okay?"

Shaking her head, Megan's eyes widened. "No! Well, maybe, I don't know. I don't really know how you are in bed. And I can't believe I started this conversation in a public place." She blew her hair out of her eyes, and Sebastian tucked the errant strands behind her ear.

"I can be patient," he promised. "It'll happen when it's right for us. We'll save New York for Valentine's Day." Megan nodded, and Sebastian leaned in for a kiss. "I love you. Because of that, whenever it happens, however it happens, it'll be perfect because it's the two of us. Don't worry about it. When the time comes, it'll be easy."

He always used the right words. Charming wasn't the only positive descriptor for him, sensitive, caring, funny, attentive, and *safe*. She felt safe with him. He was almost too good to be true, like a character in a book. But he was a living, breathing, in the smooth and perfect flesh, a man who loved *her*, the shy girl that did everything to blend in, the wallflower.

He was helping her bloom.

Twenty-Two

SEBASTIAN STEPPED OUT of a patient treatment room to find Jackie standing there waiting for him, chewing her bottom lip.

"What's up?" he asked. "Something wrong?" Biting her lip, she looked towards the waiting room. A fist-sized lump coiled in his stomach. "Is it something with Megan? Or Shannon? Is there a problem with the baby?"

"Sebastian, your father is here," she said in a hushed voice. Tension rolled through his body, turning his blood cold and his jaw to stone. He straightened to his full height and took a step back, fists clenching. Son of a bitch. What the hell did his father think he was doing? His first inclination was to refuse to see him, but then he was afraid something may have happened to one of his grandparents. Then again, Sebastian was confident his father would not feel the need to make a personal visit to his estranged son. The man never cared about Sebastian's feelings before, he wasn't likely going to start now.

But of course. This wasn't about Sebastian at all. His father must know Shannon was here. This was about getting his defiant daughter back—one that dutifully posed for pictures at political fundraisers and was previously seen around the country club with suitable men carefully chosen by her ice queen mother. Why else would his father speak with him unless he absolutely had to?

Then again, he could have come all this way to get his signature on that damned confidentiality agreement. It seemed a long way to come to do your own dirty work, but if Donovan was clipping his loose ends, he may think it was better done himself.

Sighing heavily, Sebastian rubbed his forehead.

"I could tell him you're in with patients," Jackie suggested. "We can put him off. He may be a big shot at some other hospital, but he's not at this one."

For a brief moment, Sebastian's tension relaxed a bit. He would enjoy listening to her go out to the waiting room and let his father have it, her fists clenched and fury in her eyes. Not many people were unfortunate enough to see Jackie's temper.

But the light moment passed. No one should deal with his father but him. He used to be afraid of the man when he was younger. The way his father looked at him with a cold, dispassionate gaze. It wasn't even that he looked at Sebastian without emotion so much as he looked at him as something to be crushed. If it wasn't for Sebastian's appearance, he would have questioned whether or not the man was his real father.

But of course, his father got a paternity test, so there was no dream of really belonging to someone else.

"Please have Natalie tell my next patient I'll be in in a minute," Sebastian said. Jackie arched a brow, no doubt at the mask he suddenly slid into place. The old familiar feeling of numbness rolled over him as he prepared to see the man he hoped never to encounter again. What would it take for him to be left in peace? A restraining order? It would take his father harassing him a lot more than this for that to fly.

Then again, the chief of police *was* his brother-in-law.

Handing Jackie the patient file he was holding, he turned on his heel and walked in the direction of the waiting room. A nurse sat behind the reception desk staring his father down with the distain Sebastian knew she saved for those that thought hospital rules didn't apply to them. To show up without an appointment or an actual emergency was a very large sin in her world. She ran a tight, efficient, and orderly ship. She was scary as all hell and indispensable.

His father sat in an Armani suit with one foot propped up on the opposite knee as he scrolled through his phone. Sebastian had been with his last patient fewer than ten minutes, so he knew his father hadn't waited long. Sliding his hands into his pockets, Sebastian tried to affect a casual stance, but his muscles were coiled to spring. He cleared his throat and, as usual, waited for his father's attention.

His father didn't immediately look up, and Sebastian refused to address him by name. He had stopped calling him 'Dad' or 'Father' long ago. When they worked in the same hospital, Sebastian just called him 'Sir.'

The elder Dr. Stuart glanced up, and when he saw Sebastian, he put his phone in his pocket and rose from the chair. That was unlike the man, Sebastian thought. Donovan Stuart finished what he was doing before you gained his attention—*if* you ever did. After watching his father tugging on his jacket lapels then putting his hands in his pockets and taking them out again, Sebastian realized that his father was nervous. Dr. Stuart Senior did not show a petty weakness like nervousness. He was always stoic, calm, cool, and collected. But now everything about him looked uncomfortable.

"Sebastian," he said, nodding his head and finally settling on putting his hands in his pockets. "I apologize for just showing up like this. Do you have some time to talk?"

Thrown by his father's softer tone of voice, nothing initially came out when Sebastian opened his mouth to respond, but he was quick to recover.

"Not right now, I don't. I have a full schedule of patients, and we have a few admitted. I'm afraid I have to wait until the evening covering practice comes on to take care of them. My sister needs to leave. She can't stay. Her nanny had surgery, and Jackie needs to pick up the baby from her sister-in-law."

Why was he explaining all this to the man? The inner workings of the hospital and his family dynamics were certainly none of his father's business. And he specifically referred to Jackie first as his sister. Sebastian had wanted to throw his family in his father's face—wanted his father to be reminded that Sebastian was in a place where he was surrounded by people who loved him. He even had the love of a wonderful woman—*the* woman—but Sebastian wouldn't tell his father about Megan. His father didn't deserve to know about her.

"I have a room at the hotel in town," Donovan said. "I can come back at the end of your shift, and we can have a late dinner. Please, there are things I need to say to you."

The hell? His father sounded like he was pleading with him. He must have been desperate to get Shannon back into the fold.

Though the hotel in town was nice, it certainly wasn't the five-star standard his father expected. It was clean and well-maintained, but the Waldorf it was not. Sebastian was suddenly feeling very defensive of his adopted hometown, and his father hadn't even said anything negative about it—yet.

Slowly, Sebastian nodded his head. "All right. There's a great brew pub in town. It's called Over the Hop. I'll meet you there at eight o'clock, unless all hell breaks loose here."

Blowing out a breath, his father nodded in return. "A brew pub. Well, that will certainly be a new experience. I look forward to it." Giving Sebastian a half smile, Donovan nodded again and left out the front door.

"Well, that was cryptic," Jackie said, coming out from her hiding place around the corner and just out of sight of the waiting room. Sebastian shook his head. He should have known his sister wouldn't have let him go into battle alone. "What do you think he wants to talk to you about?"

Sebastian began to walk down the corridor back to the treatment rooms. "I imagine he's trying to get Shannon back. They've probably found some Wall Street banker or hospital resident to say the baby is his. I don't know what influence he thinks I might have over her."

Following along, Jackie said, "He sounded nervous and unsure of himself. That doesn't sound like the man you told me about."

Stopping at the coffee machine, Sebastian began to brew his fifth cup of the day. *No, it wasn't like his father at all.* What could shake the man's confidence so much? A chill ran over his spine and he shuddered against it. Was his father in a twelve-step program? Though he loathed the man, he hoped he wasn't sick or in recovery. Sebastian wouldn't wish that kind of suffering on anybody. But would he be able to give forgiveness for a life without the love of the man he should have been able to emulate and depend upon?

Sighing, he rubbed his hand down his face. He warned his father in Chicago that the day would come that Donovan would regret the way he treated Sebastian his whole life and not to come calling when he did. Was that time now? But he tried to have Sebastian sign the confidentiality agreement. If it was presented to him again at dinner, Sebastian needed to decide if he would sign it and his reasons for whatever decision he made. If he truly wanted to be rid of his father and out of his iron grip, signing the agreement would be the way to go.

But again, breaking away had to be on Sebastian's terms not his father's. He'd had enough rejection from that man.

"Sebastian," Jackie said softly, putting her hand on his arm. "You don't owe that man a single thing. If you don't want to see him, don't. He has had time after time to make amends with you, and he never cared before."

"I don't think it's about me," Sebastian said, doctoring his coffee to his liking. "It can't possibly be. I'm sure it's about Shannon. He needs her to fall back into line. I'm going to text her and let her know he's here, but the question is? She has her own issues with him, but I don't think she's ready to hash them out. She hasn't had enough time to work through everything yet. Not to mention with the pregnancy hormones she can be overly emotional."

Jackie crossed her arms and leaned up against the counter. "I wonder if you shouldn't tell Shannon he's here. Stress is tough on a baby, and it might make more sense to find out what he's doing here first. He just might have come for you. People do change."

Sebastian began walking toward the treatment room that held his next patient. "Five minutes ago, you wanted to kick him out of the joint. Now you're advocating for him?"

"I'm not advocating for him," she argued as they stopped outside the room. "I'm advocating for you. You're a wonderful person, Sebastian, worthy of love and affection. People have life changing events that cause them to reevaluate their lives and how they live them. Isn't that what happened to all of us?"

"There is nothing good inside that man. I clearly take after our mother." Giving her shoulder a squeeze, he disappeared into the treatment room, ready to throw himself into work.

IF SEBASTIAN WAS stressing out, Megan was having a full-on neurological event. Sebastian had texted that he would be late because his father dropped in unexpectedly. He was likely to be emotionally drained when he got home. He would need comfort from her, which she could give. From what Sebastian had told her about his father, he was not a good man, and the visit likely wouldn't be a good one.

What could the man possibly want with the child he spurned? Megan couldn't understand having a parent like that. Her parents could be smothering at times—and that was frustrating—but that was because they loved her so much and wanted to protect her. She never had to wonder growing up why neither parent wanted her. They expressed their love for her and her brothers every day. She was always sure of her belonging.

What she wanted to do was to go down to Over the Hop and give Sebastian her support. Maybe she could pop in under the guise of hanging out with Laurie, and Sebastian would know she was there if he needed her. Was that too presumptuous? Would her gesture be unwanted? She could sit at the bar and not go over to Sebastian's table unless he requested her to. He didn't even have to tell his father who she was.

No. She would stay put. He hadn't asked for her to come and she wouldn't impose where she wasn't invited. This was a part of his life that he didn't want to touch her, and she had to respect his wishes, no matter how bad her need to go to him and support him in any way she could. This wasn't about her and what she needed. It was about Sebastian.

He was eating at the brewery, so making him dinner was out. Sighing, she looked around. She was terrible at this. Her last boyfriend was so long ago, she couldn't even remember if she was ever in the position to provide comfort. She was overthinking it. She should go with her gut.

At the knock on the door, Megan crossed the apartment and peeked through the peephole. Sebastian's sister, Shannon, stood on the other side. Stepping away from the door, Megan paused before opening it. She hadn't had a lot of interaction with Shannon. Obviously, their paths crossed living in the same building, but their conversations were short and mostly confined to the topic of Megan's recovery.

Megan pulled open the door, and Shannon stood there stoic and serious.

"Hello," Megan greeted, stepping back to allow Shannon into the apartment. Once she was inside, Megan closed the door again and looked at the other woman expectantly.

"I have to kill someone," she said evenly. "Do you think it's actually possible to kill someone with an icicle? I mean, they're very sharp, and they would be the perfect weapon because they would melt."

Sebastian had said he was specifically not telling Shannon that her father was in town until he found out what the man wanted, but she didn't look emotionally worked up. She looked serious as she waited patiently for Megan to answer.

"Um, who do you want to kill?" Megan asked.

"I don't *want* to kill anybody, but this person has to go. It's just the way things have to be."

Megan backed up a few steps. Was Sebastian's sister having some kind of episode? She didn't know much about the other woman. Maybe she had psychiatric issues she was getting treated for. Mental health was a common problem. People were treated for all kinds of conditions.

"Who is this person?"

"Darcy." Shannon sat down on the couch and tucked her ankles underneath her like she was settling in for a long girl talk. "I can't reveal the whole thing, but she's been tracking the killer for the whole time and he gets her. It'll be unexpected and a huge twist, but I got to thinking that it would be cool if it was done by icicle. No one would ever know what happened."

"Is this person ... fictional?" Megan sat down on her favorite chair, letting out a relieved breath when she remembered Shannon was a writer.

"Yes, of course," Shannon said. "I'd hardly kill a real person for research purposes."

"Research?"

"Yes," Shannon said, "For my book."

Of course. Could the woman seriously not lead with why she had a pressing need to know if an icicle could kill someone?

"Well," Megan said. It was nice to focus on something other than her nervousness on how to help Sebastian deal with the emotions from his father's sudden appearance. "First of all, I'm not sure it would be sharp enough to penetrate deep enough to cause damage, let alone death. I mean, they're cones, and as soon as you touch it, the heat from your hands, even if you were wearing gloves, it would start to weaken and melt, right?"

"Hmm." Shannon scratched her chin and looked up towards the ceiling. "Valid points. But there is documented evidence that people *have* been killed by falling icicles."

"True," Megan conceded. "But those broke off of a roof or a tree and gained speed before hitting their victim. Is your killer going to launch it like a javelin? How could he hit his target that way? They're also brittle and slippery. I don't think even wearing gloves, you could get the grip you needed to have the power required to drive it home." Megan cocked her head in thought. "Having said that, if it were used, say in a crime of passion or self-defense, then you might be able to get away with it. But it doesn't make sense for a killer who has been stalking his victim. He'd be ready with a more effective weapon."

"Shit, you're right." Sighing, Shannon grinned up at Megan. "You're really good at this."

"I read a lot." Megan said. "And I used to work in the library. That was fun to think through."

"I'm going to save it for a crime of passion. I liked that idea a lot." Looking around the apartment, Shannon continued. "This is cozier down here. Sebastian's is so manly. I came in here to take care of the cats while you were in the hospital and Sebastian was MIA. It's much more feminine. Since he pretty much lives down here now, I've basically taken over upstairs. I'm not sure what I'll do when the baby comes."

"Are you excited?" Megan envied any woman that was able to carry a baby. She had talked with her doctor at her last appointment about having children, and her doctor told her that though she would be considered a high-risk pregnancy, he didn't see any reason why she wouldn't be able to have children.

Now it was just a matter of getting over her fear of passing on the disease to said children.

"When I first found out, I have to say I wasn't." Shannon said. "The father wasn't interested; my father called me some pretty nasty names, and I couldn't fathom the ways my life was going to change. I knew I wasn't going to have an abortion, but I wasn't sure I'd keep the baby. How could someone with my upbringing and education—my pedigree, if you will—mess up so badly?" Shannon pulled her legs out from underneath her and sat up straighter.

"I'm sure Sebastian told you we weren't close growing up. We barely knew each other. Our father said that was Sebastian's fault. It was my brother's doing that we didn't have a relationship. Of course, eventually I realized that wasn't true. And when it became apparent that I needed to come up with some kind of plan, I don't know, I just *knew* he would help me. I'm still not sure I'm going to stay here for long after the baby is born. I don't know if it's our place, but I know I need to be here now." Shannon stood up and wandered around the room.

"I am excited for the baby. I wasn't before, but with my writing income, we'll be okay financially for a little while. We'll have to see how well this book sells. With Sebastian, we've got some support. Maybe I'll end up at the beach, or another city, or maybe I'll end up staying put. It's a little scary not to have that plan in place, but it'll come." Shannon cradled the small bump in her abdomen with her hand. "It's me and this kid against the world. We'll be a good team."

Smiling at the serene picture she made, Megan let her thoughts drift. She wanted that anticipation—preparing for the life that will change your whole world, and she wanted that with Sebastian. Images came to mind, and soon an evening plan formed. She just might have some surprises in store for her Dr. Delicious.

Twenty-Three

OVER THE HOP was packed when Sebastian entered. Dart night was always busy, and it slipped Sebastian's mind that it was happening here tonight. The dart leagues moved from bar to bar for their matches. Scanning the crowd to see if anyone he knew, or was related to, happened to be there tonight, Sebastian's eyes eventually fell on his father sitting at a high-top table with a beer in front of him. Donovan was watching the crowd, and Sebastian could only imagine what the man thought.

Sebastian hung back to observe his father without his knowledge. He was dressed in slacks, a dress shirt and a dark grey V-neck sweater—what he always considered a casual outfit. There were no jeans, and certainly no sweatpants, in Dr. Donovan Stuart's wardrobe. Sebastian always imagined his father slept in silk, so formal was he in his attire. The beer in front of him was full. A prop. For what? To show he can fit in?

Taking a deep breath for fortitude, Sebastian stepped into the busy pub and wound his way through the crowd until he reached his father's table. Donovan surprised him by slipping off his stool and stepping towards Sebastian. He raised his arms and Sebastian realized in a horrified moment that his father actually intended to hug him. Except his father didn't seem to know what to do with his arms and ended up enveloping Sebastian in a completely unexpected and totally awkward hug. On impulse, Sebastian's arms came up before they dropped. In Sebastian's memory, this was the first time he'd been in his father's arms. He didn't even get a hug when Donovan dutifully visited him in the hospital when Sebastian got his appendix out when he was a young kid. He had checked on him and left. The whole so-called visit took about three minutes. Never mind that his son was terrified to be in the hospital, his father had patients to see.

Sebastian fidgeted before stepping back from the strange and uncomfortable hug. His father looked everywhere else but at Sebastian.

He didn't seem any more at ease with what happened than Sebastian did. All those years Sebastian yearned for a hug from his father, and when it finally came, it felt unnatural. Clearing his throat, his father gave an awkward smile and slid back onto his stool, eyes scanning the crowd again.

"So, was everything all right at the hospital this evening?" His father asked.

"Yes," Sebastian said. "We don't typically see a lot of real serious cases. We have a surgery, and now that I'm on board, we'll be expanding to take more routine cases. Our admitted patients are often step down from surgery or they come for something like the flu or pneumonia. We've delivered a few babies. It's a nice variety and slower pace. I like it."

His father nodded, likely because he didn't have anything positive to say. Laurie showed up, slid a beer in a frosted glass in front of him, and gave him an encouraging pat on the shoulder. Megan probably told her Sebastian was having a difficult meeting.

"She didn't take your order," Donovan frowned.

"She knows I like all their beers, so she just brings me whatever and I get to be surprised," Sebastian explained. "They'll be by to take a food order soon. It's dart night, so things are busy." Sebastian glanced down as his father's beer, which did not show evidence of being in a frosted glass. Laurie had added a nice little touch to show how Sebastian was valued and liked here.

"I figured it was something like that," Donovan said looking around him. Sebastian thought he saw the first hints of disapproval.

Repressing the urge to jump to the pub's and people of Grayson Falls' defense, Sebastian held his tongue. It would be a losing battle. People like his father didn't understand the culture of the real working class—despite being raised in a middle-class home himself.

Taking a long pull of liquid courage, Sebastian put the glass back down on the table and looked his father in the eye. "Well, we're not here for small talk, so why don't you tell me what's brought you all this way. I'd have heard by phone if there was a problem with Grandma and Grandpa."

"My parents are in good health. They seem to be thriving in Florida. It was good of you to help them settle into a community that meets all their needs. Thank you for that. We were in agreement on that community."

Sebastian wasn't aware his father had taken any interest in where his parents were actually settled down. He didn't hear either his grandparents or his father talking about it. But he should have realized his father would be involved. He had a good relationship with his parents—where Sebastian wasn't involved that is.

"They raised me," Sebastian needlessly reminded him. "I would do anything for them." Sebastian didn't want to bring the conversation—whatever they were discussing—to a level of angst, but he couldn't seem to help himself.

"Well, that brings us to what I wanted to speak to you about." Cocking his head to the side, Sebastian studied his father. Donovan scanned the restaurant, and Sebastian wondered what he was looking for. Why would his father have trouble meeting his eyes? The man may have been harsh in the past, but he was always painfully truthful.

Placing his hands on the table, Donovan focused on them while he spoke. Sebastian leaned forward. "I know the kind of father I was—and *am*—to you. And I also know that you don't understand why I am the way I am. It's not something I can ever explain and have it make sense to you."

"I'm an intelligent guy." Sitting back, Sebastian crossed his arms over his chest. "Why don't you give it a try, *Dad*?"

Donovan met Sebastian's eyes when he called him "Dad." It was sarcastic and not at all affectionate. Taking a deep breath, Sebastian tried to reign in his temper. Their last meeting was hostile and, quite frankly, Sebastian was tired. He no longer wanted to fight this man.

He just wanted to be free of him. And so, he decided to hear what he had to say first and then send him back to Chicago.

"Daisy, your mother, was vibrant like a sunburst when she exploded into my life at a time I could not afford the distraction. She didn't ask anything of me other than to hang out and have a good time. She was an undergrad—or she said she was—studying to be a kindergarten teacher. Daisy was genuine, and we were friends—*not* lovers. We did not have a romantic relationship. That's what I liked about her. She was fun and wasn't looking for any sort of entanglement."

Shifting in his seat, Donovan paused when Laurie took their food order. Scanning the restaurant again, he took a small sip of his beer. It was the first time Sebastian had seen him touch his drink since he sat down. If he didn't want a beer, why didn't he just order something else?

"Then came the end of year fraternity picnic. I brought her as my date. She was the life of the party, and I started to get jealous. There was so much interest in her, and she was a bombshell. All sorts of guys were giving her drinks. In my foul mood, I started drinking. I'm not sure what my problem was. She certainly wasn't interested in any of those other guys. People were just naturally drawn to her—including me. We left the party drunk out of our minds. One thing led to another, and the next morning, she was gone."

Both men leaned back away from the table as Laurie delivered their food. Finally, Sebastian's father ordered a water, seemingly giving up on the pretense of beer.

"I didn't know about you until she put my name on the birth certificate ten months later."

Sebastian polished off two wings before responding. Nothing was different from what his grandparents told him, though his father's version had more details.

"Daisy was diagnosed with schizophrenia," Sebastian said. "I haven't met her, but Jackie, Ryan, and Ethan have. And, of course, she raised Zach with his father, to the best of her ability. She's in a care facility now. Her health is deteriorating. I don't know if it's better to have never met her or to see her even just once but only meet some shell of the vibrant person you knew." Sebastian paused to take a fortifying sip of his drink. "Why didn't you just give me up? You were never interested in being a father to me, and from what I've seen, you weren't much of a father to my siblings."

"My parents insisted I not," Donovan said with a small shrug. "Your grandmother couldn't stand the idea of having a grandchild out there in the world that she never saw. She thought once I was out of medical school and in a steady job, I would be in a position to take you back. I had intended to do that, Sebastian. I always thought, 'Once I'm making X amount of money,' or 'once I'm on X shift, I can bring Sebastian home.' The goalposts got further and further away, and I got more and more frustrated. When I got married, Valerie didn't want to raise somebody else's child. I pulled away, distancing myself. I couldn't let myself care about you. As a result, I couldn't care about any of my children. My marriage was a failure. I was a failure as a father. The only thing I had was my career, and I took that out on you."

Shaking his head, Sebastian wasn't sure he believed him. "You married a woman that didn't want anything to do with your son? How does somebody do that? How did you reconcile that? You're saying you gave up your son for that? I say bullshit."

"By the time that came around, you were well-settled where you were. You were in a good school. You had sports, after school activities, friends. I thought it was unfair to take you from a place where you were thriving and bring you to a loveless home." Donovan looked around them and lowered his voice. "I married your stepmother for her political ties, and I sold my soul for it."

Picking up a French fry, Sebastian made patterns in his ketchup. It added up, and yet at the same time, didn't.

"So, Valerie is in charge," Sebastian said. "She's calling all the shots, and you weren't man enough to stand up to her for the sake of the son you supposedly loved. I have a hard time believing that, especially when it's so easily verifiable."

"Ah, so now we get to Shannon," Donovan said, sipping his water. His food still went untouched, while Sebastian polished off the rest of his wings and fries. "I know she's staying with you. I was angry—very angry. And I said things I can't take back—horrible things. I saw her in the same position I was, and I don't want that for her. I've since realized my lack of judgment. I am certainly in no position to lecture anyone on how to raise their children. She had a bright future ahead of her, and writing is not a stable income. The decision to give up your child so he can have a chance at his best life is agonizing. I wouldn't wish it on my worst enemy. That's what I did, Sebastian. Your best life wasn't with me and in a loveless house. It was with your grandparents. I made poor choices. I don't want Shannon to do the same."

Something shifted inside Sebastian, and he found himself more affected by his father's words than he thought he would be—or even could be. He wasn't compelled to have a warm, fuzzy hug-fest with the man, but he could almost see how what Donovan said could be true. It was plausible enough.

But it didn't fix what had been done. There was no changing the past. The hurt—the pain—could be buried, but it would always be there, just under the surface.

Standing, Sebastian pulled out his wallet and threw cash on the table. While he wasn't charged to eat and drink here, he did still want to leave a good tip. It was the right thing to do. He knew Laurie gave her tips to the other wait staff to split, since as part owner of the business she already drew a salary.

"I don't know if I can forgive and forget," Sebastian said. "I don't think I have that in me. But I can let go, and that's what I'll do. I'll absolve you of your sin, but you need to do something for me. If what you said is true and you ever loved me, you need to also let go. Don't contact me. Don't send me anything to sign. Don't ask me to do any political appearances. If I want to see you, I'll contact you. We're never going to have a father/son relationship, and I think you know that. Focus your attention on reconciling with your other kids, and just let me be."

Emotion flickered across his father's face and for a split second, Sebastian was convinced the things his father told him tonight were absolute truth. But just as fast as the emotion came, the wall went up, and Sebastian recognized the tightening of his jaw, slight narrowing of his cold eyes. This man was unreachable. Sebastian accepted that. After his father gave him a single nod in acknowledgement, Sebastian wove his way through the crowd and outside.

The bitter winter air felt liberating. His breath came out in white fluffy puffs and disappeared. Sebastian envisioned each cloud to be another issue he had with his father dissolving in the air, never to weigh him down again. Stepping away from the door of the pub, Sebastian walked to his car, leaving his past behind him.

MEGAN'S PULSE RACED in anticipation as she heard the outside door close. Smooth jazz was playing softly out of the speakers, and candles cast a warm glow through the living room and into the bedroom. She would have liked to have flowers about, but she didn't have the time. Not having ever done this before, she was nervous about what Sebastian would think, but it was too late now as the apartment door was swinging open.

A weary look was on Sebastian's face as he walked into the apartment. As she suspected, the meeting with his father had hit him hard. Dying to ask him about it, but knowing he'd tell her when he was ready, she held her tongue and watched as he looked around him in interest. When his eyes fell on her, they were no longer weary, but filled with lust.

Standing there in a short, black silk nightgown and robe, Megan couldn't help but feel exposed, but something about the way he looked at her reassured her that she was in safe hands. She needn't be nervous or apprehensive. With actions motivated by love, everything would be fine, no matter how she fumbled.

As Sebastian slowly walked toward her with his eyes locked on hers, Megan licked her lips. When he reached her, he took her in his arms and kissed her painfully slow. Tipping his head against her forehead, he cupped her cheek. "How did you know I would need you like this tonight?"

Wrapping her arms around his neck, she leaned into him. "You said you were meeting with your father. I took a guess."

"Of course," he smiled lightly. "This is perfect. Can I just stand here and hold you for a minute?"

You can hold me for the rest of our lives.

Melting in his arms, Megan sighed. She had thought that he might have taken one look at her and devoured her whole. She was almost prepared for it, but not the slow pace he was setting. Realizing he was looking for comfort and love, she tightened her arms around him.

He ran a soft hand down her arm and linked their fingers, bringing their joined hands to his chest. Slowly, he started to sway and turn them.

The things this man did to her healthy heart.

Rubbing his cheek against her hair, he led them in a dance as old as time, kissing her as they continued to turn and sway. A slow burn started in her core and began spreading out through her body filling all the crevices with desire. Never had she wanted a man this strongly. Never had she *needed* a man this desperately.

"You look incredible," he murmured in her ear. "You *feel* incredible."

"I think the angry scar on my chest tells a different story."

"It doesn't bother you." He shook his head. "If it did, you wouldn't be wearing this. You'd be trying to cover it up—not that I'd ever let you. It'll always be beautiful to me—a reminder of your resiliency and the strength of your spirit, of everything I could have lost, and my greatest blessing."

His arms skimmed down her sides, coming to rest at her waist where they began making slow circles in the silk of what little she had on. He dipped her low and placed a kiss over her heart and the angry looking scar that lay there before bringing her upright again.

The slow burn in her body was heating up to a furnace. Curling her fingers into his hair, she pulled his mouth down to hers, but this kiss was not gentle. Feasting at his mouth, she slid her body along his over and over, sending her nerves into a riot. Groaning, his arms banded around her and he parted their lips to deepen the kiss.

This is what she needed. This is what she needed to give to him—what would take the hurt and pain away.

Empowered, she furiously attacked the buttons of the shirt he had on underneath.

Dear Lord, why *were there so many buttons!?*

Pushing the shirt off his shoulders when she reached the last button, she moved to unfasten his pants.

"Slow down," he whispered. "I wanted the first time be relaxed and savor it."

"Next time." Panting, she locked her lips on his again. Slow and exploratory was for another time. Maybe even later tonight. But now an inferno was raging inside her, and if she didn't let it out, she'd explode—and not in a good way.

Hopping up, she wrapped her legs around his waist and he grabbed on. Chuckling, he said, "I never figured you for the aggressive type."

"I never have been," she confessed. In fact, she had always been so concerned about her heartrate during sex, she all but just laid there for it. She didn't even know she had this tigress inside of her. But even if she didn't have the surgery, she suspected she would be this way with him. He made her feel safe, and that made her feel brave.

Stumbling and laughing their way to the bedroom, they bumped into the door jamb then the dresser and finally toppled onto the bed after Sebastian tripped on a cat. Tumbling into the fluffy pillows, they laughed freely. There was none of the nervousness she had expected with him. No insecurities existed. Everything felt so right between them.

Tugging his wallet out of his back pocket, Sebastian tossed it on the bed in reaching distance then worked his jeans off. Megan felt a slight pang in her chest as she realized there was a condom in there. Her daydream earlier about having a baby with him faded away. He was being smart, of course—safe. They never even had a discussion about having children together. Though they loved each other, and their relationship felt strong, it was still too early on to discuss having a family together.

Sitting up, she slid the silk robe off her shoulders. When she reached for the straps of her nightgown, he stayed her hands. "I really want to see your body, Megan, *really* badly, but this," he said swirling his finger at the silk confection, "is really working for me right now. I hate that some other guy saw this."

"No one saw this, Sebastian," she said quietly. "I bought this last week for you. I told you, there hasn't been anyone in years."

Groaning, Sebastian fell on top of her, careful to keep his full weight to the side and not crush her. He left lingering, open mouthed kisses along her jaw, neck, chest, the rise of her breasts, and of course, over her heart. Grabbing the silk in his fists, he raised up the material to expose her stomach and continued on, hooking his fingers in her panties and sliding them down her legs.

Settling between her legs, his first kiss sent her body jack-knifing off the bed and her head rolling into the pillow. The overwhelming sensation sent little pinpricks of satisfaction over her skin and made her eyes tear. When her release came, it was a burst of light and warmth that shimmered around her. Basking in its glow, she was surprised at the sexy sounding moan that fell from her lips.

Cradling himself on top of her, Sebastian kissed around her face as she continued to roll on the wave of contentment that engulfed her. "Mmm ... I didn't know it could be that way."

With his face buried in the crook of her neck, she felt the hum of his voice when he answered, "It's never been like that for me. And we haven't even gotten to the main event yet." He lifted his head and she ran a finger down his cheek. He grabbed her wrist and pressed a long kiss to the inside of her palm.

"Did you just take my pulse?" She asked suspiciously.

Continuing his kisses down her wrist and to her elbow, he murmured. "No. Do you feel okay? I assumed you were cleared." When she didn't answer him, he stopped what he was doing and looked up at her. "Megan?"

"He was going to clear me next week anyway, and I feel awesome. Better than awesome." It was only a matter of time before she messed everything up. Why did she say anything at all? Who cared if he *was* checking on her? Her old insecurities snuck up on her at the worst time.

Sebastian sat up on his knees and looked down at her with a frown. "Megan, these milestones are put in your recovery plan for a reason. Your heart has experienced a massive trauma. It stopped and was shocked to life three times, then it was shaved down to a fraction of its size. Just because you *feel* good doesn't mean you *are* good."

Sitting up, Megan crossed her legs and pulled a pillow to her chest, suddenly needing a shield against the growing tension. Was he accusing her of being careless? There was only concern on his face not accusation.

"*You're* the doctor that's been overseeing my care, Sebastian," she said. "I've simply been checking in with Dr. Wilson. Think like a doctor and not like a penis. Am I ready for sex?"

"That's an unfair position to be put in," he argued. "As the penis is part of the doctor."

Taking his hand, Megan slid it up to her heart. "Feel it, Sebastian. It's strong. I haven't had any negative symptoms. It's finally a healthy heart. *I'm* healthy. My heart beats for you." He flinched at her words, and she suspected there might be more at play here. "Sebastian, I think this might be less about what I'm feeling and more about what you're feeling. I'm not the only one that experienced a trauma that day. Just because yours was emotional doesn't mean it wasn't painful and it didn't leave scars. I'm *not* going to die on you." His quick intake of breath told her she was right on the mark. "You weren't worried five minutes ago. In fact, I'd wager to say you were having a good time."

Staring at the scar on his chest, he nodded. "I was having a very good time."

"Stop thinking now," she ordered. "You'll be the very first person to know if something's wrong. Tonight is about you."

"Tonight is about *us*," he vehemently corrected.

"Then let's get back to it," she said, pulling her nightgown over her head. His eyes widened in response to her now totally naked body. Her bold gesture had the desired effect as he was drawn to her like a magnet. Show a man a pair of breasts, and everything else going on disappears.

She tossed the pillow aside and took him in her arms. Together, they eased back into the mound of pillows. When she shivered, he pulled the sheets and blankets over them, though her chills weren't from the cold. Lowering his head, he kissed first one breast and then the other, lathing the peak with his tongue and sending her into distraction. Where was the conservative girl now? She was nearly swinging from the ceiling fan like Laurie joked.

His hand ran up and down her body while his mouth stayed occupied with her breasts. His hand slid down between her legs, and he used his fingers until she was dizzy with need. Just when she was about to come to pieces a second time, he left her, and this time, her body felt the cold. A wrapper crinkled, and in moments, he was back in her arms and poised to enter her.

Placing a hand on either side of her head, he looked intensely down at her. "This is about *us.*" She nodded her agreement, and he plunged deep inside her. She cried out in surprise and a little bit of pain. It had been years—nearly five of them—and she was tight.

Burying his face in her neck, Sebastian moaned long, "Holy fuck. Oh, shit, Meg. This is ... this is ..." Words failed him, and his voice dropped off.

"Yeah," she sighed in agreement. How did she explain the feeling of total fulfilment by one person, mind, body, and soul? An awareness that one person could complete you when you didn't even realize a part of you was missing.

And to think, a few months ago, she resisted this man.

Slowly, he began to move, pulling nearly all the way out and then sinking in again and again. On instinct, she wrapped her legs around his waist and was swept up in the most delicious frenzy she'd ever known. They met thrust for thrust, and as the first prickles of feeling started to build within her, her mind went blank. The sensation of falling into a hole of vibrant bliss creeped over her until she was in a free fall, but not yet ready to crash back down into reality. She became conscious again when Sebastian caught her, arms tight around her as the thrumming of her nerves began to ease.

He was above her still, panting heavily. He kissed her forehead, her cheeks, her mouth before shifting slightly to her side, rolling her just enough.

"At the risk of sounding indelicate, I need to take care of the condom."

"At the risk of sounding overeager, I put a trash can and tissues next to the bed."

He rolled to the side. When he rolled back, he took her in his warm embrace and pulled the blankets tight over them. This was how they fell asleep every night—curled up in each other's arms. But this night was different. This night was an acknowledgement that they had a love that would last. She was content now to take their time and explore every facet of this new partnership between them. Their own relationship milestones would be that much more worth it as they reached them together.

Her last thought before she fell asleep left a grin on her face. Dr. Delicious had certainly earned his name.

Twenty-Four

SEBASTIAN OPENED THE door to his apartment whistling. He needed to talk to Shannon about their father, but he was in too good of a mood and didn't currently possess the anger needed to have the conversation. He had tried to summon some of the feelings and emotions he had earlier in the evening last night, but after his night with Megan, he just couldn't get there.

The night had started out badly but ended blissfully in the early morning hours of today. She had taken him to heaven, and all he wanted to do was stay there. Who would have thought his shy, conservative girl was a vixen in bed? And he got the feeling Megan was just as shocked as he was.

Fear had briefly gotten the best of him when he found out she wasn't technically cleared for sex. He had never known true soul-crushing, debilitating fear before being faced with losing her—truly, end of life, losing her. How would he recover from that? He was a physician. He knew all about the mysteries that lay within the human body, and the shattering blows it could deal for no known reason. Just when he had seen a clear future, it had burned to nothing in front of him.

Three times.

It would take him some time to get over that—if he ever would. Perhaps the doctor might not think anything of her panting from exercise or having her pulse race from excitement, but the man that loved her would always be a little afraid something would go wrong. After all, there were patients whom the septal myectomy didn't work for. It wasn't a large percentage of patients, but it wasn't uncommon. Only time could soothe his nerves there.

Shannon wandered out of the kitchen with a steaming mug, wearing yoga pants and an oversized sweater with her hair piled high on her head. She may have looked casual, but the clothes were designer.

"Hey, there," she greeted, putting her mug down on the coffee table near her laptop that sat upon a portable desk. She looked to be setting up for a day of writing on the couch. "FYI, I heard you through the floor last night. I don't think I'll ever get that noise out of my head. Ever, Sebastian."

He couldn't help but grin, and the night played over in his mind. "Sorry, not sorry."

Sitting down, Shannon pulled a blanket over her legs and set a throw pillow on her lap. "So, what did Dad have to say?"

Sebastian's mouth fell open, but he really shouldn't have been surprised. "The town Facebook page?"

"The comings and goings of Dr. Delicious are a hot topic of gossip around here. It's like you have some kind of fan club. Did you have one in Chicago?"

"I don't think so," Sebastian said. Certainly not one that had ever been pointed out to him. "This is a close-knit community. Things are very different here." *Things were* very *different here.*

Leaning over to pick up her mug, Shannon blew on the tea and took a sip. "So, Dad? You know, we were never allowed to call him 'Dad.' We had to call him 'Sir' or 'Father.' I felt like one of those kids in the *Sound of Music* calling him that. 'Mother' fit though. A colder woman I've never met. I didn't exactly hit the jackpot in the parent department, that's for sure."

"I did in the sibling department," Sebastian said, sitting down.

Smiling over her mug, Shannon said, "I'm getting luckier there."

Crossing one ankle over his opposite knee, Sebastian settled in to explain what happened the night before with their father. Shannon listened to the entire story without interrupting. When Sebastian was finished, Shannon put aside her mug, folded her hands on the pillow, and gave him a sympathetic look.

"You know this is about his campaign, right?" She asked gently. Sebastian had already suspected that might have been the case. There would be no other purpose to his father coming to speak with him. Everything he said last night, he could have said anytime when Sebastian lived in Chicago.

"Yeah," Sebastian agreed. "I figured there was some kind of ulterior motive to be had. He kept looking around the restaurant. I wasn't sure if he wanted to be seen or didn't want to be seen." Still, Sebastian had to admit that there was a part of him that wanted to reconcile with his father for the right reasons. He still didn't know whether or not his father was telling him the truth last night. Quite frankly, the story didn't paint him in much of a positive light, so it seemed unlikely it was a lie. "He almost broke the boy you were, Sebastian. Don't let him break the man you've become."

Sebastian scratched the back of his head. Fuck it. He was done trying to figure the man out. He left Chicago to get away from him and a life he didn't want. He had everything he needed in the family he had in Grayson Falls and his grandparents in Florida. His father was nothing more to him than the sperm donor. Just like Daisy was the egg donor. Neither had done anything more for him than create him. Donavan writing a check to his grandparents every month did not make the man his father.

"What about you?" He asked. "What are you going to do if he comes to speak with you? He expressed remorse over the things he said to you."

Shannon let out a barking laugh. "He won't come for me. He'll try to summon me a few times, probably send me a confidentiality agreement like he did to you, but if he wanted to reconcile with me, he would have told me he was in town. Making up with his estranged son, who looks just like him and is in the same profession, is what looks good when running for office. A single, pregnant daughter with no plans to marry either the baby's father or anyone else definitely does not look good for his family image. It's all about the visuals for him. Eventually, the press will dig me up, and he'll have to deal with me. But I doubt he'll want to be pre-emptive there. He knows I won't marry anyone just for the sake of not being a single mom. I'm not my brother and sister."

Propping his elbow on the arm of the chair, Sebastian rested his cheek on his fist. "Do you really think there's no hope for them?"

"Yes." She nodded, picked up her mug again, and took a sip. "They never had much to do with me growing up. I'm too much like you. Driven, not willing to toe the line. They liked to tell me that, too, as if it were a bad thing. I played the part when required of me, but at home, I couldn't keep the pretense up. They'll always play the game. They're too much like our parents. Appearances and the life of luxury are too important to them. I feel sorry for them. Strange, isn't it? Feeling sorry for someone who seemingly has it all?"

"Not so strange," Sebastian said, sitting back up with a shrug. "They don't have it all, and they never will if they continue on the path they're on. They'll always be just a little bit unhappy. You said yourself Erica is in more or less an arranged relationship."

"Do you know Erica and Anderson haven't even tried to contact me?" Shannon asked. "Didn't ask if I was doing all right, feeling all right, needed any help. Nothing. It's like they cut me off when my parents did."

"It was easier for me to walk away. Once Grandma and Grandpa moved, there was nothing left there for me." Sebastian said.

"Ouch."

"If I had any inkling you needed me, Shannon, I would have stayed until I knew you were all right," Sebastian said. "I would do the same for Anderson and Erica. They may not like me, and I may not be overly fond of them, but I help my family—the family that will have me anyway."

Smiling lightly, Shannon replied, "Thank you for helping me. I've enjoyed getting to know you better. I almost feel like your sister."

"I almost feel like your brother." They shared a laugh. He found himself wishing she would settle in Grayson Falls, but of course, she needed to do what was right for her. Now that she was in his life, he could travel to visit her.

"So, what do we do about the ogre otherwise known as our father?" she asked.

"As far as I'm concerned, I'm done." Sebastian held up his hands. "He told me what I wanted to know, and I believe he told me the truth. I think his motives for doing it were disingenuous, but nonetheless, I got the information I needed. Grandma and Grandpa have always been my parents. Grandpa has been the only male influence I've needed. He taught me what it was to be a man. It took me a long time to realize all that."

"Like I said, I don't think he'll come for me," Shannon said, tossing the pillow she had been holding to the side. "Mother might, if only to express her extreme disappointment. But I don't believe I'm enough of a commodity to them now. I write under a pen name. Some enterprising journalist will probably connect me to them at some point, but for now, I'll seek my anonymity and lick my wounds. I used to comfort myself saying that just because they didn't like me, doesn't mean they don't love me. But with them, that's exactly what that means. My baby may not know them, but they *will* know family—as much family as I can give them."

Sebastian stood up. "Don't worry, Shan. Jackie will adopt you into this family and then you'll be drowning in brothers and sisters that love you."

Nodding, Shannon smiled and said, "I look forward to it."

"WELL, LOOK WHO decided to show her face," Laurie greeted Megan as she slid onto a bar seat at Over the Hop. Megan was past the lunch hour this time, after having spent the morning in bed then the tub soaking her sore muscles ... and other body parts. When she finally emerged, she lounged around the apartment reading, watching Netflix, and generally being lazy, enjoying her last few days off before she started work again next week.

She was ready to get back to her life, ready to start planning to meet her new goals. She missed Ally to bits and couldn't wait to see how much she had changed since they'd been apart. Christmas was in a few weeks, and she was looking forward to seeing how Ally reacted to all the decorating and excitement.

She was also planning on asking Sebastian to officially move in with her. His cat was already living there full-time. Sebastian himself was just going upstairs to shower and change now, leaving his sister to have the apartment to herself. True, he had a bigger place, but with his sister needing a place to stay, his apartment would be better suited for a new mother—assuming Shannon stayed in the area. Megan knew Sebastian really wanted her to make her life here permanent.

Drumming her hands on the bar, Megan boldly put in her drink order. "I'll have the Adirondack Ale, please."

If there was music playing, it would have scratched to silence.

Slowly, Laurie turned to her, looking concerned. "That's a beer," she needlessly stated.

"From what I understand, it's a good beer. I'll take one. Maybe not in a pint glass though. I feel like I should start smaller."

Leaning her elbows on the bar, Laurie studied her cousin as if she were some kind of rare artifact. "A beer has alcohol," Laurie said. "Something you avoid with the medication you have to take."

"I don't take most of that medication anymore. I'm not even on painkillers now," Megan said. "I'm over twenty-one, I promise."

Pushing herself off the bar, Laurie continued to look at her like she was an alien. Then she turned toward the kitchen and bellowed, "Justin!" Eyes still on Megan, Laurie walked to the kitchen door, pushed it open and yelled back. "Justin, get your ass out here now!"

Barreling through the door like he was expecting a fire, Justin stopped short at the bar. "Oh, hey, Meggie," he greeted. "What's up? Everything okay?"

"Who do I have to know to get a beer around here?" She laughed. "I'm trying to get a beer in my family's establishment, but the bartender seems to being having some kind of episode."

Smiling, Justin moved behind the bar and picked up a smaller glass. "I'm going to drive you home after," he said, putting the glass under a tap. "You have zero tolerance now for alcohol. I'm going to start with the wheat since it's our lowest alcohol content level. I'm also going to put in a pretzel order for you, so you have something to absorb it."

Sliding a snifter-sized glass in front of her, he turned to the computer to plug in the food order. Laurie seemed to recover herself. "Sorry," she said. "My default is to immediately worry about you. You never touched the stuff before. Are you sure you're cleared for this now?"

"My doctor told me it's all right. I'm not on any medication that will react poorly with the beer, but I have been instructed not to go on a bender," Megan said, matter-of-factly. She picked up the glass and lifted it in a toast. "Here's to my first beer and my new life."

Sipping gingerly, she crinkled up her nose. The smell was pleasant, but the taste was bitter to her. She didn't think the beer was made to taste bitter, but it was difficult to associate the beer in a different way.

"It's an acquired taste," Justin said, chuckling, "Don't tell David you didn't like his beer."

"It's not that I don't like it," Megan said, sniffing the beer and then taking another small sip. "I've just ... never tasted anything like it before."

Justin poured himself the Scottish Bastard Red in a pint glass and came around to sit next to Megan at the bar. "Cheers, sis." He clinked his glass to hers in toast. Megan took another slightly larger sip.

"Sebastian is getting me a treadmill," she announced. "I've been using one in physical therapy, and he says it will help through the winter in my marathon training. There's a half marathon on St. Patrick's Day about an hour away and a marathon in May. So far, he, Zach, and Piper are going to run with me in the half marathon. Possibly Jackie and Danny if they have the time to train, as well."

"That's ambitious," Justin said. "But count me in."

"You don't run," Laurie chided. "You don't do anything."

"Which is why I'm going to do this," Justin said. "If my sister, who had major heart surgery, is going to run a half marathon and then a marathon, then I'm going to do it, too. We'll put Gabe at the end to resuscitate me."

"That all sounds like work to me. I'm going to make funny signs and wait for you at the finish line," Laurie said. "Somebody has to cheer you on."

Smiling, Megan took another sip. She felt the alcohol starting to go to her head. Justin wasn't kidding about her having no tolerance for it. She felt happy. Now she saw why people ended up drinking too much. If consuming alcohol enhanced this feeling, why wouldn't you want to feel this way? However, she was not looking to be hungover, so she would listen to the advice of her brother and take it slow.

When her pretzel came out, Laurie slid a glass of water in front of her. She took gulping sips. When Justin finished his beer, he ruffled her hair, stole a chunk of her pretzel, and disappeared back to his kitchen to continue with his dinner prep.

"So," Laurie said, dusting liquor bottles while she talked with Megan. "You came in here glowing. You still are, and I know it's not from the beer, so spill."

Dipping her pretzel in cheese sauce, Megan kept her gaze down on what she was doing. "Who knew swinging from the ceiling fan could be so fun?"

Pausing while Laurie absorbed her words, Megan took another sip of her beer.

Laurie's eyes widened as she realized what Megan was telling her. "No!" A bright smile on her face, Laurie clapped her hands. "And how was it?"

Reliving the night in her mind, Megan sighed. Everything had been perfect. She was so scared before he got home that he wasn't going to like what she was doing. She thought she would make a fool of herself being the seductress, but she didn't give Sebastian enough credit. He loved her, and he showed her in so many ways.

"It was perfect." She knew she had a goofy smile on her face, but she couldn't bring herself to reign in her emotions. "He's everything, Laurie. I didn't even want him at first. I didn't want *anybody*, especially a doctor. He broke down the barriers, and I can't imagine going back to the way things were before I met him. I don't want to. He's the one, Laurie. I wasn't even looking for him."

"Well," Laurie said, wiping down the bar and refilling the snack bowls. "I'm happy for you, Megan. I really am. No one deserves to be happy and settled more than you. But believe me when I say, it's better you than me. This girl is in no way interested in settling down."

"Neither was I, if you recall." Megan pointed at her with a piece of pretzel before she popped it in her mouth. "They say you find your true love when you're not looking for them."

"A little sex and you become the Yoda of relationships?"

Megan laughed and let the subject drop. Just because she was happy in a relationship didn't mean everybody had to be or even wanted to be. It wasn't too long ago she was rolling her eyes when people asked why she didn't have a boyfriend or wasn't married. She wanted her brothers and cousins to find love, but she wanted them to find it at the right time.

For now, Megan had everything she wanted, and she had her eye on a future with even more.

Twenty-Five

AFTER CONFIRMING WITH Ryan that Ethan was at the farm, Sebastian headed over to Ethan and Natalie's house to talk with Natalie. He had already confirmed by text that she was home, and he was hoping that Ethan would stay at the farm long enough for Sebastian to get all the details he needed before speaking with his brother.

Natalie opened the front door as Sebastian was walking up. He didn't know if she saw him drive up or the extensive security system on the house alerted her. He knew without a doubt that Eric Davis knew he was here. Eric was the one that installed the state-of-the-art system on the house, and unless Sebastian missed his mark, the man was head over heels in love with Natalie. She, of course, didn't acknowledge Eric's feelings. She seemed uncomfortable with them—not in a fearful sort of way, but in more of a she didn't know what to do with them sort of way.

Natalie was apprehensive about forming attachments. However, to Sebastian's mind, she pretty much threw that out the window when she decided to move to Grayson Falls to be closer to Jackie and Ryan. There was no way Sebastian and his siblings would allow her to keep her distance from them. Hell, Ethan rolled right over her when he decided to move in with her. If Bravo hadn't come with the deal, Natalie likely would have refused, in which case, Ethan probably would have just camped out on the front steps until she changed her mind.

Natalie held the door opened, and Sebastian entered the living room. The two-bedroom ranch was cozy—and by cozy, he meant small. But somehow, Ethan crammed a large sectional and behemoth television into the living room. When Natalie noticed Sebastian staring at the room too long, she sighed.

"I know," she said. "It's ostentatious, but it relaxes him. They were Zach's. Ethan likes to disappear into the couch in front of a game. It helps him to zone out every now and then."

There were no pretenses between Sebastian and Natalie anymore. After that night driving to the hospital, they weren't going back to how things were. Sebastian would keep up the charade, but when it was just the two of them, he wouldn't pretend she wasn't his sister. Natalie seemed to understand that.

"Have a seat." She waved at the couch. "I'll grab us some drinks." Sebastian sank down on the couch and crossed his ankle over his other knee. Stretching an arm along the back of the couch, he could definitely see how Ethan could waste away a day on this massive piece of furniture. It did make things cramped in the little house though.

Returning to the living room, Natalie handed him a beer, clinked the neck of her bottle to his, and settled down on the catty-cornered piece of the sectional.

"Bravo's not with you?"

"No, he's with Ethan." Natalie shook her head and took a sip of her beer. "E needs him more than I do. I don't like having him around when I go places. It draws attention to me, going about town with a massive dog."

"I suspect it just looks normal now," Sebastian shrugged.

"To the people that live here, sure," Natalie agreed. "But to an outsider? Someone walks into the hospital and there's a nurse with a huge dog following her around and no one says anything? Red flag."

"People probably assume he's a therapy dog. That's not unusual."

"He's *Ethan's* therapy dog. I love the big fur ball, but I don't need him under foot. I did it to appease Ethan, but he needs Bravo more than me."

"How bad is he?" Sebastian asked quietly.

"He has good days and bad days," Natalie replied. "The bad days are worse than they've been. He's going to see his therapist, Sebastian. You don't need to do an intervention. I'm watching him. I have some experience in this area. If I think it's getting out of hand, I'll call everyone in. I asked him to go back to his therapist, and he has been. He's having nightmares. He won't talk about them, but I wonder if his dreams are starting to mix with his reality, you know? Like instead of the guys in his unit being in the Humvee, I wonder if it's us that are in there now, and it's his family that he can't save. It's just a guess. That's a common thing that happens. I can't really know unless Ethan tells me."

"I know the town thinks you two are a romantic item, thanks to Norrie," Sebastian said. Natalie rolled her eyes. Danny really did need to reign in his dispatcher. "But is he seeing anyone? He hasn't mentioned it, but he made a cryptic comment a few weeks ago along the lines of 'what makes me think he didn't have a woman?'"

Natalie started peeling the label off her bottle and gave her attention to that task. "He won't say," she said. "But there's somewhere he goes at night. I don't know if it's to see a woman or he just drives around or something. Maybe he goes to a bar in another town. But he will disappear a couple nights a week. He won't stay out all night though. He sneaks back in."

"I'm scared for him," Sebastian confessed.

"We're all scared for him," Natalie said. "That's why I watch him so closely. Superheroes have flaws, even Ethan does. I'm going to give him more time to work through things with his therapist. He's doing everything he's supposed to be doing."

"Have you locked up his guns?" Sebastian asked.

Natalie's gaze snapped up to his. "They're not here," she whispered. "He doesn't know it, but they're at Eric's. I'm giving him the space he needs, but God help me, I couldn't leave his weapons here. He'll be pissed when he finds out and I'll have to deal with that. Maybe when he's feeling better, I can bring them back without him ever knowing they were gone."

"You did the right thing," Sebastian said. "I'll back you up. He might get pissed, but at least he'll be alive and pissed."

"Let's talk about something else," Natalie said. "This topic is depressing."

Satisfied that Natalie had things well in hand with Ethan—for now—he would stay in his role as an observer. Ethan understood he could come to Sebastian if he needed help, and there was nothing else Sebastian could do. Everything that could be done for Ethan at this stage was being done. They just needed to help him get through it.

"So, Nat," Sebastian said, linking his fingers behind his head. "Tell me your real story. What was your upbringing like?"

Shrugging, Natalie turned toward him, rested her hands on the back of the couch and then dropped her chin to her hands. "Depends on which part you're asking about," she said. "After I was born, I went to a man who thought he was my father. I don't know who he was now. Daisy said Ethan and I are twins, and our father was a hockey player. My dad never talked about playing hockey. I don't know what to believe. Whoever Richard Currie was, he was not a good father. He drank a lot and was often out of a job. We moved in with my grandmother, and she wasn't much better. Richard would get sober, and things were nice. Then he'd fall off the wagon, and things weren't nice anymore. I was in and out of foster care. I knew college was my way out of that life. I studied hard in school, got a few scholarships and worked my way through school to pay for the rest. I left and never went back.

"I met a guy that I fell hard for, but then he revealed his true colors. He was just like my dad. When I talked about breaking up if he didn't change his ways, he told me he would kill himself. Then he started telling me he would kill me. When I saw the relief mission to South America advertised, I jumped at the chance to get away from him. I'm sure you know the rest."

Sebastian brought his hands back down from behind his head and picked up his beer. "I'm sorry you had to go through all that. What made you come to Grayson Falls? Why would you want to be near siblings you couldn't tell the truth to?"

Straightening up, Natalie took another drink. "Like you, I wanted to be around good family. Even if Ryan and Jackie only ever thought of me as a friend, *I* would know what I was to them. Then Ethan showed up, and he and Jackie figured me out the first time he and I were in the same room together. I know our family knows. But Sebastian, I can't stand the thought of you being used against me by someone trying to get to me. Nothing's foolproof. Eric found out about me. Juan Espinoza may be in jail, but his followers aren't. I'm on their Most Wanted list. If I'm being watched, you'd all be targets. I can't live with myself if that were the case. I've thought about taking off again—either on my own or having the Marshall's Service reassign me. But at this point, I know Eric would just find me again."

"Please don't ever do that," Sebastian said, reaching out to grab her hand. "We would miss you very much if you did. We'd always wonder how you were and if you were all right. Between Danny, Ethan, and Eric, we clearly have the resources to protect you."

"It's why I stay," Natalie said softly. "I just hate being a burden."

"You're not a burden," Sebastian insisted. "You're our sister, and nothing that happened was your fault."

"Let's talk about something else. How's Megan?"

Sebastian took another sip of his beer. That goofy feeling rained over him as he thought of Megan. She was everything. His future was laid clear before him now. But did she want the same things he did? Now that she was free of the physical limitations that set her back before, what did she want to do? No longer hampered by her body, the world was her new playground. He couldn't be one more thing to hold her back. He loved her too much not to help her spread those beautiful wings.

"She's doing excellently," he said. "I'm buying her a treadmill so she can start her marathon training. She's it for me, if she wants me."

"And women all through Grayson Falls weep tonight. Dr. Delicious is off the market."

Rolling his eyes, Sebastian stood up. "On that note," he said. "I think I'll head out." Natalie rose with him. "You let me know if anything changes with Ethan—anything at all. I'm not afraid to have the conversation with him."

"Will do," she said. "Neither am I."

After leaving Natalie and Ethan's house, Sebastian headed toward home, but when he saw Zach's SUV parked at Over the Hop, he pulled in. He seemed to be sibling hopping today. Entering the pub, he found Zach sitting at a high-top table alone reading his tablet. Zach wasn't such a novelty around town anymore. Occasionally, commuters that took the train came into the pub after work for a bite to eat and a pint before getting in their cars and driving to whatever other town they lived in. Every now and then, one would spot Zach at the pub and ask for his autograph and a selfie. Usually, Zach was happy to oblige.

Sebastian approached his brother and slapped him on the back before taking the chair across from him. Zach looked up and smiled. "Piper kicked me out. She's against a deadline and apparently just having me in the house was a distraction. I wasn't even by her. I was in the office minding my own business. Apparently, she can't resist my body."

Holding up his hand, Sebastian closed his eyes briefly. "Spare me the horrifying details, please."

"You've got a woman now. You should understand." Zach picked up his glass and took a sip.

Laurie appeared and slid a pint in front of Sebastian. "I gave you the Perfect Porter. I felt like being clever," she said. Sebastian smiled. The Perfect Porter was a beer named after Zach after he pitched his perfect game and which Sebastian named. Of all the things to go to his brother's head—going down in baseball history, a sure spot in the Hall of Fame, a legendary career in the major leagues—having a beer named after him at his favorite watering hole seemed to be what he was most proud of.

"So," Laurie said, clapping her hands together. "He's getting wings. Do you want that, too?"

"I'll take the chili loaded," Sebastian said. "It's getting pretty frigid now. I could use the warm up."

"More snow this week. Christmas is coming," Laurie said. "It's my favorite time of year. Especially this year with my new beer-drinking cousin."

Wincing at the possibility of a drunk Megan, Sebastian looked at her. "Was she all right? Did someone take her home?"

"Justin did," Laurie nodded. "She did fine. Justin gave her the wheat with a pretzel and water. She was walking straight when she left."

It should have been strange that Sebastian was busting with pride over his girlfriend having an alcoholic drink, but these little milestones were to be celebrated. Each time she did something she couldn't do before, his chest swelled.

"That right there," Laurie said, pointing at Sebastian's face. "That's the same look she had when she was here. You two are gone over each other."

"Guilty," Sebastian said. Laurie squeezed his shoulder before walking away.

"What is it about this place?" Zach asked. "First Jackie, then Ryan, then me, now you. What is in the air in this town? Who's next? Ethan and Natalie must be scared witless with all this love going around. We're all dropping like the acorns from the trees." Absently, Sebastian rubbed his head. A couple of those acorns hit him this year, and those little suckers hurt. A rain storm of acorns was not something he had to deal with in Chicago.

Glancing at the door when it opened, two men Sebastian hadn't seen around entered the pub, scanning the room with their eyes before their gazes fell on Sebastian and Zach.

"Looks like you've got some fans looking for you," Sebastian said, nodding toward the door.

Zach glanced over his shoulder. "Those two have 'reporter' written all over them. I assume they want a piece on what it feels like not be heading to spring training this year. 'Retired Pitcher Happy in His Life.' Oh, the clickbait they'll get from that one."

Sebastian laughed at his brother's sarcasm as the two men headed their way.

"Dr. Stuart," one man said, sticking out his hand. "James Colby with the *Chicago Tribune*."

Confused, Sebastian shook the man's hand. Sebastian looked over at Zach who, not surprisingly, looked just as befuddled as Sebastian felt. A feeling of dread crept into Sebastian's stomach, and he suddenly felt nauseated.

Sebastian looked from man to man. "What does the Chicago Tribune want with a doctor in private practice in New Hampshire?" But of course, Sebastian already knew.

"We're covering your father's senate campaign," the other said. The pit in Sebastian's stomach grew deeper.

"I can't help you," Sebastian said.

The first man pulled a tablet out of his shoulder bag, woke it up, and turned it so Sebastian could read what was on it. Under a headline of "Senate Hopeful Donovan Stuart Reconciles with Estranged Son," were two pictures taken of him and his father. One was of the world's most awkward hug; the other while they were sitting having dinner.

Sebastian looked down at the picture dispassionately. "You've been misinformed. I have nothing to do with to that man."

"Come on, Dr. Stuart," the second man said. "We're not that stupid. Neither are our readers or Indiana's voters. We just wanted to see if we could get a comment from you on the story and your relationship with a candidate that is campaigning on family values."

Biting the inside of his cheek to keep from laughing, Sebastian continued to stare at the pictures of himself plastered across the tablet story. The urge to laugh was soon replaced with the urge to cry. He knew his father's motives for coming here were disingenuous. He had told Shannon as much. But there was just a small part of him—maybe of the boy inside him that desperately wanted his father's attention—a part that was crushed to discover he had been used to advance the man's agenda.

Turning to focus his attention on his beer, Sebastian said, "Sorry, I can't help you."

The first man turned the tablet back around and studied it before looking back up at Sebastian. "Are you sure about that?"

"He said as much, didn't he?" Zach growled. Though Sebastian didn't need it, he was thankful for his brother's help. He was out of his element dealing with reporters.

The second reporter held up his hands in peace. "All right, don't get testy." He looked around the pub and rocked back on his heels. "So, what's good here?"

"Other restaurants," came a very unhappy voice behind Sebastian. He turned to see Justin standing there, glaring at the two reporters. "Other restaurants are good. I own this one, and I don't take kindly to my customers being harassed. There's a pizza joint down the street. Go there. I recommend the calamari."

Justin stood there and continued to glare as the two men backed up and left the pub.

Sebastian looked up at Justin. "Thanks for coming to my rescue."

Shoving at his shoulder, Justin laughed. "Just keeping an eye out on my sister's shitty boyfriend. It doesn't look like he can take care of himself." Sebastian laughed and took the joke in the spirit it was intended. Megan's brothers could give him a hard time about dating, and practically living with, their sister but they didn't. He expected a little hazing. The fact that there wasn't much was appreciated by Sebastian.

Justin returned to the kitchen, and Laurie brought their food out. "I saw what happened," she said, as she placed their food in front of them and picked up their empty glasses. "They're probably waiting to ambush you outside, but in here, we take care of our family." Winking at them, she turned and walked away.

The feeling of dread and nausea that had taken up residence in Sebastian's stomach was gone now, replaced by the warm embrace he always used to feel when he crossed the town's border for a visit. Only now, he wasn't visiting. He was here for good, and his family grew larger and larger the more time passed.

After he finished his food and beer, Sebastian said goodbye to his brother and stepped outside. Cautiously, he looked around for the two reporters. While it could be that they were stealthier at hiding than he was at his surveillance, he was reasonably sure they weren't around. He got into his car, and as he pulled out of the parking lot and headed toward home, nobody followed him. The reporters would probably poke around town looking for their answers. Sooner or later, the chief of police would hear about and it and good luck to them then.

Each time Sebastian walked into to Megan's apartment, he hoped for dimmed candlelight and soft music. But he realized that the memory of that first night wouldn't be as special if that became the norm. There were plenty of memories yet to come and he hoped each one would be unique.

Megan sat on the couch with her ankles crossed in front of her reading a magazine when he entered. Looking up, she gifted him with that luminous smile he had come to love. Everything inside of him relaxed and he determined he would leave his worries at the door.

Tossing the magazine on the table, Megan stayed where she was while Sebastian came to greet her. He started at the opposite end of couch and slid up her body, resting his cheek on her breast. Megan's fingers came up to run through his hair. Closing his eyes, he gave himself over to the sensation. Taking a deep breath, he released it and let all the stress of the day out of his body.

Short of an actual restraining order, there was nothing to do about his father. Unless things worsened with Ethan, there was nothing to do there but wait and be there if and when Ethan did need him. He had come to Grayson Falls for a different life—a slower-paced life—and he had to let go of the things he couldn't control.

Now that Megan and Sebastian were getting serious—and in truth, he knew he would ask her to marry him someday—Sebastian felt guilty not being truthful with her about Natalie. How could he allow things to go on with a huge lie between them? But Sophie and Piper didn't know, and his brothers were engaged to be married to them. If the secret ever did finally come out, there would be a lot of explaining to do. He just hoped Megan understood.

"You're troubled," Megan said softly. "What's wrong?"

"How could anyone be troubled with your perfect breasts right by his face?" To prove his point, he trailed his finger along said breasts over her sweater.

"Ah," Megan said. "So, we're evading tonight. All right. I'll wait until you're ready to talk about it."

He rubbed his cheek against her sweater. "I appreciate it. I just want to put it all out of my mind for now. Tell me about your first day back with Ally."

"She's amazing!" Megan gushed. "I've missed her so much. She's changed a lot. I've barely saw her since I had the surgery. I was almost afraid she wouldn't remember me, but she did. I fell right back into my old routine, and it felt nice. I was back on ground I understood again." She paused then said more quietly. "Spending time with her makes me look forward to the day when I have my own baby."

Sebastian froze. Was she starting a conversation or just making an innocent comment? He relaxed back into her body. "Do you want to have your own baby? No adopting?"

"Yes, of course," Megan said. "Things are so different for me now. Things I couldn't think about before I can indulge in daydreaming about all day. Of course, I'm nervous I would pass my disease on, but I'm also worried my kid would get my nose."

Sebastian propped his chin on her chest and looked up at her. "Your nose is adorable."

"You just want to get laid."

He tightened his arms around her. "Yes, but that doesn't mean your nose isn't still adorable. I stand behind my compliment."

"Do you ... want kids?"

So, she was definitely starting a conversation. Sebastian was okay with that. He'd put all his cards on the table and answer all her questions. He didn't want to leave anything open to assumption.

"Eventually," he said. "I want to travel a bit first. Once you have kids, everything changes. I know in theory you can just pack up a kid and make off to parts unknown, but the reality is, once they start school, things like that are more difficult. They have homework and activities and things they can't miss. Not to say I don't want to take my kids places, but I think I want to hit the romantic hotspots before I'm trudging to Disney every year."

Propping himself up on his hip, Sebastian looked over at her. "And I'd want kids if you were their mother." Megan's eyes widened just slightly as she took in his meaning. "What do you say, baby? Do you want to have kids with me in the distant future?"

Nodding her head slowly, Megan smiled. "Yes, I want to have children with you in the distant future." Sebastian was about to seal the deal with a kiss when she stopped him. "But only if you move in with me in the present."

"Like, in here?" he asked.

"Well, with the baby coming I think Shannon would be more comfortable in your place, don't you think? Or do you want to go somewhere else entirely?" He didn't answer right away and her face paled and her jaw dropped. "Or do you just not like the idea? You're here all the time anyway. I thought it would make sense." Megan dropped her face into her hand. "I'm such an idiot. I am really no good at this. I can't even ask you to move in with me."

Grabbing her hand away from her face, Sebastian kissed her fingertips. "That escalated quickly. Remind me not to wait more than three seconds to respond to major life decisions."

"What does that mean?"

"I thought leaving my cat here permanently was a sign that I wanted to be here permanently, too." He said gently.

"I thought maybe you didn't want him anymore because he's an asshole."

"Well, he is an asshole," Sebastian conceded. "But for better or worse, he's my asshole now and I love him."

Smiling tentatively, Megan said, "So, we're doing this then? Officially?"

"As soon as we can get all my stuff down here. Is there any furniture or anything you want from up there?" He asked. Technically, he really didn't need to leave Shannon with anything. She had money to buy her own things, and he assumed she would want to do so at some point. But Megan's place was smaller. All he really wanted was his stereo system and record collection. Maybe Megan would agree to look for a new place together for them. He wondered if he could get them into a house or if that would be too presumptuous.

"I do love the couches," she sighed. "And mine are showing their age, but I can wait until Shannon figures things out."

Propping himself up on his hands, Sebastian kissed her. "You make me very, very happy," he said. "From that very first meeting when you hated me, I knew you'd be important to me. I hoped for it."

"I didn't hate you. I just didn't trust you."

Sebastian shrugged one shoulder. It didn't matter anymore. Megan's strength and resilience inspired him to have the fortitude to break ties with his father and leave a childhood of pain and endless disappointment behind.

"So, we're doing this? Together?" Sebastian asked.

Wrapping her arms around him, she pressed her lips to his. His heart picked up pace as she smiled. "Together."

Epilogue

MEGAN'S CHEST BURNED and her breaths came in short pants. Her heart was pounding so hard she could hear it's thumping in her ears. She wanted to die. She wanted to fall down and just die. People did this voluntarily?

Every muscle in her body ached. The impact of each step on her knees rattled through her legs. Sweat soaked clothes clung to her skin—which was chafed in some unpleasant areas.

"Almost there, Meggie." Justin was on one side of her; Sebastian on the other. Jackie, Danny, Zach, and Piper were around her, all laboring along with her. They had just passed the twenty-five-mile marker of the marathon. Only one point two miles to go.

Everyone had some physical issue going on, and the complaints were legion along the race course. But the energy of the group rose each step closer to the finish line.

The finish line. That most glorious of places where a medal, a bottle of water, and a banana waited for her.

Along with professional massage therapists.

How she was going to move her body tomorrow was a mystery to her. At least Danny and Jackie had arranged a few days off to recover from the race. Everyone would be walking strange tomorrow—if they could walk at all.

"Note to siblings," Sebastian said through his panting. "Megan doesn't get to pick the next group activity."

They were all in agreement.

"I'm glad there's doctors among us," Justin said, pushing his hand into his side. "I think my kidney or spleen or something is going to pop out of my side. Maybe I have appendicitis. Do you think I have appendicitis?"

"No," Jackie and Sebastian answered simultaneously.

Though they all ran at different speeds, they agreed that if they were going to do the race, they were going to do it together. It was slow going at times as Megan and Justin were new runners, but even Zach, who was in amazing shape, struggled at times. Twenty-six point two miles was just a long way to go.

Why, *why*, didn't she stop with the half marathon? They said if you can run a half marathon, you can run a full. Why wasn't that knowledge good enough? What did she think she was trying to prove?

They all groaned at the approaching hill. Hills were the spawn of Satan and meant to be avoided. If it wasn't for the victory party Laurie was planning at the pub, Megan would have called it quits and gotten into an ambulance miles ago—if anyone would have actually let her.

They leaned on each other to get through it. Jackie's leg cramps stopped them for a few minutes while Danny and Sebastian massaged them out. Piper's stomach derailed them another few minutes. While stopped, they all took a good hydration and stretching break. It didn't matter to them how long it took them to cross the finish, just as long as they did before the police car came to clear the course of runners taking too long to complete the race. They still had another hour or so before that happened.

Both Justin and Megan needed ambulance stops for band aids. During that stop, Sebastian did a quick assessment of her to make sure everything was normal. She had never felt better.

That wasn't true. She was miserable. She wanted to fall into a bathtub and lie in a nice whirlpool tub for a few days before collapsing into their soft bed with its Egyptian cotton sheets and weighted blanket.

But she was almost there. Her goal of running a marathon was almost complete. Something she had never given a second thought to before because it was unattainable.

Not anymore.

Sebastian taught her how to ski over the winter, and they had fun as she stumbled and snow-plowed down the slopes then warmed up inside with hot cider before going out for more tumbling down the mountain—sometimes on her face. But she loved every minute of it.

Each time her heart rate sped up without pain or anxiety was a win for her. She wasn't a daredevil by any stretch. She did keep her exercise within a reasonable limit for the most part, but once she thought of doing a marathon to celebrate her new life, the idea held, and she was more and more determined to make it a reality.

A super painful and exhausting reality.

She decided to focus on the signs along the course. They had proven to be entertaining so far. The people holding them looked happy and refreshed—not a bit in pain as they called out encouragement for the runners, or just let their signs do the talking.

This is a lot of work for a free banana!

Toenails are for sissies.

It's too late in the race to trust that fart.

Some were entertaining; some were gross, and some just didn't make sense.

"There it is!" Danny called out. "Mile 26! Shit, I haven't run like this since the Army." Nearly dizzy with glee, Megan whimpered. The torture was almost over. It was almost time to lie down and put her feet up, or soak them, or rub them. It was almost time to do anything but stand up. She never wanted to stand up again.

"At least you're not hauling all the gear," Zach said. "This should feel like a dream."

"Yeah, Porter. That's exactly what it fucking feels like, a dream." Danny shot back. "More like a fucking nightmare."

If Danny was feeling the pain, Megan could only imagine what her body would feel like when she stopped moving. She wondered idly if there was some kind of shot Sebastian and Jackie could give them for the coming pain. Did she have any painkillers left? Each time she lifted a foot in the air, she wanted it to stay there. It was the only millisecond of relief from the stabbing pain in her shins and ankles. Throbbing knees and an upset stomach rounded off her current list of ailments.

And she definitely wasn't going to ever run another marathon. She can check the experience off her bucket list and concentrate on something else.

Running was stupid.

"Oh my God, I see the finish line!" Jackie yelped.

Sebastian moved closer to Megan and took her hand. Their fingers slipped together and nearly apart again from the sweat. She'd never felt less attractive in her life. But it wouldn't matter to him. The sweat glistening off him made him look like a god. Adonis come to life. How come *he* got to look like the most magnificent looking person on the planet and she was a smelly hot mess?

Eye on the prize, Megan. Eye on the prize!

The finish line came closer, and Megan's legs felt like they were going to buckle. How many runners actually crawled across the finish line? Had anyone in this race already done it? She didn't want to be the first of the day.

The crowd began screaming Zach's name. It happened a few times over the course of the race. A few days before the race, it was released that Zach would be running the race with his family. He waved a hand in acknowledgement over his head before taking Piper's hand. They spread across the road, holding hands and crossed the finish line together. Megan looked at her companions in hell. They all put up a good front, smiling through the pain. Adrenaline and a magnificent feeling of accomplishment pouring over them.

Or maybe that was just the sweat.

Or liquid awesome, as Jackie had started calling it.

The euphoria that spread through her was all-consuming. She had just finished a full marathon. *Her.* The poor little girl with the heart problem. She felt lightheaded, and her legs pulsed. Goose-stepping around and shaking her legs, Megan took in the rest of their group. Zach had put Piper up in a piggy back. Tears were streaming down Piper's face, and Megan didn't know if it was from pain or joy. Maybe both. It was a little hard to tell the difference.

Laying on the ground, Justin moved his legs around in a random pattern, no doubt trying to move around the lactic acid building up. Jackie and Danny hugged before Danny swept her up into his arms, and she squealed about how sweaty he was.

Whooping and hollering, Sebastian picked Megan up and swung her around. Their bodies were slippery. Megan enjoyed the brief time off her feet, but knew they had to start walking around a bit to cool down and stretch, before getting to the massage therapists.

"Congratulations," he said, smiling radiantly at her. "How do you feel?"

"Amazing," she said, knowing this time he wasn't asking as a doctor. "I feel invincible, but I know we're going to be miserable in a few hours."

"By then we'll be showered in beer and glory at the pub." He set her gently on her feet. "Let's get the banana and hydration. We need to replace a lot of water." Jackie was back on her feet, but Zach continued to carry Piper. Her head rested on his shoulder, and Megan wondered if she was having a problem or Zach was just being his usual overprotective self. Large crowds weren't Piper's scene.

A photographer spotted them and led them over to a race banner for a group picture. Zach was positioned in the middle and Piper lifted her head and gave a small smile. The rest of them beamed. Pulling Megan close, Sebastian slid an arm around her waist. He smelled awful. But then again, that could have been her. At this point, it was tough to say.

"I love you," he said in her ear so no one else could hear. "And I'm so fucking proud of you. You inspire me more every day."

Now that she was stopped, her body was starting to throb. She knew soon she would feel like every single part of her body ached. But for now, she felt like she could take over the world.

THE END

A Note from the Author

First of all, I must thank my friend Alicia for telling me the story of her Nana. To hear the story first hand is much more funnier than anything I could have done with it, believe me.

Also making an appearance in this book is my cat, Java. All those stories about him are true. He stole all that food, and he is a bit of a jerk. But he's also the most loving and loyal pet I've ever had. He looks at me with unconditional love and he's such a comfort to me ... except when he's smacking me awake at ridiculous hours of the morning and yelling in my ear. We have a complicated relationship.

This is book four of the Grayson Falls series and my fifth published book. I can hardly believe how much I've done so far and how much more I have to go. I wish I could be one of these authors that brings you a book a month, but I'm just not that fast of a writer. I take my time, so I can bring you the best story possible the way I see it in my mind.

Thank you for picking up Sebastian's story, and I invite you back to Grayson Falls for Christmas with Ethan and Brooke.

ABOUT THE AUTHOR

Anne Marie received a Bachelor's of Fine Arts in Creative Writing from Southern New Hampshire University. She writes in the contemporary romance and fantasy genres and *The Good Race* is her debut novel. She lives in the Richmond, Virginia, area with her husband, son, two dogs and cat.

To keep up to date on the Grayson Falls and Guardian series, follow Anne Marie at:

Website: https://www.ammahlerauthor.com/
Facebook: https://www.facebook.com/AMMahler3206/
Twitter: https://twitter.com/AMMahler3206

Also by A.M. Mahler

Grayson Falls Series
The Good Race
The Slow Lane
The Perfect Game
Breaking Free
Guardians of Eternal Life Series
The Guardian
The Scholar

35262166R00153

Made in the USA
San Bernardino, CA
08 May 2019